Love is inevitable—
even under the oddest of circumstances . . .

It was the distress on her face and the shimmer of unshed tears that impelled Jason's next response. "Ah, love, don't," he begged, enfolding her, towel and all, in a one-armed embrace and cupping her chin in his other hand. As his mouth descended to cover hers, he was treated to a view of silky black lashes. She wouldn't look at him but she hadn't pulled away, he thought exultantly before abandoning thought for sensual pleasure. The desire to kiss her had been growing more insistent from the moment this afternoon when she had demonstrated the technique of whistling for a rapt little girl and an equally enchanted husband.

At first she remained utterly still, almost unbreathing, but then as he took that luscious lower lip between his and pressed tiny kisses at the corners of her mouth, moving with deliberation, she exhaled gently, melting into his embrace. Flames licked along his nerve endings as her lips warmed and clung to his, seeking and giving pleasure. He released her chin in order to wrap his other arm around her with an inarticulate growl of satisfaction.

The Abducted Bride

Dorothy Mack

A SIGNET BOOK

SIGNET

Published by New American Library, a division of
Penguin Group (USA) Inc., 375 Hudson Street,
New York, New York 10014, USA
Penguin Group (Canada), 90 Eglinton Avenue East, Suite 700, Toronto
Ontario M4P 2Y3, Canada (a division of Pearson Penguin Canada Inc.)
Penguin Books Ltd., 80 Strand, London WC2R 0RL, England
Penguin Ireland, 25 St. Stephen's Green, Dublin 2,
Ireland (a division of Penguin Books Ltd.)
Penguin Group (Australia), 250 Camberwell Road, Camberwell, Victoria 3124,
Australia (a division of Pearson Australia Group Pty. Ltd.)
Penguin Books India Pvt. Ltd., 11 Community Centre, Panchsheel Park, New
Delhi - 110 017, India
Penguin Group (NZ), cnr Airborne and Rosedale Roads, Albany,
Auckland 1310, New Zealand (a division of Pearson New Zealand Ltd.)
Penguin Books (South Africa) (Pty.) Ltd., 24 Sturdee Avenue,
Rosebank, Johannesburg 2196, South Africa

Penguin Books Ltd., Registered Offices:
80 Strand, London WC2R 0RL, England

First published by Signet, an imprint of New American Library,
a division of Penguin Group (USA) Inc.

First Printing, August 2005
10 9 8 7 6 5 4 3 2 1

Chapter One

"Why, Robert? Why will you not tell me where you are going?"

The request seemed reasonable, her tone mild, but the hint of anxiety underlying the young woman's words alerted the man leaning over the bed. Glancing up from his packing, he produced a quick smile.

"It is not *will not* but *cannot,* Amy, because I do not know my precise destination. As I just told you, I am going to take *Zephyr* out to pick up an old friend who has been traveling and—"

"Traveling in France?"

"Now, where did you get that nonsensical notion?" he asked, laughing easily. She, however, from her position leaning against one of the bedposts, had seen his hands pause in the task of folding a knitted garment, and so she was neither abashed by censure nor fooled by playacting.

"From that other 'old friend' who arrived here yesterday all travelstained but unable even to remain for dinner, and who introduced himself to you as being from the Foreign Office," she retorted, her eyes meeting his defiantly when he looked up in annoyance.

"Still listening at keyholes, I see. Father should have taken my advice years ago and packed you off to a school where they might—and, mind you, I do not presume to put it any higher than might—have succeeded in teaching you how a lady comports herself."

"Before she died, Grand-mère taught me all I need to know about how a lady comports herself," she riposted, her delicate chin firming to a fair approximation of her brother's square jaw, "and you well know I could not have gone to school and left Papa all alone with you away in the army. His spirits required constant support, and I was the only one who could restore him after one of his—his bad spells—"

"After one of his prolonged bouts of drinking, you mean," her brother amended grimly. "But all your devotion couldn't prevent him from drinking himself to death in the end. I'm sorry, love," he added hastily, spotting the sheen of unshed tears before she turned her face away. He abandoned his packing and put a comforting arm around her shoulders, handing her the handkerchief he'd been about to include.

"None of it was your fault. No one could have saved our father from his fate," Robert assured his weeping sister earnestly. "He seemed to be driven to the one end, and you were left to cope with this by yourself." He grimaced in self-reproach. "Your loving family has done poorly by you thus far. First our mother died after your birth—"

"But there can be no blame attached to anyone for that sad event!" Amy interrupted in protest.

"Not for that, no, but you were scarcely out of leading strings when Grand-mère descended from the north, and a greater martinet I never met in or out of the army. Of course, having had the good fortune and foresight to be born male, I soon escaped to school, making you the sole recruit upon whom to exercise her power for most of the year."

Satisfied that the little chuckle this evoked signified that his sister had recovered her composure, Robert stepped back and resumed his packing, but he continued in the same serious vein. "Father treated you like a favorite pet, spoiling you rotten when he was sober and reviling you when in his cups."

"He never mistreated me, you know," she assured him, "and he was always sincerely sorry afterwards. It was just that he would sink into such a spell of the dismals that he

could not bear human company. We merely intensified the irritation of his nerves, even I who so longed to comfort him."

Robert nodded. "I can see clearly in hindsight that I did
you no service either by letting you tag along with me every-
where, especially after Grand-mère died. Instead of allowing
you to learn to be a young lady, I turned you into a hoyden
and then compounded the damage by joining the army and
leaving you to your fate. I am ashamed to admit that I would
not be here now if Father's death had not forced me to sell
out lest the estate go to rack and ruin with only old Barton to
manage things."

"Well, if you truly regret abandoning me, do not do it
again—do not go off on this trip," Amy said lightly, taking
out of his hands the shirt he was crushing.

"This is one thing I must do, love," he replied, compelling
her glance when she would have looked away. "You see, the
man I am going to meet *is* an old friend—at least, I met him
first in Portugal two years ago and we became good friends
thereafter. Before I left for England I had heard that he was
captured in France. I may be the only person who can identify him if the French are trying to slip an agent into the country."

"Then let me crew for you. I can handle *Zephyr* as well as
Tom, and I—"

"Unthinkable!" Robert said flatly. "Nothing would persuade me to run my sister into possible danger. I am leaving
Tom with you and taking Sim Upchurch as crew this trip."

"But Sim is not nearly as handy on the boat as Tom!"

"He is strong and willing, however, and I will have the
peace of mind of knowing Tom is here to take care of you
while I am away."

"Why should Tom have to take care of me?" she demanded, giving him the neatly folded shirt. Her pure green
eyes stared narrowly into a startlingly similar pair until his
shifted away.

Apart from the rare eye color they shared, there was little
family resemblance between brother and sister. Amy was
slender and scarcely of middle height with lightly tanned fair

skin and rich, chestnut-colored hair, while her brother was tall and strongly made, almost stocky, his sandy hair streaked with gold and his skin burned to a ruddy hue by the Iberian sun. Their speech held a similar cadence, and both displayed a tendency to illustrate their words with hand gestures—graceful on her part and forceful on his.

Robert turned to her now, his hesitation betraying his reluctance to reply. "These are dangerous times," he said at last. "If we have people in France, you may be assured that Bonaparte has agents here. You must not speak of this trip to anyone—anyone at all. I should be back within a sennight, but if anyone shows any curiosity about my whereabouts, tell them I've gone to London to visit my bootmaker—anything but the truth. Do you understand?"

"Y-yes. When do you leave?"

"Tonight. Tom will hide Pegasus after I have sailed so it will look as if I've gone off on horseback."

"Won't people notice that *Zephyr* is missing from her mooring?"

"I spent some time in a tavern on the quay in Rye this afternoon bemoaning the fact that I'd let myself be talked into lending her to a friend for a fortnight just as the weather is turning so beautiful. If you should be asked, the friend's name is Middleton. Remember that—and the identity of anyone who might seem curious about this subject."

Amy's eyes grew round, and fear rushed into her brain as she listened to her brother's instructions.

Robert broke into a grin. "Where is that vaunted spirit of yours?" he teased. "I'll be back before you have time to miss me, and you and I will make a bolt for the metropolis, shall we? We'll order you a new wardrobe and maybe look around for a house to hire for a few weeks for the little season. There are a number of my former schoolmates in town whose families will be happy to receive my sister."

"B-but we are still in mourning," Amy stammered.

"Now perhaps, but by the autumn we should be able to exchange visits at least. It will be a good way to ease you into something resembling a normal social life for girls your age.

At one-and-twenty you are already older than most of those making their comeout. Do you have enough money on hand?"

Amy blinked at the change of subject, her face a picture of confusion as her brother strapped his baggage together. "Money for what?"

"Emergencies . . . I don't know." He flung his hand out, palm up as she continued to stare at him; then he fisted his fingers and brought his hand to a pocket in his waistcoat from which he withdrew a small key that he held up to her eye level. "This is for the strongbox in my desk. All my papers are there, my solicitor's direction, some money."

When Amy made no move to take the key, he reached for her hand and placed it on her palm, closing her fingers around it. "I must go, my dear. Time and tide wait for no one, and there is still much to do before I sail. Do not look like that," he chided, holding her arms above the elbows and administering a gentle shake. "I'll be home within a fortnight at the latest, I promise."

She'd have clung to him then, but he put her aside after a quick embrace and strode to the door, catching up his pack as he circled the bed. "Wish me Godspeed," he commanded with a jaunty grin, "and no weeping, mind."

Her lips obediently formed the words, but no sound had come out by the time he vanished around the closing door. The hall carpet muffled his footsteps, but a gay snatch of whistling floated back to her straining ears.

Whistling! Amy frowned fiercely as a rush of anger ousted fear for the moment. He was heading off into deadly danger on what was most likely a fool's errand, and he was happy to be going! Men were stupid, insensitive clods who brought nothing but misery to the women who loved them! She balled her fists in impotent fury, then gasped at the sudden pain. She opened her hand, surprised to see that the key Robert had given her had bitten into the flesh.

As she eyed the offending piece of metal balefully, anger drained away to be replaced by a pervasive dread. All during his army service a sense of fear had dwelt in a corner of her mind, moving forward periodically when news of battles arrived in England, but Robert had been part of a large army then, surrounded by comrades undergoing the same experience. And she'd had her father's company throughout the period, plus his worsening physical condition to occupy her mind toward the end. In contrast, the present situation would be one of continual, stark, unrelieved fear for her brother's safety, compounded by the need to conceal his mission from everyone.

Over the next few moments, the initial paralyzing panic gradually subsided as Amy came to realize that she also was on a mission and hers was twofold: she must disguise her own fear by maintaining a posture of equanimity, and she must take every opportunity to throw sand in the eyes of anyone seeking to learn of Robert's whereabouts. Her expression was sombre as she began to pick up discarded garments and restore order to her brother's bedchamber. He had not gotten around to engaging a valet since selling out of the army, depending on his sister's supervision of the laundresses to care for his clothes and his own efforts to dress himself and keep his belongings in order in his quarters.

At the door she glanced one last time around the large chamber that had been her father's. Everything was neat once more, nothing out of place on top of the tall dresser and no wrinkles marring the smooth surface of the coverlet. The new bed curtains and window drapes she'd sewn before Robert's return from the Peninsula hung in soft folds, and the lovely old carpet with its faded tree of life design was free of lint.

Her nerves jangled as her eyes lighted on the strongbox key lying on the bedside table, and she darted across the room to snatch it up. How could she have forgotten that she had laid it down in order to smooth the coverlet with both hands? A fine chatelaine she'd make if she could not even keep track of a vital object for fifteen minutes!

Amy hurried down the hall to her own room, feeling woefully inadequate for the role thrust upon her. By the time she had locked Robert's key away in her grandmother's leather jewel casket and buried that key in a jar of potpourri on her writing table, however, she felt some faint stirring of her intellect again. After examining her countenance closely in the glass over the dressing table, she was relieved to find that the recent ordeal had thus far left no visible signs on her face. She dusted a few clinging petals from her fingers and tucked a couple of straying strands of hair back into the neat coil at the back of her head. She straightened her shoulders and took a deep sustaining breath in preparation for donning a carefree persona.

As Amy made her way to the kitchens, the house felt oddly unfamiliar, echoing with even greater emptiness than during the weeks following her father's death while she had awaited her brother's return. She increased her pace, comforted to hear the chatter of the kitchen maids cleaning up in the scullery as she headed for the housekeeper's room.

She knocked briskly, lifted her chin and poked her head around the door. "Sorry to disturb you, Mrs. Fenton—oh, good, you are here too, Fenton," she said directing a smile at the butler, who was enjoying a cup of tea with his wife. "No, do sit down, both of you. I just wanted to let you know that my brother has gone to London for a few days, so you need not bother setting out any meats with breakfast. A coddled egg and toast will be fine for me."

She was pleased that her voice sounded completely normal in her own ears, but was instantly on guard when the buxom, gray-haired housekeeper said in surprise, "Gone off, has he? Did Tom Watkins go with him? I haven't laid eyes on that one since breakfast this morning. He was supposed to do some weeding in the kitchen garden today."

"No, Tom hasn't gone with Mr. Robert," she replied, improvising rapidly, "but I believe he's been doing various errands for my brother all day. I will help with the weeding tomorrow."

"No, that you won't, Miss Amy," Mrs. Fenton declared with all the authority of an old servitor who had helped raise her employers from the cradle. "You'll be ruining your complexion and your hands with all that gardening. If your granny could see you now as brown as a field hand, and dirt under your fingernails, I'll be bound, she'd turn over in her grave, she would."

"And sit me down inside sewing samplers all summer into the bargain," Amy agreed with a rueful smile that masked her relief in getting safely past the question of Tom's activities today.

"I'm thinking somewhere in the stillroom there might still be some of that lotion she used to make up. She swore by its bleaching properties for the skin. I'll search it out for you, tomorrow, dearie."

"Thank you, Mrs. Fenton. I promise to wear a hat now that the sun is heating up. Good night, good night, Fenton. I'm going to read in the library for a while before going to bed."

"Now don't you go ruining your eyes reading all hours by candlelight. Nothing good ever came from too much reading—it addles the brain, my old mother always said."

"I will use a good lamp, Mrs. Fenton. Good night." Amy whisked herself out the door before her self-appointed guardian proposed tucking her into bed, but tonight she welcomed the feeling of normalcy and security that accompanied the dear soul's fussing.

The Fentons had been fixtures in her life from earliest recollection, and she bore them great affection. After her grandmother died and Robert went into the army, many of her happiest hours were spent in the kitchen and stillroom learning every aspect of domestic management under the housekeeper's patient—and garrulous—tutelage. Perhaps the proudest moment of her life occurred the day Mrs. Fenton declared that her pupil's apple pie had eclipsed her own for perfection of form and flavor. Certainly she could not recall Grand-mère bestowing any such heartfelt accolades on her performance on the pianoforte or for her skill with her needle. Praise from her grandmother had been sparing—even grudging would not be too strong a description—and was nearly always accompanied by a qualification or outright caveat that diluted the satisfaction she might have felt in the original compliment.

Her grandmother had been a woman of strong character and equally strong prejudices. She had embraced a code of the strictest morality and duty but was not equally fervent about forgiving the trespasses of others. Sinners in search of pardon or mercy would have to seek it from a higher authority. She had formed no cordial bonds among the local populace in all the years she lived in Kent, and though respected for her good works, was not liked personally. Amy had always found it sad that her grandmother held no affections, preferences or enjoyments in any comparable degree of pleasure to the intensity of her dislikes and prejudices.

Immersed in a reflective humor on entering the library, Amy did not immediately act on her stated intention of reading. Her eyes were drawn to the fireplace where a cheerful little fire burned, though the evening was mild. She wondered if the blaze was evidence that Fenton had been unaware of his master's intention to go away. Of course Robert might have told his butler something of his plan. Fenton might have decided that a fire would add cheer to her lonely hours in the shabby but comfortable room where she and Robert spent most of their evenings together reading or playing chess. In any event, though not cold, she was grateful for the comfort implied by a fire, and she pulled a wingback chair a little closer to the fireplace.

She was still sitting in the same spot when the tall case clock in the corner chimed a quarter past midnight, though she was no longer making any pretense of reading. She'd sent Fenton to bed an hour earlier after permitting him to lock up the house, but she'd unlocked the French doors leading out to the rose garden once the butler's footsteps had faded.

She heard the soft tap on the glass and flew out of her chair, reaching the doors just as they opened to admit a tall, massively built young man who snatched off the cap covering a shock of straw-colored hair.

"Well?" she demanded before the young giant could speak.

"Mr. Robert sailed on the evening tide." His speech was soft and very deliberate, almost faltering.

"Did anyone take any notice of *Zephyr* when she left?"

"She was already away from her mooring at Rye Harbour so's I could paint her trim this week over in the cove near Sim Upchurch's place. I didn't see anybody around when she sailed."

"The tide was hours ago. Where have you been, Tom?"

"I was bringing Pegasus somewheres he won't be seen for the next while."

"Come over to the fire and get warm. I haven't scattered it yet. Where did you hide Pegasus?"

Amy had gone back to her chair before Tom emerged from the shadowed area near the doors and edged closer to the fireplace. He kept his face averted as he replied, "Mr. Rob said best you not know, Miss Amy; then you won't have to tell lies."

"Hah! He didn't seem to mind me telling a lot of lies about this . . . situation from his instructions before he left."

"I promised, Miss Amy." He turned toward her in his earnestness and the reason for his earlier reticence now became apparent. Tom Watkins possessed only half a face in the strictest sense, for almost the entire right side consisted of luridly colored scar tissue. There was no eyebrow on that side, and his right eye was half-enclosed in a web of tissue. Likewise, his mouth was pulled down and scarred in a way that made it evident that it must require a Herculean effort to enunciate intelligibly. To come upon him suddenly would be to receive a shock that no amount of discipline could disguise. The tenderest heart must recoil in revulsion initially. Amy had witnessed small children run screaming from his presence. Fifteen years ago she had done the same on encountering him for the first time in the village.

It was many years since she could recall any of those feelings about Tom Watkins. They had been replaced by tremendous admiration and respect for the courage and endless patience with which he met both deliberate and unthinking cruelty from the greater portion of humanity. He possessed a natural dignity and a generosity of spirit that would always be an example to all with whom he came into contact. The integrity of his character was manifest in all his actions, and she would trust him with her life, as her brother obviously did.

"You have been engaged on this business from dawn, Tom. You must be starving as well as tired. Come into the kitchen and I'll find you something to eat."

"Thank you, Miss Amy, but I had a bite before I stabled Pegasus. I'll be glad to get to bed, and that's a fact." A weary half smile distorted his features further. "There is one more thing though . . ."

"Yes?" Amy inquired, biting the bullet, for his hesitation told her the "one more thing" would not be to her liking.

"Mr. Rob said I was to go wherever you go and not to let you out of my sight while he's away. He said to tell you this is an order."

Tom's speech was always difficult to comprehend, and because he had hurried in his eagerness to get the task behind him, it took Amy a moment to grasp the full import of her brother's command.

"That's ridiculous," she exploded in due course, fixing a furious stare on the unfortunate soul her brother had designated as her keeper. "I am not a child to require a nursemaid, nor some fine London lady who never stirs outside her house without a bewigged footman in attendance! A fine ninny I'd look in the village with you tailing after me into Mrs. Carey's dry goods shop. Robert must have hit his head on a spar! The last thing we desire is to draw attention to my actions while he is gone. Well, never mind, Tom," she added with a kind smile for the patiently suffering servant. "We'll just assume my brother did not think the situation through. No doubt his mind was so focused on his mission that he couldn't concentrate on anything else. You go to bed now. I will scatter this fire."

She suited her action to her words and bent to her task, her ears at the stretch for the sound of the door closing—an event for which she waited in vain. Not one to give up easily, she drew the fire screen across the opening and dusted her hands together before turning at last to face the silent man.

"Good night, Tom," she said pointedly.

"I promised, Miss Amy."

The simple words and the man's dogged and weary presence doused the flames of her temper. "Very well," she said on a sigh. "Go to bed. I will see you in the morning."

"Yes, ma'am. Good night, Miss Amy."

Amy watched his quiet departure, aware that his broad-shouldered form had a decided droop to it after what must have been an extraordinarily long and difficult day. Her expression was penitent as she tucked her book under her arm and took up the lamp after extinguishing the candles on the big mahogany desk purchased by her long deceased grandfather. Her besetting sins had always been a quick flaring temper allied with an intemperate tongue. Her grandmother's strictures had fallen on deaf ears, despite the many punishments imposed to correct these faults over the years.

Amy liked to think her basic nature was rational and trusted that she was never so blinded by temper that she failed to see the reason in others' arguments or decisions. Fortunately, she was not too proud to apologize for her shortcomings, but she must still be a sore trial to those with her best interests at heart. She acknowledged this with regret as she entered her bedchamber in a chastened mood and with little expectation of true repose.

Amy stood gazing out her bedroom window, her face a study of indecision. Should she or shouldn't she go through with her plan? If only she could be sure it would do no harm.

Robert had been gone for six days. She reminded herself repeatedly that she had no reasonable expectation of hearing anything in the interim, but she was finding the constant need to project an image of untroubled complaisance while wracked by anxiety to be a trial beyond bearing—at least beyond bearing with good grace. She had caught herself being short with the servants on more than one occasion, and she prayed for patience during the restless hours before dropping into a numbed sleep from which she arose unrefreshed. The most innocuous intercourse with those around her set her teeth on edge as she held onto her temper with hard-won patience. She had no desire for the most ordinary human contact; she begrudged the effort required to perform her share of the social contract.

Tom was the only person with whom she could share her fears and drop her guard, but there was scant relief in this. The day after her brother's departure, she and Tom had reached the unsatisfactory conclusion that both were too well known in the area to seek information about *Zephyr* lest their interest should reach the wrong ears, especially when neither had any idea of whose were the wrong ears. Rye had long been a center of smuggling activity, and its citizens historically had a strong connection to the sea. The war with France had bolstered the government's sporadic attempts to suppress the smuggling trade that had lately been consolidated into a land guard as well as a naval blockade with a strong presence in Rye.

As the dreary days had crawled past, the enforced inactivity frayed at Amy's temper while the unregulated mental exercises, speculation and abortive planning that went on in her head resulted in a frenzied desire to do something to further Robert's cause or at least confuse any shadowy enemies.

Each day Tom asked her if she desired to do any errands or make any visits in the neighborhood, and each day she replied in the negative, still resentful at having to accept his discreet but unwelcome oversight. This morning she had again expressed her disinclination to leave the house but told him she had an appointment with a dressmaker in Rye for the next day.

Neither statement had been true. Many fruitless hours of cogitation had produced only one idea that might be useful, but she knew Tom would object. It would be necessary, therefore, to give her faithful watchdog the slip in order to execute her plan.

She told herself that a little guilt at deceiving Tom was a small price to pay for the only chance to learn if there were any rumors circulating concerning her brother's expedition. Taking a deep breath, she walked over to the dressing table and examined the figure in the mirror with some confidence.

Gone was Miss Amy Cole, daughter of this or any house. Looking back at her was a slim youth dressed in well-worn breeches topped by a neat blue jacket and a belcher neckerchief. Heavy stockings and shoes were obviously country-made. The garments had belonged to her brother at varying times during his school days, and this was not the first time she had appropriated them for ease in tramping about the marsh in solitude when her life with her father had become trying. Today was the first time she would be trusting the garments to disguise her sex in public, however. She had pinned her hair securely atop her head, and now she pulled on a peaked cap of brown corduroy at a jaunty angle. She revolved slowly, trying to judge her appearance through objective eyes. At least a casual inspection should reveal an ordinary youth—beardless but ordinary, she concluded hopefully as she turned toward the door.

She had pleaded a headache after her meeting with Tom and told Mrs. Fenton not to send up any lunch to her room. With a little luck she would be back before dinnertime without her absence being discovered.

Amy had no difficulty effecting an invisible departure from the house and grounds, using a grove of trees to put distance between herself and Tom Watkins. The fact that she could not saddle her horse or take out a carriage without his knowledge had stymied her at first, but Rye was less than four miles away if she kept to the coast paths, a distance that held no challenge for someone accustomed to following an older brother around for long hours on end.

Amy set off at a brisk pace, aware of cool clean air that wafted a sensation of blessed freedom with it, despite the anxiety that had taken up residence in her heart.

Chapter Two

At the height of mackerel season, emptying the Kettle nets resulted in carpeting the foreshore with thousands of the wriggling silver-toned fish, as if a giant sea god had pulled back the ocean bed and unrolled it again, spilling its treasures onto the land. The spectacle generally attracted a crowd of gawkers, mostly youths and idlers from the town. A holiday atmosphere prevailed, not surprising on a glorious summer day that would have poets reaching for their pens and their similes. A light breeze off the water swept the skies clear of clouds, leaving a dazzling azure firmament to grace this little corner of creation.

The fishermen, dealing with nets and harvest with long-practiced efficiency, ignored the gratuitous advice of those with nothing better to do and the noisy horseplay of the youngsters. But when the boys snatched up fish and threw them at each other, this behavior prompted growls from the fishermen, driving the boys back temporarily.

In this scene of diverse busyness one figure stood out from the rest by virtue of his stillness. Atop the dunes above the beach a man sat on the back of a magnificent chestnut stallion, watching the activity below. None of the scene's bustling animation seemed to find an echo in the horseman who might have been a statue erected on the spot. His thin cheeks and aquiline profile might have been cast in bronze.

Only his eyes held life as they embraced all details of the lively pantomime below, from the squirming sea of silver fins to the antics of the rowdy boys and the scattering of idlers, some of whom were engaged in a brief exchange with a youth in a brown cap. That lad detached himself from the group presently and moved off toward Rye without a glance at the other boys, his determined stride soon reducing him to a small speck in the distance when next the rider glanced down the beach.

After several moments of immobility the chestnut grew restless and tossed his head in the breeze. "Sorry, boy," the rider said, patting his strong neck, "let's go down. Easy now, you can do it," he added when the stallion took exception to the shifting terrain. Aware that their arrival on the hard-packed shore had attracted all eyes, Sir Jason Archer swept a neutral glance over the interested spectators and said, nodding toward the heap of slithery creatures, "Quite a haul. Is it always this good?"

"In high season," said one loafer.

"You must be a stranger to these parts," another observed.

Sir Jason admitted he was indeed a stranger, and found that he was now the chief object of interest at the scene, or at least second to Samson. The interrogation that ensued elicited the chestnut's history and lineage from his owner. The horse's good nature was amply demonstrated by the patience with which he endured the pats and attentions of a half dozen eager boys.

Into this amiable encounter Sir Jason ventured a few casual questions of his own. Was this cove close to Rye? He was assured that Rye Harbour was a short way farther along and the town proper on top of the rock. Nobody could miss Ypres Tower which had stood squarely on the Rock of Rye for hundreds of years. Did all those gathered around the mackerel catch reside in the town, he wondered audibly and discovered that all but two of the men and one lad lived outside of Rye. Could anyone recommend a decent inn? It seemed every man jack could, sparking a lively, not to say contentious discussion of the merits of several hostelries until someone with a discerning eye commented on the quality of the stranger's clothing and the beaver hat he sported. Instantly the George became the unanimous choice of his advisers.

Sir Jason thanked them gravely and remarked that he was hoping to find an old friend in Rye, a Mr. Armand Martin who had a slight foreign accent and might be accompanied by a lady with green eyes and reddish brown hair. Two among the helpful citizens offered up a Josiah Martin and a Will Martin but admitted that they spoke the King's English like everybody else. All denied knowing any green-eyed ladies; in fact, some voiced doubts of the existence of green eyes in humans of any persuasion.

"Well, if that don't beat all—and here's that young'un what just left not more'n ten minutes since with eyes as green as grass," exclaimed a tall reedy fellow with a missing front tooth and a head of coarse ginger-hued hair that curled around his ears.

This claim was greeted with jeers and reminders that the claimant, referred to by his naysayers as Felix, had called Sukie Symms's hair yellow also, when anyone who had two good eyes and wasn't loony over the girl could see it was as dull a shade as a wren's breast.

Sensing that there was material here for an extended debate, Sir Jason proceeded to detach himself from the group with repeated thanks for all information, initiating a chorus of expressions of mutual goodwill on all sides.

The amiable expression Sir Jason had shown to those on the shore faded the instant he turned his back on them and directed Samson toward Rye Harbour. His face was set like flint, his eyes dark gray stones in a taut, sun-browned visage. He might have weighed in on Felix's side back there, he thought, his mouth twisting into a bitter line. Who better than he could testify that eyes "as green as grass" did indeed exist—though he had once likened them to emeralds.

"Idiot!" He must have uttered the epithet aloud, for Samson turned his head and whickered a bit in response.

"Not you, boy—your fool of a master," he explained, patting the stallion's long mane. Only a fool or a schoolboy in the throes of calf love could have been so completely taken in by a pair of cool green eyes and a vulnerable air of a lost little girl. At thirty, he was well past his school days, and he had never considered himself a fool, even at his most callow stage.

That was before he met Désirée Ryder of course.

The sunshine, the balmy, sea-scented breeze and the soothing rhythm of the tidal movement were all lost on Sir Jason whose ears and eyes were directed on internal scenes, none of them pleasant if the rigid set of his jaw was any indication.

Even someone as self-absorbed as Sir Jason could not ignore the looming gray presence of a stone tower as he approached the harbor area in the marsh below what was obviously the town of Rye. He was aware that Rye had been one of the Cinque Ports that constituted England's eastern defenses in bygone days and recognized that this must have been one of the old Martello Towers erected back in Norman times. Since he obviously wasn't going to get Samson up the steep flight of steps leading to the tower area, he cast an eye about the harbor, looking for a path that would lead upward.

There were a number of boats moored near the quay and plenty of activity going on around them. He made a mental note of a tavern on the quay, a logical place to inquire for Martin and Désirée, if as he suspected, they were planning to leave the country.

Movement on the periphery of his vision brought his head around to include a slender figure crossing from the quay to the steps. Something about the boy seemed familiar. As Sir Jason narrowed his eyes on the brown cap, he had his answer. It was the youth who had been talking to the men in the cove earlier, the lad with eyes "as green as grass" according to the man called Felix.

"Wait, boy!" Sir Jason called, giving way to a sudden impulse. He urged Samson toward the stairs, pulling up just as the youth, who had already begun his ascent, stopped and looked over his shoulder.

For the space of one harsh, indrawn breath, Sir Jason stared into a pair of wide green eyes nearly on a level with his own. By the time he'd summoned up a voice, he was staring at the boy's back as he streaked up the steps. His "Stop!" was ignored by the youth but caused some interest in a couple of men exiting the quay, who looked his way.

Jason flung himself off the stallion's back and, sparing a thought for his belongings in two saddlebags, thrust the reins at the nearest man. "Here, hold my horse for a few minutes. You won't lose by it, I promise you." Still in the grip of an irresistible impulse, he set off at speed up the steps after the fleeing youth.

Ten minutes later, Sir Jason acknowledged defeat and started back down to the harbor, his rapid breathing slowly returning to normal as he marveled at the speed of his youthful quarry. By the time he'd reached the top, the lad had disappeared into one of the narrow hilly streets of the town—or perhaps into a building where he could remain out of sight until his pursuer gave up the chase. When Jason had asked an old man in the square if he had seen the boy, the dotard had acted as if he were deaf or demented.

Sir Jason sighed with relief to see Samson at the foot of the steps, still wearing his saddlebags. He hurried down the last few and pressed a crown into the outstretched hand of the horse minder, at the same time discreetly feeling the offside saddlebag, which seemed full, hopefully of his possessions. He thanked the man and listened carefully to the Sussex version of English directing horse and rider to the George Inn.

It was long past midnight when Sir Jason finally sought his bed at the inn. He had learned in the last fortnight that simple tiredness was no guarantee of sleep. Unless wearied to the point of exhaustion, his brain refused to shut down and permit his body to restore itself. Likewise he had learned that the nature of his quest demanded that he seek out the company of others, though his frame of mind was such that human society was anathema to him of late. Again today during an afternoon stroll that had acquainted him with the town and an evening devoted to eating and drinking, he had assumed an air of conviviality and initiated a number of elaborately casual rituals of acquaintance designed to elicit information. He had honed his techniques with practice and developed patience in pursuit of knowledge, still hoping to avoid scandal if possible. He had also paid for a lot of drinks for habitués of taverns along the way and learned to limit his own consumption of spirits without appearing to do so.

Again today his exhausting efforts had produced no positive results. Désirée and the Frenchman had not been noticed in Rye's environs. He would try Dover next, but not quite yet.

He had told himself it was vital to get his laundry done, which was true, and he'd made arrangements with a laundress this afternoon. He'd been dirtier on countless occasions in Portugal with no laundresses to be found, which might account for his current appreciation of clean linen and brushed leathers. The question of laundry aside, however, he could not deny that his decision to remain another day in Rye had been made the instant he had lost sight of the elusive youth with eyes every bit as green as Désirée's.

Even now, many hours after the event, he could still summon up the shocked sensation that he was looking at Désirée's face when the boy had turned his head. And he had not mistaken the fear that had leapt into those eyes when they met his. He would take his oath that his instinct to seize the boy had been correct, only not quick enough. He'd sat there stunned a moment too long. Tonight during his perambulations from tavern to tavern he'd hoped to spot one of the men who had talked to the lad this morning so that he might question his identity, but here also he had been unsuccessful.

Jason almost fell into the sturdy bed provided by the George, thankful for the fresh scent of clean cool linen as he stretched aching limbs and sought a comfortable position for sleeping. As on every other night of this hellish odyssey, thoughts of a green-eyed temptress immediately filled his tired brain to bursting.

Désirée claimed she was the only child of a French mother and a British father, but Désirée had told him other things that had turned out to be untrue—that she loved him, for one. Instinct told him her resemblance to the strange boy was too strong to be coincidental; this must be a brother, a younger brother. Had he been away at school when they met this spring? Why lie about it in any case? He had been besotted enough to willingly take on the care of a dependent sibling.

Numb with the effort of pursuing yet another profitless line of speculation, Jason tossed and thrashed about until sleep finally overtook his weary body in the hours just before dawn.

Amy barely got home in time to scramble out of her masculine costume before one of the maids knocked on her door to see if she required assistance in dressing for dinner.

"Is your headache better, Miss Amy?" the girl asked, looking sympathetically at her flustered mistress.

"Much better, thank you, Minnie," she lied, aware of a steady beating in her temples as she closed the door of the armoire where she had just tossed the garments she'd worn in Rye. "Perhaps you might brush my hair for me if you have time."

Looking pleased, the maid bustled about, pulling the chair out from the dressing table with an inviting gesture. She glanced at the scattered pins on the tabletop. "Were you trying to arrange your hair yourself, Miss Amy?" she asked innocently, taking up a brush.

"Yes," Amy replied, piling lie upon lie, "but I think I will merely have you tie it at the nape for tonight, Minnie. My scalp is still a little tender."

That at least was the truth, she thought with a sigh, settling onto the chair. After many hours with her hair being tethered by numerous pins, her tortured scalp delighted in the gentle brushing motion. After a few minutes she felt her nerves and muscles relaxing for the first time in hours.

At first she had enjoyed her break for freedom this morning, physically delighting in the exercise as she strode down the beach, the sea breeze cooling her cheeks. She had been a bit nervous about keeping her voice husky and was relieved that no one she spoke to looked at her suspiciously, and that she had managed to stay away from a group of youngsters who might have seen through her disguise.

As far as her mission was concerned, however, she soon discovered that it was beyond her capabilities to lead an offhand conversation around to the subject of smuggling, spies or the coastal blockade. She never got past a few comments on the state of the fishing industry. Happily, there were no reports current about any missing boats, and she decided to go into Rye and buy a meat pie to eat on the way home.

She'd had plenty of time on the harrowing trip home to relive and try to make sense of the brief encounter with a stranger who had sent her fleeing in panic—hours to analyze an incident that had lasted a second or two at most.

There had been no premonition of danger when she had turned at a hail just as she was leaving the harbor area, but danger was what she had seen in the fierce black eyes of an unknown horseman. At the time she had fled instinctively, aware of nothing save mindless terror, and no amount of rationalization once she'd escaped had persuaded her that her panic was self-induced or inappropriate to the situation.

She had hidden behind a barrel in an alley for uncounted minutes, not stirring until long after she'd seen her pursuer walk past the alley on his way back toward the Baddyng steps leading to the quay. Even when her heartbeat had returned to normal and her nerves had quietened, she had been reluctant to leave her dirty sanctuary. Every step had required an act of courage until she had left the town behind. There was no question of returning along the shore. He must have come the same way she had; she had a vague recollection of a horse above the beach with the fish. Even going the long way home by the road was frightening, given that the man was mounted. She had not ceased looking over her shoulder until a farmer came along and offered to take her on his wagon for part of the way.

Who was the man, and why had he hailed her? Did he know who she was? He'd called her "boy," but if he had not suspected her, why chase after her, leaving his horse down in the harbor? Was he a French agent waiting to waylay Robert on his return with his friend? He was dark enough to be foreign, and his skin was burned even browner than that of the fishermen of the area. Amy shivered at the thought as she had each time it had popped into her head this afternoon.

"Is something wrong, Miss Amy? Did I brush too hard?"

"No, no, Minnie. It was quite soothing actually. I believe there is a black ribbon in the drawer over there if you will just tie it back now."

Amy thanked the maid and walked downstairs with her to the dining room where she ate another solitary meal. Having missed lunch and expended considerable energy during the day, she did full justice to the kitchen's offerings and gratified Mrs. Fenton into the bargain. That good woman would have been less pleased had she known that the young mistress was merely putting food into her mouth indiscriminately to satisfy hunger while her brain continued to wrestle with the mystery of the day's events.

Her first reaction on reaching home safely had been to cancel her plan to return to Rye on the morrow. Though it seemed far-fetched, the frightening horseman may have suspected she was Robert's sister, in which case it would be folly to go back to Rye as herself. The proposed trip was unnecessary in any case. She had invented an appointment with a dressmaker for tomorrow to throw Tom Watkins off the scent of her plans for today, which had worked, at least from this standpoint. She had learned nothing, but no news was certainly preferable to rumors of missing boats, she assured herself.

Amy spent the evening in the library, alternately pacing about the room and sitting with an open but unread book in her lap while debate raged in her head. As the minutes and hours ticked by until Tom would appear with his nightly summation of events on the estate, the scales began to tip in favor of returning to Rye. She had never seen the horseman before, of that she was certain. That hawkish countenance was not one she would have forgotten. If she had never seen him, then he could not have seen her before either; ergo, it was safe to appear in Rye in feminine dress. The fact that she would be dressed in black gave her an additional sense of security since people tended to overlook those in mourning. The definitive argument for keeping to her plans was the consideration that accompanying her would give Tom a reason for being in town and provide him with an opportunity to put his ear to the ground also.

The long hours outdoors had taken their toll on her muscles and her spirit, and she longed for her bed. Thankfully, Tom arrived by half after ten.

"I hope you are feeling better, Miss Amy," he said upon entering through the French doors. His obvious sympathy elicited another guilty pang for her continued deception.

"Yes, thank you, Tom," she said, mustering up a smile. "Did anything of moment happen today?"

"No, ma'am. I went over to exercise Pegasus earlier this evening. He's lonely but in good condition."

They spoke quietly for another minute or so and settled on a time for the drive to Rye.

When Tom left, Amy trudged upstairs, still chasing after something niggling at the back of her mind about the horseman. As she blew out her candle and slipped between the sheets it came to her in a disquieting flash. She had seen and reacted to the ferocity of the man's expression, but there had been something else that had registered fleetingly on her senses at the same time: he had looked dangerous indeed, but he had also looked like a man who had just received a shock. She could make nothing of this as she lay in her bed, where, to her dismay, she spent another restless night despite being exhausted.

*   *   *

Tom Watkins put Amy down in Mermaid Street in front of the dressmaker's. "I will put the gig in the livery stable and come back to wait for you, Miss Amy."

"By all means, leave the gig at the stables, Tom, but I will not have you standing outside Clothilde's like a jailor," Amy said firmly. "I shall be here at least an hour. Go and have yourself a meal." She pressed money into his reluctant hand. "I mean it," she repeated, hardening her heart against his unhappy expression.

He ducked his head and the gig started forward at a snail's pace. When he looked back over his shoulder, she made an impatient shooing motion with her hand before turning to go into the shop.

As it turned out, Clothilde was engaged with a customer. Feeling as if she had been reprieved, Amy told the modiste she would be back in a few minutes and quickly backed out of the shop. Aware that she had been sharp with poor Tom and that the headache with which she had awakened was still present, she decided on the spur of the moment to slip into the church in the hope of achieving a feeling of peace and balance.

She set out at a brisk pace, bowed to an acquaintance on the other side of the street and hurried around the corner to avoid being drawn into a conversation. The result of this maneuvering was a minor collision with someone coming the other way. Her lips parted to apologize as she looked up—straight into the dark burning eyes that had panicked her yesterday on the quay. She lowered her gaze quickly and tried to brazen it out.

"I beg your pardon, sir," she began, taking a step to the side to get around him.

"And so you should, for a number of reasons, my dear Désirée," he said with cold composure, blocking her path, which brought her head up again in protest. "Why did you not tell me you had a brother?"

"You have obviously confused me with someone else. We do not know each other. Please let me pass," she insisted, giving him stare for stare now as her temper threatened to ignite.

He laughed harshly. "Well, part of that nonsense is true; you certainly do not know me if you imagined you could hide by tricking yourself out in mourning and browning your complexion like a gypsy—not with those green eyes. Where is he? It is time I met your lover." He reached for her arm.

"Sir, you are clearly deranged!" Amy gasped, pulling back from his hand, "but since you have the appearance at least of a gentleman, I shall warn you just once that if you lay a hand on me I shall scream very loudly. There are a number of citizens on the street, as you can see. I am known in this town and I shall be believed. Do not come near me again!" She spun around and headed back the way she had come, but his stage whisper was perfectly audible.

"You'll see me again very shortly."

Amy looked back before going into Clothilde's shop, shuddering in relief when the figure rounding the corner turned out to be a ragged-looking boy, not a dark commanding lunatic. She would be safe here until Tom came for her. If only the throbbing in her temples would go away.

Amy would have been less sanguine about her safety had she been privileged to spy on the "lunatic's" activities after she left him fuming on the pavement.

Sir Jason's anger stopped short of inviting scandal, but his determination remained undiminished by her intransigence. She had scarcely achieved the corner when he caught the arm of a passing youth. Holding up two crown pieces, he said, "One now, one later. Follow the young lady in black who just went around this corner. Tell me where she goes. I'll be in the stables of the posting inn on the next street."

Sir Jason moved off on the words, running ideas through his head as he strode into the stables. He sent an ostler off to the George to pay his bill and bring his saddlebags, now full of clean linen, to the stables. By the time his arrangements were set in motion the eager-eyed youth had returned with the lady's location.

Sir Jason produced another coin and promised more if the boy reported when the lady left the shop and the direction she took. There was one additional preparation he needed to make that entailed a visit to an apothecary. He set off on this errand, still working out his plans. As he waited for his purchase a few minutes later he frowned in concentration as a major objection presented itself. Considering her defiance of him just now, there was no likelihood that Désirée would get into the carriage with him without creating a scene that would make him a laughingstock even though his will would prevail in the end. Likewise, the sight of Samson tied to a chaise would alert her to his presence.

While puzzling over a solution, he happened to overhear an exchange between the clerk and a woman standing a few feet away. Apparently she did not have enough money with her to pay for her purchase, and the clerk refused to trust her for the rest. Jason swept an assessing eye over the woman's rather flashy clothing and over-rouged cheeks. The beginning of a plan formulated in his brain, and he plunked some money down on the counter in front of the clerk. "Allow me, madam," he said softly, touching his hat.

"Thank you, I'm sure," the middle-aged female said, favoring Sir Jason with a coy smile and then turning on the clerk with a disdainful sniff. "Now, that is my idea of a true gen'lman, unlike some I could mention."

The clerk regarded her stonily as he handed over the package. She turned a haughty shoulder and flounced out. Sir Jason paid for his order and followed the woman, catching her up within a few yards. It was worth a try, he decided, smiling at her and doffing his hat.

"Ma'am, I wonder if I might impose upon your good nature for a moment?"

"Go ahead," she invited.

"I find myself with a problem of a delicate nature . . . concerning my wife," he added when the woman stiffened and her eyes hardened, "and it occurred to me that you might be willing to assist me in the matter . . . for a consideration. . . ."

"What kind of consideration?"

"Twenty pounds," he replied, encouraged that her preeminent interest was in finance rather than his problem.

"And what is the nature of your problem?" she inquired.

He took heart from the avid gleam in her eyes and launched into a tale. "My wife and I had been married only a short time when a minor disagreement escalated into a quarrel that resulted in my bride's returning to her mother's house. I came here hoping to resolve the issue and take her back with me. Do you agree that a woman's place is with her husband, Mrs. . . . ?"

"Mrs. Greyson," the lady supplied. "Yes, of course a wife's place is with her husband."

"Unfortunately, my mother-in-law would not agree with us. She is a widow, and my wife is her only child. She delights in having her back under her roof. I believe she has intercepted my letters to my wife and destroyed them. She has refused to admit me over the doorstep or even permit me to see my wife."

"Tsk, tsk, selfish, that's what she is, coming between man and wife for 'er own comfort." Mrs. Greyson shook her head, dislodging a fall of brassy-hued curls over her forehead from beneath an enormous straw hat.

"I have a post chaise waiting to take my bride home, but I fear she would not get in it if I asked her, so—"

"She wouldn't get in with you even to talk it over?"

"I fear not. I bumped into her on the street a while ago, and she would not speak with me."

Mrs. Greyson's shrewd brown eyes studied his set face and averted gaze. After a moment, she said, "So, if I understand you rightly, my job would be to lure your little bride into this post chaise for you?"

Uncomfortable at this unvarnished description of his request, Jason hesitated briefly, then slammed the door on scruples and regrets. "You are very perceptive, Mrs. Greyson. That is it in a nutshell. Will you do it?"

She nodded. "I'll take half of that 'consideration' now if

you please, sir, to show good faith, and the rest when I deliver your bride to you."

After inspecting the ten pound note he proffered, Mrs. Greyson stuck out a lace-mittened hand that Sir Jason solemnly shook to seal their bargain.

Chapter Three

While Sir Jason was seeing to the final details of his brazen plan, Amy was concluding her business with the dressmaker. Having taken shelter in Clothilde's shop, she had felt constrained to order something to avoid the necessity of explaining her reluctance to leave the premises. Her wardrobe was soon to be enlarged by the acquisition of a new driving dress of half-mourning for later in the summer. Clothilde had enthused over a leghorn straw bonnet she'd noticed in the milliner's window a few doors up on the other side of the street.

"Tiny lavender roses round the crown it has, Miss Cole, that would look a treat with your new gown. Why not pop over to have a look?"

Amy stole a peek at the watch pinned to her dress, and her nerves jumped to note that there was still more than half an hour to wait before she could expect to see Tom. To conceal her agitation, she walked slowly to the front of the shop and glanced out at the street. A woman walked by holding a little girl by the hand, and two youths loitered on a step across the street. All seemed very normal and unthreatening.

"Not that way, Miss Cole. Back up the hill. You cannot see it from here, but you must know the place. The Fuller sisters have run it for ten or twelve years," Clothilde said from just behind her, causing Amy to start.

"Oh, yes, of course. It had slipped my mind. Well, thank you, Clothilde. I'll be on my way now." Amy left the shop on lagging feet and crossed the street, noting that one of the boys from the step ran off as she approached. Her confidence returned as she neared the milliner's shop. There were always people circulating about the town. The man who had accosted her would not dare to force himself upon her notice again. She was being henhearted to wish for the sight of Tom's unsightly face.

Amy pulled up in front of the hat shop, delight chasing away nerves. Clothilde had not been exaggerating. The hat was perfect for the new gown. For that matter, it would complement most gowns and enhance the appearance of most females.

Ten minutes later she exited the shop, bandbox in hand. The hat provided an excuse to return to the dressmaker's. She would model it for Clothilde and see it beside the fabric they'd chosen for her gown. Then she would casually announce that she might as well wait for her servant there.

Amy was heading back toward the dressmaker's when a post chaise came up the hill and pulled over to the pavement on the narrow street. As she walked past, the window in the chaise came down and a square-faced matron in an appalling hat appeared in the opening and beckoned to her.

"I wonder if I might ask your assistance," the lady said, displaying large teeth in a smile.

"How may I help you, ma'am?" Amy asked politely, stepping up to the window.

"It's very addlepated of me, but I've never gotten the hang of reading a map properly," the matron confessed. "I thought Edgemere Street was in this quarter, but I am sure we have been going in circles." She shrugged, producing a large creased paper. This she thrust toward Amy who took it unthinkingly in one hand. As she bent to lay her bandbox on the ground, the matron protested, "Oh, you must not dirty your box on my account. Here, come sit inside for a minute while you show me where we are." She brushed aside Amy's demurs. "No, no, I insist. You are being so very obliging."

As she spoke, the woman opened the carriage door and moved over, indicating the other bench with another toothy smile.

Good manners warred with disinclination and triumphed. Amy handed in the bandbox and climbed up into the chaise, assisted by the postilion who suddenly appeared at her elbow and closed the door after her. She glanced in surprise from the door to the woman who seemed absorbed in opening out the paper to its full size. Amy cleared her throat and admitted, "I do not believe I recall an Edgemere Street, ma'am. Are you certain it is in this quarter?"

The woman murmured an assurance that was lost in the noise produced by the chaise wheels as the vehicle moved off. Astonishment, disbelief, fear, then fury marched through Amy's brain at a quickstep as she struggled to keep her voice level. "What is the meaning of this, madam? Be so good as to halt this chaise at once."

"Now, there's no call to get all hoity-toity with me. This is by way of doing you a service in the long run, my dear, I promise you."

"A service! You tricked me into getting into this carriage, and now you are taking me somewhere against my will. Pray tell me what sort of service you imagine this is to me?" Amy asked, truly mystified.

"No one knows better than me that wedlock isn't all beer and skittles; it takes some getting used to at first, but you hadn't ought to—"

"Wedlock! Ma'am, you have mistaken me for someone else. I am not married. This is all a mistake. Please take me back to Mermaid Street," Amy begged, feeling as if she had wandered into Bedlam.

"Now, dearie, running home to your mama doesn't change the fact that you have a husband—and a proper gen'lman he is too, and handsome with it, though I don't generally favor such dark-avised men myself. No matter what your mama has told you, he is pining away to have you back."

The woman stopped, suddenly blinking as Amy stared at

her in dawning horror. She could feel the blood draining from her head, and she summoned all the strength of will at her command to present a calm facade.

"Ma'am, do I understand that—that you have lured me into this carriage at the request of a man who has told you I am his wife?"

"Well, yes, but you shouldn't look so frightened."

"He lied to you, ma'am! I swear to you that I saw that man for the first time yesterday. My mother died when I was born. I have lived all my life at my home, Marshland, near Romney Marsh."

"Then how do you know just the man I am talking about?"

"Because a dark-complexioned man accosted me on the street today, but I got away from him," Amy cried, seeing disbelief in the woman's fleshy countenance. "I do not even know his name!"

"Nor do I, for that matter, but he certainly knows you."

"He doesn't know me! He is clearly deranged," Amy argued, more frantic than ever as she sensed the horses slowing down. "Please, ma'am, you said you thought to do me a service, but you have done just the opposite. My name is Amy Cole. Please, at least go to Marshland. Tell them what has hap—"

The door opened before she could finish, and a gloved hand assisted the flustered matron to descend. Amy could not see the man's face, but she glimpsed a tall beaver hat just as the carriage began to roll again. She scrambled for the other door but lost her balance as the chaise jolted into a rut. Her head struck the door with an impact that would have done real damage had her bonnet not given her some protection. As it was, the pain that shot through her head left her gasping and weak.

Amy stayed on her knees on the floor of the chaise, leaning her head against the opposite seat for long minutes, tears of self-pity spilling unheeded down her cheeks until the initial pain in her head gave way to discomfort from her awkward position. Slowly she pushed herself up off the floor with one hand, feeling for the seat behind her with the other. Her movements were far from graceful, but eventually she was seated, facing the direction in which they were traveling. She pulled off her bonnet and ran tenuous fingers over her scalp, wincing as they discovered a lump behind her ear.

It was time to master her emotion, ignore her fears and begin to take stock of the situation with her faculties. The result of this exercise was a bleakness that settled over her mind and spirit after a very few minutes.

She had been kidnapped.

She was in a post chaise behind a team of fast horses, being carried farther away from her home and her life with every minute that passed. Despite the stuffiness of the closed carriage, a chill feathered down her spine. She told herself to disregard it and concentrate her thoughts.

Secondly, she was in the power—temporarily—of a man who might or might not be a French spy, but who was certainly of unsound mind. The chill spread to her chest, and it became more difficult to ignore the unpleasant sensation.

Of lesser importance but not to be forgotten, she was in this carriage with approximately two pounds and a few shillings in addition to the clothes she was wearing and a beautiful new hat. Obviously, the sooner she made an escape from this madman, the better her chances for getting back home on her own.

But she was not really on her own, she reminded herself. Tom Watkins would be looking for her soon. Checking her watch, she saw with a sense of unreality that it still lacked five minutes until the time he had planned to return for her. Tom would leave no stone unturned in his search. She clung to one more little grain of comfort, recalling her plea to the woman who had trapped her for the kidnapper. Amy was persuaded the woman was neither evil nor heartless. From what she had said during the short drive to the outskirts of Rye, it was easy to see the man had told her a whole farrago of lies about a runaway wife. If the woman learned that Tom was searching for her or simply had an attack of conscience, she might very well go to Marshland and tell what she knew.

Amy took what comfort she could in the possibility of eventual rescue until she considered herself calm and alert enough to put these thoughts away and shift her focus to planning her own escape. Occasionally she could distinguish the hoofbeats of a horse besides those of the team pulling the chaise. She deduced that the kidnapper was accompanying the chaise on horseback, though he had not crossed her line of vision since he had helped his accomplice descend from the carriage. She knew they were on a tollroad, and she thought from the position of the sun that they were heading in a southerly direction. The team would probably be good for two stages, but she had no idea where or how far he planned to take her.

Obviously she could not leap from the moving chaise without risking injury, recapture or both, which left the changes at the post houses as her only opportunity to escape before they reached the abductor's destination. She could not expect to be left unattended during the changes, which seemed to leave subterfuge or trickery as her best weapons. She might pretend illness or injury to get away from the chaise and nearer to other people who might come to her aid. Meanwhile, it would do no harm to conceal her money about her person and hide her watch, though she could not think how a timepiece might aid her efforts. She put her bonnet on again and removed the money from her reticule.

Amy had recourse to her watch, now pinned on the inside of her gown, more times than she cared to admit over what seemed like an eternity but was actually less than two hours before she felt a slackening in the vehicle's speed. The anxiety that had been her constant companion flared into full-blown apprehension as the chaise drew to a halt amid noises of horses and harness that proclaimed this a posting inn. Footsteps approached the chaise, and the door was pulled open.

Amy clasped her hands together in her lap and straightened her spine as the man she had expected to see climbed into the chaise and sat down opposite her. She met his burning gaze bravely, firming her lips to control their tendency to tremble. In the close confines of the carriage he seemed even more powerful than he had looked on the street in Rye. Bareheaded now, his thick wavy hair appeared nearly black, as were straight brows over dark gray eyes. He seemed to suck all the air out of the carriage, and his bold gaze roving over her person increased her sense of being smothered, but pride and temper kept Amy silent as she vowed she would not let him see her fear.

After an interminable, fraught silence, he said with soft menace, "Well, here we are, my dear Désirée, as promised."

She let this challenge pass. Her voice was even but husky as she asked, "Who are you? Why are you doing this to me?"

She thought there was a flicker of surprise in his eyes before he said impatiently, "Are you still at that game? What do you hope to gain by pretending we are strangers?"

Her eyes flashed with scorn. "You told that poor woman I was your wife to make her your accomplice. That was a vile and cowardly thing to do!"

Swift color scorched under his cheekbones and a muscle twitched in his jaw, but he hung on to his temper, saying with a sneer, "This is the first time I've ever known you to show a concern for anyone other than yourself. Cowardly am I because I preferred not to cause an uproar in Rye by airing our . . . domestic problems in public? It is my name that you dishonored, after all, by eloping with a lover."

"And what name would that be, sir?" she inquired, ignoring the accusation.

"Don't be absurd," he snapped. "This change has been accomplished. We'll be traveling with only a pair of horses from now on because of Samson. We'll have something to eat at the next change if you will agree not to create a scene." He opened the door and extended a booted leg.

"I'll agree to nothing," she snapped in her turn.

"You might be hungrier in two or three hours," he said over his shoulder, a gleam of what might have been humor in the dark eyes as he ducked his head and exited the coach.

Quickly she scooted over to the other door, but again the

chaise jerked into motion. She didn't bump her head this time, but she did not get the door open either.

Amy settled back with a sigh, her mind a jumble of impressions. Apparently she had a few hours to try to evolve a workable plan to escape the instant the chaise stopped. All she could think of was to run fast and hide completely until her captor gave up the search. It would still be full daylight at that point, but she quaked at the thought of the distance they would have covered by then. Even slowing the pace for the sake of this Samson, who must be the horse she could hear occasionally, would mean she would be nearly fifty miles from home at the next change. She gritted her teeth and fought to deny the tears that crowded behind her eyelids.

It was difficult to remain optimistic in the face of the implacable purpose that radiated from the mysterious man. Yesterday she had feared his presence on the quay had something to do with Robert's mission. When they met on Mermaid Street today his mention of her brother had seemed to confirm this. Even a kidnapping was not beyond belief if a French agent hoped to coerce Robert into giving up his friend in exchange for his sister.

But this theory bogged down when some of his other statements and actions were taken into consideration. He'd called her Désirée in Rye and again just now. It was certainly a French name, but if this Désirée was in truth his wife, she could not be Robert's sister also. Confusion threatened to addle her own brain at this point, and she settled deeper into the seat, closing her eyes and trying to disregard the throbbing in her head.

The most disturbing observation she had made in their two short encounters today was the utter certainty with which her captor had addressed her as his wife. Just picturing the conviction in the dark eyes that had tried to pierce her soul increased her heartbeat uncomfortably. Unless he really was as mad as a bedlamite, she must bear a strong resemblance to his wife. But he had examined her at length from less than two feet away. He *must* be able to detect differences! His conviction spoke to a definite imbalance in his mind.

It was vital that she reverse this conviction. Perhaps if she ceased opposing and challenging him, and calmly told him who she was, she could shake his assurance. He had asked her no questions save passing rhetorical references to a lover and a brother. Nor had he deigned to reply to her repeated questions about his identity and intentions except with a sneer that had set up her back. This time she must remain calm and present him with a detailed autobiography.

Alas for good intentions.

Amy was poised for escape when the chaise pulled into a stableyard for the next change. She had a door open and was nearly out of the vehicle when her captor came around the back of the chaise. She made the mistake of jumping down and would have gone sprawling in her eagerness had he not scooped her up bodily. Shaken, disappointed and frightened, she screamed, "Help me! Someone, please help!"

She was bundled unceremoniously back into the chaise before the words had died down, but not before she'd seen two stable boys, who had looked over at the yell, sent on their way by the postilion.

"That was rather foolish of you, my dear," her captor said, standing outside the door. "Errant wives receive little sympathy among the working classes. Spare me the tears, I beg you," he added wearily, spotting the moisture she dashed away from the corner of one eye. "Surely you had overplayed that card within a month of our marriage. That's better," he said as she glared at him. "At least your anger is sincere. I will bring you something to eat."

"Do not trouble yourself; I want nothing."

"Neverless, you will eat something, either voluntarily or forcibly fed."

She was at the other window the second he turned away, but this was blocked by the postilion's girth. Turning, she saw that an ostler now stood guard on the far side.

She was pale but in command of herself once more when her alleged husband returned a few minutes later carrying a tray that he put on the seat opposite her. Her stomach churned, and the look she cast him from under curling dark lashes was a mute plea that he read and ignored.

"You have five minutes to eat it and drink the tea. It is the way you prefer it—strong with just a little sugar." His mouth twisted as he turned away.

Amy eyed the tray with apprehension. Ordinarily she was untroubled by the motion of a carriage, but a slight feeling of nausea was taking possession of her insides. It was a relief, therefore, to see only a plate of buttered bread under the cover. For a second she experienced a fleeting gratitude that he had not piled the tray with greasy meats. She managed to eat two slices of the bread, which she found good, and she thirstily gulped the tea. It was strong as advertised, but tasted rather strange. Still, it was hot in her stomach and she had drunk most of it when he returned.

He made no comment on the food remaining on the tray, saying only, "Finish it," when she would have handed him the mug.

"I cannot," she replied faintly, thrusting it onto the tray and turning away. She tensed at the pause that followed while he evidently debated whether to insist. When he walked away at last, her nerves relaxed somewhat, but she drooped with the resumption of the drive into the unknown. She longed to stretch her legs and walk around a bit. Her muscles rebelled at the hours of confinement, and she found herself twisting and turning in a vain effort to find a comfortable position.

How much longer would this ordeal last? She thought they were headed westward but could not venture a guess as to their destination. She had learned nothing from him and had thrown away her chance to proclaim her identity in a futile try for freedom. She couldn't help but wonder what would happen when the call of nature became insistent. Heat rushed into her face at the thought of discussing her bodily functions with this loathsome creature. The throbbing in her head had diminished to a dull beat, thank heavens, but the bump behind her ear was very tender to the touch. The sound of the wheels had receded to a distance, and the sun was lower in the sky and quite large and blurred. She blinked and had difficulty in focusing on the shining ball outside the window; in fact, it was nearly impossible to keep her eyes open. Sudden fear coursed through her mind, and she twitched with the effort to fight the inertia settling over her body.

That strange-tasting tea! It was not sugar but some kind of drug! Terror came then, but from a far distance. Before she could scream it aloud, sleep overcame terror and claimed her.

It was full dark when Sir Jason entered the chaise and eased his tired body onto the seat across from his sleeping wife. He sat motionless for a time with his eyes tightly shut, all the while knowing the balm of sleep would surely be denied him. Fortunately, Samson had had a long rest in the stables last night for he was pushing him hard today, even though the pace had eased off considerably with nightfall. The moon was nearly full, which was a blessing. It would be nearly morning by the time they reached Oakhill.

His eyes opened and automatically fixed on Désirée, slumped in the corner of side and back supports. He'd taken a pillow from the last inn to place beneath her head and a blanket that he leaned over and rearranged more securely about her now. A shaft of moonlight illuminated her face at the moment. She stayed unmoving in her drugged sleep, her breathing reassuringly regular.

A spasm of pain or anger contorted his own features as he studied the lovely modeling of her face, heart-shaped beneath a widow's peak with marvelous high cheekbones, a perfect nose and a delicately rounded chin. This was not what he had envisioned six weeks ago in Portsmouth when he had married a wistful orphan by special license, against the advice of his solicitor.

He had met Désirée Ryder only three weeks before, shortly after his return from ten years in the army, having sold out when word of his father's death had reached him in

February. After paying a visit of condolence to the family of a fallen comrade, he had wandered into the cemetery in Portsmouth, looking for the graves of two naval acquaintances, and had found a beautiful girl weeping at the grave site of her recently deceased mother.

From that instant, the urge to stand between the lovely orphan and all of life's adversities had emerged as fully grown as Athena from Zeus's head. Her exigent circumstances— essentially penniless and staying with a former schoolmate—had dictated the speed of their courtship. Would the fever in his blood have run its course had their meeting and courtship proceeded according to society's approved practices? It was a question that had tormented him this past month, but in balance, he thought not. He had been hell-bent on winning the right to be protector and all things to a girl whose beauty filled his senses and whose charming manners and appealing airs enchanted him.

The enchantment had ended on their wedding night when he had discovered that his bride was not a virgin. She had not prepared him for this shock, and when he had demanded the circumstances of the seduction, she had claimed, amid much weeping, to have been violated by a drunken youth at a friend's home. He had not entirely disbelieved her on this occasion and, truth to tell, had been ashamed at the depth of his own revulsion. In his own defense, however, he had still hoped the marriage could become solid in time. That was before his bride's subsequent behavior had so thoroughly given the lie to all the high-flown sentiments she had mouthed before the wedding. When a woman set out to spend her husband's money with a vengeance, begrudged him his conjugal rights and showed herself indifferent to all his tastes, opinions and comforts, a man would have to be an imbecile not to know that he had served his only intended purpose the moment he made her a married woman. Within a sennight his home was an armed camp; within a month he came home from a day of riding about the estate his father had nearly brought to ruin, to find himself a deserted cuckold.

His initial reaction had been pure relief at the absence of hostilities. The local families had tactfully left the newly wedded couple alone during this supposed honeymoon stage, so there were no immediate explanations and humiliation to endure. The anger had come later as he considered his present situation in life. He was a married man with none of the privileges of that state. He had hated being an only child and wanted more children than just an heir. For this he obviously required a partner. Even if he divorced his unfaithful wife, he had to know how to find her and the identity of her seducer.

And this was the result of a fortnight's quest. Jason's gaze that had been trained out the window at shadows, shifted back to the sleeping figure opposite him; he marveled that she could still look so . . . "untouched" was the word that came to mind, after everything she had done in her short life. One hand was outside the blanket, still gloved. On an impulse, he leaned over and drew it off, a bit surprised to find that she had taken off her wedding ring. Most women running off with a lover would continue to wear a ring to reinforce their pose as a married couple. If she had not repulsed him so adamantly today that he feared she would disappear again, he would not have had to improvise this melodramatic abduction. Nor would he have had to relegate Désirée's seducer to the status of unfinished business. It had really gone against the grain to be obliged to postpone a reckoning with the cur, but taking her beyond her lover's reach had been his primary objective in Rye. He had not used his own name at the inn or the posting houses either, partly to shield Désirée if they decided to try to save the marriage, but that might well prove to have been an unnecessary precaution. The fact that there was a man for whom she was prepared to lose her reputation was evidence of even more deception than he would have believed possible.

Obviously he had not known her at all when they married, but neither had he known the black side of his own nature. Not in his wildest imaginings would he have believed himself capable of drugging his own wife, but today he had deliberately purchased laudanum as a practical measure for subduing a recalcitrant bride, and he had used it without a qualm when she had tried to escape him at the first opportunity.

Bitter thoughts and regrets occupied Jason's mind during the long hours of darkness as the horses ate up the miles to Hampshire. Sleep was impossible. He despised coach travel in general because it made him feel like a caged animal. Being in enforced proximity to the woman who had trampled on his dreams and insulted his manhood multiplied the torment tenfold.

In defiance of his brain's repeated orders, his eyes kept returning to that beautiful countenance with its illusory impression of innocence. Every look at her sent thoughts that defied reality circling endlessly in his tired brain, and he longed to be outside in the fresh night air.

Concern for Samson, however, kept him out of the saddle until the very last stage when he thrust himself out of the chaise with controlled relief and climbed onto the stallion's back for the rest of this accursed journey.

Chapter Four

The sun had barely crested the horizon when an unshaven Sir Jason carried his still-sleeping wife back into his ancestral home from which she had fled over a fortnight since.

The sounds of the chaise's arrival had brought his butler to the entrance hall from the nether regions, and he could hear someone cleaning out the grate in the small room off the hall where he received tradesmen and paid bills.

"Welcome home, sir, and her ladyship too. I trust she is not ill?" The portly man, who had been a fixture at Oakhill since his grandfather's day, looked askance at the unconscious young woman.

"Recovering," Jason said shortly, heading for a magnificent oak staircase with his burden. "Send Mrs. Natwick to her ladyship's room and tell one of the boys to take Samson to the stables. I have already paid off the chaise. Oh, and send someone to lay a fire in my wife's room."

"That will not be necessary, sir. The room has been ready since . . . all along, as has your own."

"Thank you, Hatcherd." The thanks were mostly for the man's tact, Jason acknowledged, as he continued up the stairs. He shouldered open the door to Désirée's bedchamber and deposited her on the bed, frowning down at the unmoving figure in a crumpled black dress and sturdy half boots. He removed her shoes and pulled back the coverlet and blanket. When she still did not stir, he started on the buttons of her walking dress and presently pulled it over her head, completing the undoing of the coiled arrangement of hair at her nape that rubbing against the chaise upholstery all night had begun. Sliding his hands under the slender back, he lifted her enough to place her between the sheets in her petticoats and shift. He pulled the covers up over creamy shoulders and caught himself before his hand strayed to the silken chestnut tresses released from their confinement.

There was heat in his thin cheeks and a grim set to his mouth, which he made a conscious effort to ease when he heard the housekeeper's labored breathing as she came puffing into the room, setting down Désirée's bandbox that he had left inside the entrance door with his hat and gloves before going back to lift her out of the chaise.

"You're back at last, sir, and with her ladyship, praise be, but what is wrong with her?" The housekeeper moved over to the bed, staring down at her sleeping mistress.

"Nothing serious, Mrs. Natwick, but she suffered a blow to her head in a fall, and it has had a strange effect on her memory. The doctor assures me she will regain her memory in time, but at present she cannot recognize me, and she thinks she is someone else entirely. She has invented a whole new history, in fact, and grows disturbed if people try to tell her otherwise. For the time being there is nothing we can do for her except try to see that she does not become agitated. Also, someone must know where she is at all times because she might try to wander off. Another blow could have serious consequences, so she must be protected from herself."

"My land," Mrs. Natwick said, clasping her hands to her bosom, her eyes starting, "the poor child—her poor brain! What a thing to happen! Mercy on us, what next? There is no fever, thank goodness," she added, laying a hand on the girl's forehead.

She was now wringing her hands, and Jason said quickly, "She will probably sleep another hour or two and will be ready for a good breakfast by then, I imagine."

"Yes, sir, I'll alert the kitchen. Will you be wanting your breakfast now?"

"I may try to snatch an hour of sleep myself. I'll ring when I want to eat and come downstairs. That is all for now, Mrs. Natwick. Let the staff know about her ladyship's condition, will you please, so everyone will help to look out for her?"

"Of course, of course. The maids and cook will be eating about now. I'll go right down if there is nothing here that I can do for her ladyship. Shall I send one of the maids up to unpack for her later?" She glanced around the room, her eyes lighting on the solitary bandbox and returning to her master's face with a question in them.

"I arranged to have everything sent on later," he said. "I just wanted to get your mistress back to familiar surroundings as soon as possible."

"I see. Very good, sir."

Hopefully, that was the main hurdle crossed. Jason sighed, watching the housekeeper close the door behind her. He'd had time during the long drive to anticipate some of the problems Désirée's intransigent attitude would create among the staff, but he still felt like a man walking over a minefield. It was odds on that he had only delayed the inevitable in any event. His fists clenched, and he looked down as something pricked his finger. He was surprised to find he was still holding the bundled up dress Désirée had been wearing. Curious, he moved his fingers through the folds of the offending garment before shaking it out and discovered a small watch pinned to the inside. His eyes flew to the sleeping girl. She had deliberately hidden the trumpery piece, so its value must be sentimental. On closer inspection, it appeared to be a perfectly ordinary timepiece with no hidden compartments. A gift from her lover perhaps.

He slipped it into his pocket and went over to light the fire. She might feel chilled on waking from a drug-induced sleep.

Fatigue washed over Jason in a wave as he rose from the hearth and headed for his own bedchamber adjoining his wife's. But first there was one additional precaution to take. He detoured over to the hall door and locked it, pocketing the key. Purposely averting his gaze from the four-poster bed with its rich brocaded curtains, he entered his own room, leaving this door ajar, and proceeded to lock the one communicating with the hall. He was a firm believer in anticipating the moves of an adversary.

The chore of divesting himself of his top boots was made easier with the aid of the bootjack in the corner, mute evidence that he had not yet engaged the service of a valet since returning to England. He dropped onto the bed after stripping off his neckcloth and shirt.

Before closing his eyes, he noticed on the coverlet the black dress that he intended to consign to the fireplace at the earliest opportunity. Glancing at the door between the bedchambers, he decided on one last precaution. He stuffed the dress under his pillow along with the keys and fell instantly asleep.

Ten years in the army had conditioned Sir Jason to come to full alert at the least noise. A slight rustle of fabric brought his eyelids up while the rest of his body remained still. His roaming eyes settled on the source of the rustling. His wife, her slender form wrapped in a sheet, was intent on searching through the pockets of his discarded coat.

"What a very wifely occupation to be sure, my dear Désirée, rifling through your husband's pockets. Is this what you are seeking?"

She had gone rigid at his first drawled words, but she recovered quickly and went on the attack, swinging to confront him as he sat up against the pillows holding up a key. Though color flooded into her throat at the sight of an apparently naked man, she advanced a step, saying angrily, "Do not bother to deny that you put some sort of sleeping draught in that tea yesterday. Where have you brought me? Why is the door to that room locked, and what have you done with my gown?"

"You seem to have acquired a foul temper during your little escapade," he drawled, admiring the proud set to her head and the wealth of chestnut hair that she swept behind her shoulder with an impatient hand.

"Sarcasm is the refuge of those with neither reason nor right on their side," she cried, green eyes flashing.

"By all means, let those who may claim sweet reason for their side," he said mildly, refusing to allow her the satisfaction of seeing that her accusations had struck a nerve. "I have no intention of denying I drugged your tea. You were being very foolish in trying to run away again with neither money nor the assistance of your lover at your command. Secondly, you can see that I have brought you back to your home and your position as mistress of a sizeable, though admittedly encumbered estate. Thirdly, you were locked in to prevent you from embarrassing yourself by ill-considered rantings to the servants. You may have the key whenever you wish it, but there is something you should know first, and might I suggest that you make yourself presentable before you leave your room, delightful though you appear *en déshabillé.* Oh, by the way, do not bother to ring for Simmons to assist you. She admitted that she passed you a letter from your lover and helped you to pack and leave here. I do not keep disloyal servants in my employ."

She regarded him with a stony face. "It seems to be a waste of breath to reply to any of your wild remarks, sir. Where is my gown, please?"

"It should be a pile of ash by now," he replied disingenuously, pushing farther back against the pillows covering the item in question.

"What! You destroyed my gown? You had no right! Do you hope to keep me a prisoner by robbing me of my clothes?"

"Do not be absurd. There is an armoire full of the dresses you ordered before you left in such haste. They arrived from the modiste the next day. Martin's timing was off."

"I cannot wear another woman's clothes!" she cried, aghast. "Besides, I am in mourning!" For the first time during this contretemps, she looked more unhappy than furious.

"You ceased wearing mourning for your mother even before we were married, but I grant you it was a clever disguise. Had I not bumped into you and looked straight into your eyes, I might have walked right by you in Rye, especially with your hair hidden like a nun's and that unspeakable tan."

She appeared not to understand him, saying only, "I am in mourning for my father, not my mother."

One eyebrow escalated. "So you not only forgot to mention a brother but a father too. Are there any more relatives I should know about?"

"I never mentioned a brother," she said, all the life draining out of her face as she turned and walked back toward the door.

"You forgot something," he said, losing interest in baiting her. He got out of bed and followed her, stopping her in the doorway with a hand on her shoulder. She shrank away from him and he removed his hand, imposing a rigid control over his features. "The key," he said, holding it out. "Take it," he persisted as she did not move but stared at him in perplexity. He dropped his own gaze, took her limp hand and placed the key in it. Large green eyes seemed to question him, but he could not decipher the question, let alone provide an answer.

"I should warn you that I have told the servants that you have had a blow to the head and don't remember your identity. They won't believe any story you tell them, and they will prevent you from leaving the grounds. You would do well to accept that you will not leave here again without my agreement that we should part. We'll talk later."

Without a word she entered the other room, head held high, trailing the ridiculous sheet while still managing to look like a young queen falsely imprisonned.

As she closed the door between the bedchambers, Amy's eyes lighted on the key in her other hand and went instantly to the lock. Her hand moved forward and stopped. Could she lock the door without making a sound? If there was a sound and he heard it, would he take it as a challenge of any sort? Her arm fell to her side and she gnawed on her bottom lip. He had not actually threatened her with bodily harm, but just now when he had followed her to the doorway wearing nothing but breeches, the musculature of his chest and arms had warned her of the great disparity of strength between them.

Never in her life had she felt so desperately alone and unsure of what to do. This was her idea of a waking nightmare. Yesterday she had been abducted and put in a carriage heading she knew not where. Today she'd awakened in a luxurious bed in a beautiful room, but the room was locked and she still did not know where she was, nor the identity of her abductor. Moreover, he had destroyed her only gown and evidently spun a tale to the servants that ensured that no one she might encounter would believe her or help her to escape him.

As his wife had done. The thought sprang into her head unbidden, but it was ludicrous to feel any sympathy for his situation. *She* was entitled to leave. *She* was the injured party here, but of course the man in the next room did not know that. Even though he intimidated her and heaped scorn on her for the sins of another woman, she had glimpsed the pain beneath the anger more than once.

Good heavens, what was she thinking? She could not afford to feel sympathy for someone who had wreaked havoc on her life, just as she could not afford to worry about her lost reputation should this episode ever come to light.

Amy wandered around the room, glancing indifferently at the tasteful appointments while she attempted to marshal her wits and plan her next move. Her head felt full of cotton wool and her throat was as dry as the Sahara. She needed food and she would dearly love a bath, or at least some warm water for washing. She walked over to the mahogany armoire and pulled it open, gaping in admiration at the array of garments within. He must have been a generous husband, at least, to permit such a large expenditure at one time, she mused, fingering the soft silk and cotton fabrics. She experienced an uncharitable satisfaction that the unfaithful wife had been obliged to abandon her new wardrobe when she decamped. Certainly the thought should help assuage her guilt at wearing the clothes. As proof, she pulled out an exquisite cream-colored robe of a gossamer silk, lavishly trimmed in lace, and slipped it on before pulling the bell cord that would summon a servant.

Amy could not resist taking a peek in the long mirror between two windows. The robe fit as if it were intended for her, something that gave her an uneasy jolt. She turned hastily away and returned her attention to planning her escape. Obviously she must acquaint herself with her surroundings, inside and out, as quickly as possible and take stock of anything that might aid her flight. Perhaps a horse, she thought with a surge of optimism.

"Come in," she called, her heart racing as a young maid entered carrying a can of hot water.

"Good morning, ma'am," the girl said, directing a look of wide-eyed curiosity at Amy before taking off the can's cover and pouring water into a white china bowl on the washstand.

"And you are . . . ?" Amy had no choice but to ask.

"I'm Elsie, ma'am. You really do not remember me?"

"I'm afraid not, Elsie. Do—do you not find me . . . different than before?"

"Oh no, ma'am," the maid replied with the evident intention of being reassuring.

The actual result of her goodwill was to unnerve Amy who had been so positive that her alleged husband was allowing his wishes to influence his judgment. Now here was another presumably disinterested person who saw nothing out of the way about the appearance of the mistress of the house.

Amy turned away and applied herself to bathing her face and arms, feeling that she was plunging ever deeper into a nightmare.

"What do you wish to wear today, ma'am?"

"What? Oh, you may choose, Elsie," Amy said, still shaken as she rinsed her face and began patting her skin dry. She said nothing as the strong-limbed, plain-faced servant selected a morning gown of a delicate willow green organdie that would not have been out of place at a garden party with its low-cut bodice and double flounce at the hem. She was no longer shocked when the garment fit her like a glove. It was just one more chink in the foundation of reality.

"Would you like me to try to arrange your hair, ma'am?"

"Yes, thank you, Elsie," she said faintly, sitting down at the graceful dressing table.

"I'm sorry I don't have the experience to create the wonderful arrangements Simmons did, ma'am," the girl warned.

"Never mind, Elsie. I prefer just a simple coiled bun at the nape."

"Very good, ma'am." The girl set to with a will, brushing the heavy fall of hair with strong strokes. At one point, Amy winced and put up her hand to her head.

"Oh dear, I am so sorry! Did I hurt the spot where you were injured?"

"Pray do not look so frightened, Elsie. It was the merest touch, that's all. No harm done. If you will just wind it around for me, I will put the pins in. There," she said, after making quick work of securing the chignon and jumping up from the chair. "Thank you. Will you lead me down to wherever breakfast is being served?"

"Of course, ma'am." The maid still looked so downcast that Amy found herself chattering inanely in an effort to restore her spirits.

"It seems like a lovely day."

"Yes, ma'am."

"Goodness, this is a very large house," Amy said involuntarily as the bedroom corridor debouched into a landing with two other wings.

"Yes, ma'am."

Amy sighed. "It is alright, Elsie. I am fine, truly. Perhaps you might be so obliging as to show me around the house after breakfast?"

The maid brightened at this. "Of course, ma'am, if Mrs. Natwick permits."

"And Mrs. Natwick would be . . . the housekeeper?"

Amy hazarded a guess and was praised like a child who had recited his lesson correctly.

"That's right, ma'am. She has been housekeeper at Oakhill for a score of years, I reckon. They do say as she was Sir Jason's nurse afore that."

Amy swallowed dryly. It seemed her "husband" was Sir something, which meant she was supposed to be Lady something. It could have been worse, she told herself; he might have been a duke. Small wonder he had been so intent on avoiding a scandal.

Eventually they arrived at what Elsie referred to as the little dining room. The maid ushered Amy in and asked if she might go to request the housekeeper's leave to conduct the mistress on a tour of the house.

"Yes, certainly, Elsie." Amy smiled at the girl who backed out of the room just as a rotund man with a dignified bearing came in from another door.

"Good morning, Lady Archer. May I say how pleased I am to see you looking yourself?"

"Good morning," Amy said faintly. Archer—her name was supposed to be Archer, and this must be the butler, but again she was at a loss.

"I am Hatcherd, ma'am," he said, seemingly reading her confusion, "Sir Jason's butler. May I say that all the staff are very sorry to hear of your injury and wish to be of service to you in any way possible."

"Thank you, Hatcherd. Please thank everyone for their kind thoughts."

To her surprise Amy made a very good meal despite her ever-present and escalating anxiety. In a beautifully proportioned room with good furniture that was showing its age in the light from a large oriel window, she more than made up for yesterday's deficiencies of diet. When she left the room her outlook must be marginally improved by a full stomach, and the woolliness had left her head already.

Elsie returned as she was finishing her second cup of coffee. Amy smiled at the girl's posture of barely controlled expectancy as she dutifully presented Mrs. Natwick's compliments and a counteroffer to conduct her ladyship personally if that should be desired.

"No, Elsie. Doubtless Mrs. Natwick is extremely busy today, what with the master's unexpected return. I am persuaded you will do splendidly," Amy said, rising from the table. "Shall we begin by going out the main entrance so I might see what visitors see on arriving at Oakhill?"

This brisk suggestion was well received, and Amy followed in the maid's wake, turning down an offer from Elsie to go back upstairs for her mistress's bonnet to shield her from the sun. She did not permit her eyes to stray into the rooms they passed en route, though she could not help but utter an exclamation of admiration for a grand old oaken staircase in the entrance hall.

A vast parkland studded with enormous trees stretched before them as they descended the few steps to the carriage drive. Amy headed straight forward, not turning to look at the building she had just quitted until they had gone several dozen paces across the smooth lawn. "My word!" was her only comment on her first sight of the weathered brick structure that filled her vision.

Oakhill was large and quite beautiful, also very old, at least part of it, she guessed, noting the very tall windows to the left of the central entrance bay that proclaimed the location of the original great hall. Twin wings ending in oriel windows hinted at the H-shaped design typical of houses from the Tudor era before subsequent additions denied further interest in symmetry. She felt a tingle of anticipation for the glories of the interior which she attempted to deny, reminding herself that this was simply a ploy to acquaint herself with the layout and exits of what was, after all, her prison.

With this in mind, Amy suggested to the willing maid that they continue around the perimeter to see the gardens and stables and other offices. She was conscious of the contrast between the idyllic setting on a perfect summer day and her present plight. If she were the real Désirée Archer, this beautiful setting would be hers to relish. How could the woman have run away from this place? The beauty of the day dimmed for Amy as she considered the owner of this lovely estate. He must have been a wretched, cruel husband to drive his wife into such a reckless act. But if that were so, why was she freely walking around the property at this moment? Why was she not locked in a room with meals sent in and no one to talk to? She had been conscious of the anger smoldering beneath his cold politeness, but he had removed his hand from her shoulder as soon as she had shown the fear she had tried to conceal. Amy brought herself up short at this juncture. It was pointless to try to fathom the mind and heart of this person. Her business was to escape from him and get herself home as soon as possible. Her gaze, which had been on the pathway through some shrubbery at the side of the house, fastened on her companion.

"Elsie, where are we?" she demanded.

"Why, we're coming around to the stable block, ma'am. You said you was wishful of seeing it."

"No, I mean where is Oakhill? Near what town or city?"

"Well, I reckon Petersfield would be the nighest, but—"

"Petersfield! Do you mean we are in Hampshire?" Amy bit her lip to keep back a cry of consternation.

"Yes, ma'am." Elsie's plain, honest face took on a look of concern. "Is something amiss, ma'am? Do you wish to go back indoors?"

"No, I am fine," Amy assured her hastily. "Is that the stable block ahead?"

Elsie nodded and continued forward.

Amy found the Oakhill stables disappointing. Also, she realized that the dress she was wearing was inappropriate to the setting, and she was aware of being under surreptitious scrutiny from two men cleaning harness and a boy mucking out the barn. The big chestnut called Samson was cropping grass in one field and four grays that Elsie said were carriage horses occupied another pasture. "Are there no other riding horses?" Amy asked, trying to sound offhand.

"Seems as if I heard tell in the servants' hall that the old master sold off all his stable afore he died, except for the old bay gelding he rode. The young master put him out to pasture when he came home."

"Came home?" Amy wafted the delicate question into the air, and her curiosity was rewarded.

"From the war . . . this spring. He were a colonel and knows Lord Wellington," Elsie reported with vicarious pride.

As the young women made their way back to the house through the kitchen garden, Amy was quiet, her mind rapidly turning over this latest nugget of information about her captor. Her wits must have gone begging to have failed to connect his swarthy complexion with service in the Peninsular. And this morning she had been too busy averting her gaze from his naked chest like some prissy Bath miss to appreciate that there had been a line of demarcation below his throat. Surely this news should put a period to her fears that he might be a French agent, if she'd had any lingering doubts after learning that he was a titled member of the gentry. His mentions of her brother had made her instinctively loath to acknowledge Robert's existence, but now that she was thinking more clearly, it seemed obvious that his references must have been to the "boy" he'd hailed on the quay at Rye. He had certainly seen her eyes then and had commented on their color the next day. She'd been told all her life that the green eyes her father had passed down to his children were very distinctive.

Amy continued her careful noting of the layout and exits of the big house as she allowed herself to be led around by the accommodating Elsie. Her personal situation was no less perilous because her captor was not a French spy; if anything, it was more vital to escape from him unless she could convince him that she was not his wife. It had sounded like a threat this morning when he'd declared that they would "talk later," but as the day wore on, Amy became increasingly anxious to get this crucial conversation behind her.

Sir Jason did not appear in the small dining room where Amy was served a delicious light meal that she toyed with in solitary state. Her spirits began to sink by midafternoon when she realized that even if they had their talk before dinner, it was extremely unlikely that her captor would send her home with apologies today.

Amy had spent time in the long picture gallery after lunch, examining a collection of paintings that consisted almost exclusively of what appeared to be ancestral portraits, most of them by undistinguished artists. She could tell by the spaces and differences in wall color that a significant number of works had been removed from the walls at some point. When considered with the fact that some wings of the house were closed off and most of the furnishings and draperies were showing the effects of many years' use, she could well believe that Sir Jason had spoken truly when he'd said the estate was encumbered.

She could not help speculating whether he had married an heiress in the time-honored tradition of the great landed families whenever they had suffered reverses in their fortunes. Was that why the marriage had failed? Had his wife found someone else while he was off fighting for his country?

After leaving the picture gallery she had taken a turn about a pretty but neglected garden, leaving when she became aware that a servant was observing her from a doorway. Someone had been outside the gallery also, she now recalled. It had not been an idle threat when he had warned her she would be watched.

Feeling discouraged and agitated, Amy went back up to her bedchamber. The unknown Désirée Archer fascinated her in a morbid sense. She defended her obsession by arguing that anyone alive would be curious about another person walking around with one's own face. She looked through the armoire in vain for a riding habit, her shoulders slumping in disappointment. The only shoes she was able to find were light slippers made to match an evening gown. Her black half boots would look ridiculous with anything Lady Archer had ordered, but she shrugged that off. She would be wearing her own footgear when she left this place, she vowed, trying to keep up her spirits.

Amy was equally unsuccessful in locating a shawl or other wrap to wear with the dinner dress she selected. Like all the clothes in the armoire, the ivory silk garment was beautiful and elegant but cut much lower in the bodice than anything Amy had ever owned, and she could not will herself to be unself-conscious in it by any amount of lecturing. She could not discover that Sir Jason's bride had left so much as a handkerchief behind that she might have tucked into the bodice somehow or other.

Elsie came to her mistress's room with information about the dinner hour and a promise to escort her to the anteroom where the baronet and his lady met before dining. She helped Amy to dress and repinned her hair in its chignon, bemoaning the fact that there were no ornaments or feathers with which to dress it.

A very minor blessing, Amy admitted as she stepped reluctantly into the saloon a few minutes later, but not having her hair tricked out like one of Astley's ponies was one indignity less to endure in this forced impersonation.

Chapter Five

"Do come in, my dear Désirée." Sir Jason turned from his contemplation of a portrait over the mantel and regarded Amy with an assessing eye as she took a few steps into the room and stopped. "Don't be shy. You look beautiful as always, despite the way you have scraped your hair back from your face, but I trust you won't think me insufferably Gothic if I just mention that the décolletage of your gown, though flattering to your charms, might not be considered quite the thing in the best circles."

"I know that," she said through gritted teeth, "but all the gowns are the same and there are no shawls or scarves. If it offends your sensibilities, I'll have a tray in my room." At his mocking laugh, she spun on her heel and headed for the door.

"Had a change of heart, did you, or did you select the clothes exclusively for Martin's delectation?"

Amy stopped in her tracks, making up her mind to get the inevitable confrontation behind her rather than suffer him to salve his wounds by a barrage of insults at every turn. She walked with deliberation to a bergère chair and sat down, clasping her hands loosely together in her lap as she faced him squarely. "I did not select the clothes at all, as you—"

"Yet they seem to fit as if made for you alone," came the purring interruption. "How do you explain this?"

"I cannot explain the apparent resemblance to your wife, sir," she began quietly. "At first, I thought you were mentally unbalanced, but the servants' reaction and the way the clothes fit have convinced me that a—an uncanny resemblance must exist. For your sake I am sorry that I am not the woman you seek, but I too have a life and it has been cruelly uprooted by your error. You have not allowed me even to tell you who I am."

He disregarded the pleading in her eyes. "I do not recall any serious attempt to proclaim another identity yesterday, but of course you have had many hours since to create an elaborate fantasy."

"So you will not hear my story, which, by the way, is neither fantastical nor elaborate?"

"Oh, I am perfectly willing to be entertained by you; in fact, I have missed your entertaining little ways that have been in abeyance of late. I'll just arm myself with another drink," he said, heading for the bottle on a tray placed on a side table. He held it up. "May I offer you a glass of sherry?"

"No, thank you," Amy replied, holding on to her temper while he went through this polite charade and sauntered over to stand between her chair and the fireplace. "Would you mind terribly if I asked you to sit down?" she asked with a fair assumption of his pronounced civility. "I am getting a crick in my neck from looking up."

His laugh as he dropped into a chair opposite hers sounded natural, and Amy, her eyes locked on his, was amazed at the difference it made in his appearance. The vertical grooves in his cheeks faded and his mouth softened. The thin, aquiline nose would never convey an impression of softness, nor would his rocky jaw, but the gray of his eyes had lightened from near obsidian to pewter. The hint of boyishness was fleeting and vanished as he informed her with a trace of impatience, "You have my undivided attention."

"My name is Amy Cole," she began, imposing a stern discipline on her voice which tended to wobble. "I have lived all my life at my family's modest estate called Marsh-

land near the Romney Marsh. My mother died when I was
born and my—"

"Your mother was English?" he interrupted abruptly.

"Of course," she said, surprised. He looked as if he might
say more, but closed his lips, and she resumed her tale. "My
father's mother came to help raise my brother and me until
she died six years ago. My father died three months ago,
which is why I am in mourning."

"Go on," he prodded when she ceased speaking.

"This is my life. I told you it is not fantastic or elaborate."
She spread her fingers, palms up.

"You say your mother died when you were born?"

She nodded.

"Your brother appeared to be several years younger than
you when I saw him in Rye Harbour," he pointed out with a
lifted brow.

"That . . . that was me—I—you saw on the quay," she
confessed, going pink at his incredulous stare. "My brother
is older. I would often wear his clothes when we would go
hiking or fishing." Stung by his obvious disbelief, she said,
"I can prove I was the one you saw the other day. I saw you
first at Mackerel Beach sitting above on a chestnut horse.
You followed me to Rye and hailed me. I wore a brown cap.
You said, 'Wait, boy!'"

"I did not follow you. Why did you run away?"

"Because I was dressed like a boy! Naturally I did not
wish to be exposed as a girl," she said emphatically, but she
could not sustain his piercing look. Her gaze wavered and
she clasped her hands more tightly together to keep her posture straight.

"This is a pack of lies made up out of whole cloth that
would not convince a child or a simpleton. I am disappointed in your powers of invention, my dear Désirée. They
seem to have peaked before our marriage—"

"My story can be easily proved," Amy protested quickly.
"Write to Marshland, please; I beg of you. They will be so
worried about me—just disappearing off the face of the
earth like that!"

"Who will be worried—the older brother? What is his name?"

"Robert, but he is in London at present, though he may have returned to Marshland by now."

"Where in London?"

"I—I am not precisely certain of his direction. He had some business to attend to."

"What sort of business?"

"I am not in his confidence in matters of business."

Sir Jason stood up suddenly, putting his glass down on a table. "As I said, a pack of lies. Ah, here is Hatcherd to announce dinner." He extended a hand, and she allowed him to pull her to her feet but stepped back immediately, saying, "I beg you will excuse me, sir. I find I am not hungry this evening."

"*L'appétit vient à manger.*"

"*Je n'ai pas faim,*" she repeated, using French as he had.

He smiled in the sneering fashion she had come to detest. "*Ah, je vois que tu parles français comme ta mère.*"

"*Je parle français comme ma grand-mère, la mère de mon père, et ne me tutoyez pas; nous sommes des étrangers.*"

"You seem to be a stranger to basic manners," he said in her ear as the butler went ahead into the dining room. "I will not have you display your lack of breeding by creating scenes like a bad opera in front of the servants."

After one smoldering look at his implacable granite expression, Amy subdued her rising spleen and masked her disappointment. There was no point in courting his displeasure by trampling on his family pride. She walked into the small dining room without a word and, with a great effort, produced a smile for Hatcherd as he seated her at one end of the handsomely appointed table.

What ensued was the oddest dinner table experience of her life. Amy accepted enough of the food Hatchered presented to leave the impression of partaking of the meal, even sending her compliments to the kitchen on the quality and attractive presentation of the vegetable dishes. She brought her fork to her mouth when Sir Jason stared pointedly at her plate and managed to swallow a few morsels, though her throat threatened to close up. For the first half of the meal her physical and mental energies were almost exclusively dedicated to maintaining a pleasant air of attention, but the facade was fragile at best. Her distress at the failure of her explanation left her enervated to the point where each response to her supposed husband's conversational advances required a heroic feat of concentration. An original observation would have been beyond her powers, but this was not demanded of her.

After a while she realized that he was delivering a placid monologue concerning estate matters requiring his attention, interspersed with questions to her that needed no more than a simple assent or a choice between alternatives. He said nothing that did not relate to her own activities today — about which he was obviously well-informed — such as her visit to the picture gallery. She could appreciate that to Hatcherd, coming and going with trays, it might well seem like a real conversation, and she awarded her captor a grudging respect for cleverness.

She was going to need some cleverness herself to get away from here since he refused to really listen to her. He did not strike her as unintelligent or unreasonable by nature, so *why* would he not listen? A thoughtful crease split Amy's forehead as she studied his strong features until she became aware that he was doing the same. Like a *coup de foudre*[°] it hit her that he did not listen to what she said because he trusted what he saw instead. She must change that and make him doubt the evidence of his eyes.

"I—I beg your pardon. I fear I was woolgathering."

"I was wondering aloud if you were looking for a pet today— a cat perhaps?"

"A—a pet?" she echoed, still at sea.

"I understand you were out at the stables today. Since you do not ride, I wondered if you went to see the barn cat's new litter?"

[°]lightning strike

"Don't ride?" she repeated, seized with an inspiration. "But of course I ride!" Her eyes widened.

His narrowed, but his tone was smooth. "I can see I have been very remiss in not acquiring a mount for you. If you would be willing to try Solomon, my father's bay gelding, for now, I'll have the groom locate my mother's old saddle. We might ride together tomorrow, if you like."

"I would like that very much, but there is no habit among your wife's clothes."

He sent her a furious look as Hatcherd, eyes on the tray he carried, left the room once more.

Amy was unmoved in the face of the master's displeasure. He had announced to the servants that she was out of her head; now, let him live with the consequences. She took a sip from her water glass and then a mouthful of chicken in a delectable wine sauce. She began to eat with renewed interest, a sure sign that her spirits were on the ascent once more.

They soared higher as he said, "I believe my mother's habit is among some items in a chest in the attic. She was taller than you, but very slender. Some alteration might be possible to make it fit. I'll have Mrs. Natwick bring it to you in the morning."

She thanked him demurely, and the strained dinner came to an end without further conflict. Amy rose from the table with a sense of release that evaporated when Sir Jason, remarking that he had no interest in drinking port by himself, followed her to the door to the saloon where they had quarreled earlier.

"I am rather tired this evening, sir, and would like to retire if you have no objection."

"I have multiple objections. Sit down," he said, motioning her to a chair as he closed the door to the dining room.

Amy glanced around swiftly, taking note of her surroundings, which she had been unable to do before dinner, so concentrated had her attention been on the dramatic meeting with the man who persisted in thinking himself her husband. The door to the hall, which he closed now, was the only other exit in a room of moderate size whose furnishings had obviously been chosen more for comfort than elegance. In addition to the pair of well-cushioned wing chairs on either side of the fireplace, there was a sofa covered in faded blue velvet behind a polished but scarred tea table. Extra chairs flanked a console table against the wall opposite the windows. Wall sconces and candelabra on side tables would keep the shadows away later, but were not needed this early in the evening.

Her eyes were drawn to the portrait of a woman over the mantel, a woman with a lovely, serene face and kind eyes that seemed to look back at her with gentle acceptance. Though past the first blush of youth, she was still a young woman, dressed in the style of two decades ago. Her unpowdered head was bare, and only a glimpse of blue ribbon invaded the gleaming raven tresses as she sat at a desk, a pen in one graceful hand.

Aware all at once of complete silence, Amy looked over her shoulder straight into dark eyes studying her. "Is . . . this your mother?" she asked a trifle breathlessly, making a small gesture toward the painting.

"As you say." His eyes were hooded.

"I do not believe I have ever seen such kind eyes," she said to keep the uncomfortable silence at bay.

"Does this mean you have changed your mind about relegating it to the picture gallery and refurbishing this room?"

Amy's lips parted to refute the charge, but what was the use—he believed nothing she said. It was all so hopeless. She looked at him in troubled silence and became wary as he leaned toward her.

"Why did you marry me, Désirée? Was it only because you were so poor after your mother died? You must have known Martin even then." His voice was quiet, and his eyes were willing her to reply.

"I . . . did not marry you, Sir Jason. I am not your wife," she said, full of regret for his unhappiness and her own miserable situation.

It was as if a curtain came down between them or an invisible wall. He sat back in his chair and regarded her impersonally. "What do you hope to achieve by keeping up this ludicrous pose of denial? Are you trying to protect Martin? You will not succeed. How do you think I found you so quickly?" He paused, but Amy, with nothing to contribute but another useless repetition of her identity, sat silent and unhappy.

"I went to Portsmouth to see if your friend Lucy Miller was sheltering you again as she had after your mother died," he went on, his eyes never leaving her face. "She denied knowing your whereabouts, but told me a man calling himself Armand Martin had called on her a few days before, asking your direction. Is Martin French? Mrs. Miller said he spoke with an accent."

Amy held her breath at the mention of a Frenchman. As he stared narrow-eyed, waiting, she mustered up a voice, saying woodenly, "I have no idea of this man's identity, nor the woman's."

"So you are telling me you were not in Rye with Martin looking for a way to get to France?"

"I was in Rye to visit a dressmaker where I ordered a gown of half-mourning for later this summer."

"Given your present attitude, I can see you will not tell me Martin's whereabouts, but no doubt I should expect a visit from him presently."

"If this Martin eloped with your wife, I find that highly unlikely."

"Enough of this fencing! Let me make it clear that whether I decide to divorce you or try to muddle along with this marriage, my honor demands that I demand satisfaction from Martin. You cannot prevent that."

Amy stood up. "As a disinterested party, I would have to point out that your wife has already decided the marriage is over. It is my misfortune that she could not have found a less cowardly way to make her decision known to you."

He was out of his chair with the quickness of a panther and the same feral appearance that struck terror into her being as he gripped both her arms above her elbows and pulled her up against his body. "Do not try my patience too far," he warned with soft menace.

Comprehension flared in her eyes, and her quick tongue betrayed her prudent regard for her safety. "Oh, I see. *You* may abuse your wife at great length, but an outsider is not permitted to voice an unflattering opinion of her conduct. Does that not prove that you have noted differences between us—that you no longer believe I am your wife?"

Her eyes flashed a challenge, and she fancied there was a flicker in his before that impenetrable mask came down again. "There is another way of proving who you are and I am sorely tempted to take it, but you need have no fear tonight," he added as she blanched and started to struggle in his grasp. "I have no intention of touching you until all chance of your carrying Martin's child is past."

This time she succeeded in breaking away from him. She ran out of the room and bounded up the stairs as if pursued by all the furies. In her room she quickly located the keys where she had hidden them inside her half boots and proceeded to lock both doors with fingers that still trembled. Only then did she draw a ragged breath of relief, though her heart continued to pound while she strained her ears to hear any sounds indicating that he had followed her upstairs.

Amy had no idea how long she remained by a window listening for danger—she had not remembered to ask him for the return of the watch she'd pinned to the inside of her gown—but the sun was sinking toward the horizon when she turned her back on a picturesque scene of rural tranquility. Her surroundings, both inside and out, were totally at odds with her emotions. The greens of the lawns and trees were repeated in the brocaded bedcover and window draperies as well as in the leaves of a soft floral-patterned rug. It was a serene, uncluttered space, but her thoughts were in a turmoil as she glanced around at what was both sanctuary and prison. With a sinking heart she wondered how long she would have to remain in this beautiful but alien setting.

She had considered rescue: where was Tom Watkins at

this moment? Had he learned anything in Rye that would point him in the right direction? She had considered escape: as long as there were horses in the stables and no bars on the windows or locks to which she did not have keys, there was a chance of being able to outrun pursuit. But, she admitted dolefully, she had never considered the possibility that when she got the opportunity to explain her identity she would not be believed. Granted, the incident of her masquerading as a boy had been embarrassing to explain, but she had certainly proved that it was she and not some younger brother he had met on the quay. He had made it seem as though Robert did not exist simply because she had not been quick enough to invent a temporary location for him in London. He had even turned the fact that she spoke French against her.

Apparently his beastly Désirée was half French. The more she learned about her putative double, the more she disliked the wretched creature, Amy decided, wearing a sour aspect as she paced about the room, too restless to sit down. When she had speculated that the marriage must have been an arranged affair with a rich young woman bartered for a title, she had felt a certain sympathy for her, but it had become clear during their talk tonight that Lady Archer had been recently orphaned and quite poor when they married.

Amy stopped her pacing to chase an elusive fragment of memory. Sir Jason had accused her of knowing this Armand Martin before they married, and surely Elsie had said that he had returned this spring from the war following his father's death—she recalled thinking it was the same as with her brother. When his marital situation was put in the context of the time frame, it seemed to Amy that the courtship, marriage and the bride's subsequent elopement must have all occurred in less than three months' time. Could this be possible?

Unless she had forgotten how to count, it would seem that Sir Jason had come safely home from fighting a war, only to be immediately caught by a scheming female who already had another victim in her sights. When the marriage did not turn out as she wished, the bride had expeditiously run off with her second choice. This stark chronology of events was subject to various interpretations, of course. Amy was aware that she had put the most uncharitable light possible on Désirée Archer's behavior. What had her bridegroom done or not done that had alienated her so thoroughly in such a short span of time?

Amy dropped into the small upholstered chair in the corner of the bedchamber, her mind seething with unbecoming but irresistible conjectures about the private affairs of strangers. None of these affairs were any of her business, she reminded herself in the interest of fair play. On the other hand, she was in the unenviable position of having the consequences of another woman's actions visited on her head. It would be stupid to close her eyes and mind to any information or argument that might assist her to extricate herself from this quagmire with the least damage to her person and reputation.

It would be idle to deny that she had been badly shaken this evening. Sir Jason was tall and strongly muscled. When he had pulled her up against his chest, she had been frighteningly aware of his anger, but she had also been aware of the grim control he exercised over his actions. Truth to tell, a significant part of her distress had been the result of shock and embarrassment at the raw intimacy of his words. She had not realized before to what extent the odd circumstances of her life had sheltered her in the area of male and female interaction. She had been acquainted with many local families, and two—no, three—young men had shown an interest in her over the past three years. With her father's declining health at the forefront of her thoughts, she had swiftly discouraged the would-be swains. That she had not seen this as a sacrifice was demonstrable proof of her lack of interest in any of them. This evening's events had left her humiliatingly conscious of her inexperience, gaucherie and lack of any feminine wiles. Not that she wished to be alluring in this horrible situation, of course, but it was lowering not to know even what constituted feminine allure.

Disturbed by this aberrant line of thought, Amy glanced

around the now-shadowed room for something to take up
her mind, but there was not a single book among the pretty
ornaments on the tables. She had begun yet another mental
search for clues to Lady Archer's character when she was
rescued by a knock on the hall door. She raced over to un-
lock and open it.

Rescue had come in the roly-poly person of a smiling
middle-aged woman who wheezed into the room ahead of
Elsie. Amy knew at once that this must be the housekeeper.

"Well now, ma'am, what are you about, sitting up here in
the dark without even a candle? Elsie, see to the lights so
that I can show her ladyship what Sir Jason and I have unearthed in the attics," said Mrs. Natwick.

Her speech was difficult as she was still wheezing. Amy
led her to the chair she had just quitted and pushed her
gently down. "You are dreadfully out of breath, Mrs.
Natwick. Do not try to speak for a moment. I can see that
you have brought what must be the riding habit Sir Jason
spoke of at dinner. May I?" At the woman's nod, Amy relieved her of the garments in her lap, holding up the skirt of
a hunter green habit. "It looks awfully long," she said doubtfully.

"Aye, but her ladyship was dreadful thin her last years,
just wasting away she was, the poor soul. Taking up a hem
is no great thing. Try on the jacket. There, you see?" she said
as Amy obeyed. "Look now, if I didn't say that would fit a
treat to Sir Jason when I saw it again in the trunk. The
sleeves need taking up is all."

Amy left the housekeeper nodding in satisfaction and
headed for the mirror between the windows, her heart beating in quick step at the thought of having something that
would not draw undue attention to her escape. Yes, this
would do nicely. She turned, disguising her glee with a de-
mure smile. "Thank you, Mrs. Natwick. I believe this will
be fine. I'll get started on the alterations right away. I see
that Elsie has brought a workbox too," she added with a
smile for the maid who had finished lighting the candles and

a lamp and was bringing a pile of cloth to the housekeeper, who looked horrified.

"You'd ruin your eyes trying to work on that dark fabric at night, ma'am. Elsie will pin up the hems now and we'll take it to my room and pick out the seams and press the new hems in tonight. Between the two of you, you can do the sewing in the morning and be ready to ride with the master before noon."

"That will be wonderful, Mrs. Natwick. Thank you both very much." Amy submitted to Elsie's ministrations in removing the ivory gown and assisting her into the habit. She stood patiently while the maid marked the new hems with chalk and pins, under the watchful eye of the housekeeper.

"Sir Jason rooted out one or two of his mother's favorite shawls and such," Mrs. Natwick said, sitting comfortably while the pinning went forward. She held up a long length of spangled white gauze that was duly admired by Amy, and then a magnificent piece of black lace. "This is called a mantilla," she explained. "Sir Jason brought it back to his mother a few years ago from that heathenish place. That wasn't long before she died, poor thing. The ladies over there wear them on their heads, he says, but they make a fine shawl."

Amy admired this too, without mentioning that she already owned a fine mantilla of white lace that her brother had brought her from Spain. She was even more pleased when the housekeeper produced a card of thread lace and some delicately pleated organdie from the workbox, innocently repeating that the master had said as how his wife was displeased that the dressmaker had made the necklines of the new gowns too low.

When the fitting was completed, Amy thanked the servants with warm sincerity, firmly declining any further assistance at bedtime from the willing Elsie.

At the door, Mrs. Natwick stopped short. "There now, if I didn't nearly forget to tell you. Sir Jason asked me to go into the village tomorrow to buy some new shifts and petticoats and hose till your trunk arrives, ma'am. Of course, they won't be the quality that you are used to, but at least they'll do until your trunk arrives."

"That is very kind of you, Mrs. Natwick," Amy said faintly, relieved to be closing the door on her helpers lest there be any more revelations of her alleged husband's active concern for every aspect of her wardrobe. She turned from the door after relocking it and walked over to the table where Mrs. Natwick had left the thread lace and organdie. It was too bad the maid had taken the workbox with her, or she might have made a start on filling in the neckline of one of the morning gowns.

As she went to put the items in the armoire with the shawls, the sense of this practical musing hit her like a bolt of lightning and she stopped short. What ailed her that she should be considering altering Désirée Archer's wardrobe to suit herself? If all went well with her plans, she would be leaving this place by tomorrow night at the latest. She had already been away from home for two nights, and she dared not hope to ride the whole distance back in one day. The thought of sleeping in a field or coppice was disconcerting, but she did not wish to put in an unaccompanied appearance at any inn, nor was she sanguine about her decidedly limited funds.

Considering the problems she might encounter in finding her way home made her wonder how Tom Watkins was faring. Was he somewhere between Marshland and Oakhill right now? Had he been able to trace the journey she had made by asking questions at turnpikes and posting inns? She realized with a sinking heart that there was only one place along the entire route when she had been seen by anyone — the inn where she had tried to get out of the carriage and had screamed for help.

There was not much comfort to be derived in thinking about Tom's difficulties or Robert's potential dangers. Amy's spirits, which had perked up while Mrs. Natwick and Elsie were with her, descended again as she made herself ready for another night of captivity, carefully keeping her gaze away from the door to the baronet's room. Alone once more, she gave in to the need to weep that she had been battling ever since she had foolishly stepped into a carriage to help a stranger. Her pillow was soaked with tears before she slept that night.

Chapter Six

Morning brought sunshine and a renewal of optimism. When Elsie entered the bedchamber with hot water, Amy greeted her with a smile and a casual suggestion that if she were to have a light breakfast in her room they might get an early start on the sewing. "If Mrs. Natwick can spare you from your usual duties?"

"Of course, ma'am." Elsie shot her a quick look and went back to pouring water in the basin.

"I would not like to keep the master waiting," Amy added, feeling some explanation was called for.

"Now, ma'am," Elsie said in mild reproof, "you know the master never cuts up stiff when you are late. Now, you come over here while the water's hot for washing, and I'll go back to the kitchen for a breakfast tray."

"Bring enough for yourself too, Elsie," Amy said, glancing up from the basin with water dripping down her face.

Halfway out the door, the maid paused to cast her a horrified look at the solecism but forebore to argue, whisking herself away.

Feeling chastened and cosseted at the same time, Amy continued with her ablutions, her thoughts winging back to the missing Désirée. From what Elsie had said, she deduced that tardiness was not uncommon with the baronet's lady. When Sir Jason sent word of when they were to ride she must take care to be prompt in order to illuminate the difference between his wife and herself. His caustic remark last night about her wishing to banish his mother's portrait to the gallery was an admission that he had noted *some* alteration in his wife's customary behavior. Of course he would claim she was purposefully trying to deceive him, Amy realized, sighing as she patted her skin dry, but what possible reason could his wife have for denying that she rode?

With a shake of her head she turned her mind to formulating a plan for her escape. She was not so addlebrained as to expect she could outrun him during their ride, especially on an old horse that had essentially been put out to pasture. She would be content simply to familiarize herself with the surrounding area so she would know where to find Petersfield, which must be her first objective. Best not to dwell on the difficulties of traveling clear across Sussex with the North Downs a barrier almost at the beginning of the long trek eastward. Of a certainty she would never reach her goal if she were too frightened to start out!

Amy was ready when Sir Jason sent word that the horses were awaiting their riders. Working efficiently together after hemming the riding habit, she and Elsie had managed to fill in the neckline of the willow green dress with pleated organdie that finished in a becoming little frill at the throat. She left the maid adding a row of thread lace to the bodice of the ivory silk evening gown and ran lightly down the stairs to meet the man who insisted she was his wife.

Thanks to Mrs. Natwick, who had suddenly remembered where the military-style hat that matched the habit was stored away, her outfit was now complete to a shade. Amy saw admiration in Sir Jason's eyes as she came forward, and she averted her own gaze, disconcerted by the little surge of pleasure this gave her. It went without saying that the admiration was meant for another woman, but there was no call to feel guilty, she reminded herself. She had not chosen to usurp Désirée Archer's position and would not apologize for the fact that her face seemed not to be unique after all.

She gave him a cool greeting, her chin elevated.

"You certainly look the part of a horsewoman," he said gently.

She mistrusted the little smile that accompanied this placatory comment, but resisted the urge to retaliate. He would see, she promised herself as they headed for the entrance.

The elderly Solomon was not as decrepid as Amy had feared. He was naturally cast into the shade in the company of the enormous and powerful chestnut pawing the ground, but he was well groomed, his coat sleek and glossy from brushing. His alert eyes followed her movements as she approached with an extended hand. He accepted the cube of sugar on her palm and her pat on his neck with becoming dignity.

Amy grinned at him and looked up to see Sir Jason watching her with an unreadable expression. "Why Solomon?" she asked quickly.

"My father always held that he was born wise." Sir Jason bestowed an affectionate pat on the old horse, then laughed as Samson nudged him with his nose.

"Are you jealous, boy?" Amy crooned, moving to lay her hand on the chestnut's neck. "You know you are a handsome fellow and expect some attention too, don't you?" She gave him another pat before turning back to whisper to Solomon. Suddenly aware that her actions were being observed by both grooms and Sir Jason, she said guiltily, "Have I kept you waiting? I am sorry."

"Not at all, my dear. I'll give you a leg up," Sir Jason replied, motioning away the groom who had stepped forward, presumably to perform that very service. He tossed her into the saddle where she settled easily, gathering the reins and watching while he shortened the stirrup to her liking.

Sir Jason dismissed the grooms with thanks, and the couple set off at an easy pace.

A sensation of simple joy at being on a horse again stole over Amy, obliterating for a time all her concerns for her brother's safety and her own perilous situation. The amiable Solomon's placid acceptance of a sidesaddle left her free to indulge her interest in the countryside through which they were riding. Used to low, flat marshland and acres reclaimed from the sea, she was enchanted by the undulating terrain with its verdant fields and hedgerows teeming with plant and animal life. Ox-eye daisies and heart's ease jostled each other along the roadside and delighted the eyes. The sweetness of honeysuckle tantalized the nose as they passed by. The hedgerows vibrated with the rustling of unseen creatures and erupted with a flutter of wings as a pair of blue tits flew up and away at the approach of the horses.

Turning her head to follow their flight, she saw that Sir Jason was watching her with that peculiarly intent stare that never failed to unnerve her.

"What did you whisper to Solomon before you mounted?" he asked to surprise her.

Amy laughed but looked a little sheepish also. "I didn't wish to hurt Samson's feelings," she confessed, "so I whispered to Solomon that I have always considered bays the most beautiful horses." She glanced away quickly, relieved when he suggested they stretch the horses' legs over the rising ground opening up ahead of them on the left.

Amy nodded and followed his lead, putting her trust in his judgment and Solomon's experience. Horse and girl cleared the narrow section of hedge with no danger of parting company and galloped over the rising ground in pursuit of the stallion.

Exhilarated and flushed by the exercise, Amy arrived at the top of the hill and pulled reluctantly to a stop beside the man watching her steadily. "That was marvelous; shall we go on?" she invited, privately acknowledging a feeble desire to prolong the visceral pleasure and avoid conversation.

"I hoped you might find the view pleasant from this spot where you've never been before."

His mild admonition was unnecessary, for Amy had looked away from him almost immediately and now sat spellbound, her eyes drinking in the serene panorama of summer lushness spread out before them.

"It's lovely, a perfect little Eden," she said after a long

moment. "We have nothing like this in the marsh country."
Sensing his impatient movement in the saddle at the reference to her home, she added, pointing to a delicate spire in
the distance, "Where is that church?"

"In Petersfield."

"And that is west of here?" Amy said, her nonchalant
tone at variance with her suspended breath as she awaited
his response.

"A bit south actually. Do you not recall that we passed
through it on our way to Oakhill after our marriage?"

"And the road going east?" she inquired, ignoring the re-
minder. "What lies that way?"

"Midhurst is the first place of any size. Shall we ride on?
Samson is eager to stretch his legs, and Solomon, I fear, will
nod off if we tarry much longer."

Amy signalled her assent by bringing the bay's head up,
and they descended from their lofty eminence to the lane
once more.

During the remainder of the ride, Amy received the distinct impression that Sir Jason deliberately selected a route
that kept to the northern and western areas of his property,
but she made no demur and displayed no disappointment.
Indeed she felt none, for she had already learned what she
needed to know in order to direct the course of her escape.
The one word—Midhurst—had triggered a memory that
had set her spirits soaring.

Less than two years ago the daughter of a neighboring
family had married and gone to live on an estate lying between Midhurst and Stedham. A few moments of cudgelling
her brain had dredged up the groom's name—Lenhurst! Instantly, a daunting journey of nearly one hundred miles had
been reduced to less than fifteen. With the Lenhursts she
would be safe from pursuit while arrangements were made
for her return to Marshland.

Amy's intellect was not so taken up with relief and jubi-
lation that she failed to note that between short bursts of information or references to points of interest, Sir Jason's
expression became brooding, for want of a better descrip-

tive. This had the effect of increasing her wariness. She took care to respond with the measured approval or appreciation of a disinterested stranger, though finding it strangely difficult to squelch an impulse to please him by confiding her honest delight in the natural beauty of the estate.

Sir Jason's penetrating glance returned often to her face, but he imposed no additional tests of her horsemanship during their outing. Nor did he refer to his wife's obvious failure to mention—if not outright denial of—the accomplishment. Amy, more than a little piqued at this omission, challenged him on it as they drew within sight of the stable yard.

"You expected me to land in the hedge earlier, did you not?" she asked with a lifted eyebrow.

"I thought it a possibility at least," he admitted coolly. "If you are looking for praise of your equestrian prowess, you may have it with my good will. You are obviously an accomplished rider."

"You know very well that I was not fishing for compliments!" she snapped, her eyes stormy. "You as good as admitted last night that your wife does not ride. Now you have seen that I do. Why will you persist in denying the truth? I am *not* your wife! You do not know me!"

"I don't know my wife," he said, turning away from her to hail the groom who had materialized in the stable yard at the sound of hoofbeats.

Amy had much to mull over as she trudged upstairs to her quarters a few minutes later, the skirts of the gabardine habit weighing heavily on her arm. She pulled off the hat that was beginning to feel like an iron band around her head and breathed a sigh of relief, wondering why she should feel so bone weary after a ride of little more than an hour. Granted, she had not been on a horse in a fortnight, but she was used to riding for hours on end at home without fearing she had left her youth far behind her.

It was dealing with the man who insisted against all reason that she was his wife that brought on this crushing weight of futility, fatigue and sadness, she decided with a spurt of petulance. He was the most obstinate, provoking creature it had ever been her misfortune to encounter. From little things the servants had said in passing, from his unadmitted but manifest surprise at her demeanor and, most telling of all, from his own description of his wife's conduct, it must be obvious to the meanest intelligence that she was nothing at all like Désirée Archer under the skin. Equally obvious was the fact that he *wanted* her to be his Désirée. Considering that the brief marriage had been a spectacular failure by any yardstick, this struck her as absurd—no, worse—as insane. And so she would tell him before they were a day older, she vowed, still in the grip of sheer frustration.

Fortunately her thoughts were given a happier direction when she entered her bedchamber and saw her temporary abigail filling a bath with hot water.

"Elsie, you angel! You must have read my mind!" she declared, casting aside the hat and stripping off her gloves.

"Well, ma'am, I reckoned as how you might be aching in a few places if you had not ridden for a spell," the maid said, blushing with pleasure. "You will have to hurry a bit, though, if you intend to go down to lunch."

"I do not wish to hurry," Amy declared. "I intend to sink into that bath and soak until my skin wrinkles—or until I congeal."

"Yes, ma'am," Elsie replied, eyeing her mistress's impish grin doubtfully. "Shall I order something from the kitchen for your lunch after I help you to disrobe?"

"I can get myself into the bath unaided. You may go to the kitchen and tell the cook that I am feeling quite peckish after all that riding."

"Yes, ma'am; I'll say you have worked up an appetite."

"Thank you, Elsie," Amy said meekly, accepting the unspoken rebuke as her due. She waited until the maid had closed the hall door before going over to satisfy herself that the door between the bedchambers was still locked. That done, she lost no time in getting into the bath, sighing with pleasure as the warm water caressed her skin.

Amy did manage to lose herself in pure sensual bliss for a few moments, but her brain refused to stay quiescent.

This evening she would make one final attempt to persuade Sir Jason to question the evidence of his eyes and listen to his rational side, leaving his heart out of the equation entirely: a tall order, based on his reaction to all her efforts thus far, she admitted with a grimace.

Failing this, she must be prepared to leave Oakhill tonight, which brought her smack up against the first of two critical tasks: leaving the house without being detected. She would have to wait until everyone was abed of course. Last night she had noticed the heavy bar across the front door. Though she did not doubt she possessed the requisite strength to lift it, she did fear making a noise that might rouse someone. The hall door in the kitchen quarters posed no such problem, but the housekeeper's room was located too close to it for this to be a completely practical choice if she should be a light sleeper. Still, she would liefer take a chance on this exit than use the door in the library, which was directly beneath Sir Jason's bedchamber. He had come suddenly awake the other morning when she had crept into his room looking for the key, though she had thought her movements essentially soundless. Therefore her choice must be the exit farthest removed from him.

Once safely away from the house, she would have to get a saddle from the tack room without waking the grooms who slept nearby. Solomon would be in the field where she had seen him yesterday, and though she could ride bareback in an emergency, she'd prefer to have a bridle at least. Beggars could not be choosers, however, and she would have to do what the situation dictated at the time. If only she dared slip out to the stables this afternoon and bring a bridle back to her room, she would gladly forgo the saddle. She preferred to ride astride in any case.

With the bathwater cooling rapidly, Amy considered her chances of accomplishing this feat in daylight and reluctantly decided against making the attempt, since detection would alert Sir Jason to her intention to escape. At least she could plan to sleep for an hour or two after lunch in preparation for a long night of traveling, she thought. She finished her bath swiftly and reached for the towel Elsie had left on a nearby chair.

That evening Amy entered the saloon, refreshed by a two-hour afternoon nap. She was again wearing the ivory gown in its more modest reincarnation, and she carried her head high in a show of bravery that was contradicted by a racing pulse and uncomfortable flutterings in her stomach. Conscious that this could be the last time they would ever meet and that each previous meeting had ended in a less than amicable fashion, she was determined to do her utmost to keep her dignity and contain her temper this evening.

This noble resolve was shaken at the outset when in response to her greeting, Sir Jason snapped, "Will you please stop 'sirring' me like some little maidservant! How do you think that looks to my staff?"

About to retort that upholding his pride in front of the servants was not an object with her, Amy swallowed her spleen and allowed her better nature to prevail, saying merely, "Very well. How did your wife address you?"

His compressed lips told her this was not an entirely felicitous compromise, but he chose not to resume hostilities, although the tone in which he said, "By my name," was dry as dust.

"Good evening, Jason," she parroted obediently.

"There, that was not so difficult, was it?"

"No." Amy walked over to the chair she had occupied on the previous evening and sat down, her eyes following his movements as he poured a glass of sherry from the decanter and held it up in mute invitation.

"No, thank you," she said as she had night before, watching as he took the chair opposite her and sipped from the glass.

His gaze roamed over her still figure, and his lips softened into a faint smile as he observed, "I see your needle has been busy altering more than the riding habit."

"Yes," she agreed serenely.

His smile twisted a bit when nothing more was forthcoming. "You have changed, Désirée. You were never one to let a silence grow. I used to wonder if you had an inexhaustible supply of charming little platitudes to fill any awkward conversational voids."

She shook her head and fixed him with pleading eyes. "Jason, I believe you know that I am not Désirée. We are two different people."

"You are three different people," he countered wearily. "The innocent girl I courted became another person on our wedding night when I discovered you were not a virgin, and now you seem different once again. Who are you really, Désirée? I confess I do not know. Do you?"

Amy, her wide eyes locked on his, could not have produced a syllable to save her life, so perhaps it was fortunate that Hatcherd appeared in the doorway at that moment to announce dinner. She blinked but made no other movement until Jason rose and extended his hand to her. She blinked again and took it, allowing him to pull her to her feet. She made no effort to assert her independence and was surprised to find her hand still clasped in his when she reached her chair in the dining room. She mumbled a thank you when he seated her, slowly coming out of the state of shock brought about by his incredible revelation about his bride.

Given the inauspicious beginning, the dinner period passed quite smoothly, enlivened by none of the verbal fencing that had rendered the previous evening intolerable. Sir Jason offered a description of the genteel families in the area and their proximity to Oakhill. For her part, Amy no longer felt any desire to cross swords with him. Jason's disclosure of his wife's ultimate deception had aroused both pity and dismay in her breast. The compassion would have been shared by anyone with an ounce of humanity, but the dismay was the product of what she recognized as an irrational desire to make it up to him somehow for another woman's betrayal.

This must be the result of being cast in the role of the betrayer with all the accusations and unspoken pain of the victim raining down on her own innocent head, she assured herself. Thank heavens she would be leaving here tonight, because it was becoming increasingly difficult to refrain from shouting out that *she* could never be so dead to all tenets of morality and propriety as to act as Désirée Archer had.

The appearance of amity at the dining table lulled Amy into a state of passivity that was shattered at the meal's conclusion when Jason followed her into the saloon, saying in an offhand manner that did not ring true that he had something to discuss with her. Concealing her trepidation that something might yet happen to prevent her escape, Amy murmured, "Of course," and sat down near the fireplace. She glanced involuntarily at the portrait over the mantel as if seeking assistance from the gentle face of the baronet's mother.

"I have spent the better part of the past two days going over the post that accumulated during my absence."

His voice brought her head around and she assumed a look of polite inquiry.

"There is one communication that is of particular interest because it pertains as much to you as to me." In the pause that ensued, Amy read tension in the taut lines of his countenance. He meant Désirée, of course, she thought, quenching the little spurt of hope that his words had engendered.

"You may recall that I mentioned writing to announce our marriage to my great-aunt, Lady Glenallan, when you first took up residence at Oakhill." Amy stared at him blankly, and after visibly clenching his jaw, he continued, "Great-aunt Martha was childless, and my mother was her favorite niece. Mama would take me to Glendale for a fortnight during the summers of my childhood. The old lady put up with a scrubby brat quite graciously, considering that she really couldn't abide boys. Actually, she held the entire male sex in dislike, her late husband included."

Amy's eyes were drawn to the reminiscent smile that softened his well-cut mouth for a second before he continued. "I was a bit surprised when she did not reply to my letter within a few days and would have written again had I not been so preoccupied with our . . . situation. The letter that arrived during my absence was written by my aunt's companion, Miss Chistleton. Evidently Aunt Martha's health has been steadily declining since the winter. . . ."

"I am sorry," Amy said softly when he stopped. "You are fond of her?"

"Yes. She is unique—arrogant, officious, outspoken to a fault, prejudiced—but also widely read with a rational mind and a dry sense of humor. All of these qualities are more readily evident than her intrinsic kindness, which she seems determined to conceal from the generality of humanity as if it were a weakness or a flaw to be ashamed of."

"She . . . certainly sounds like an original." Amy found herself smiling until Jason's gaze on her mouth became intent, which instantly aroused her defenses, erasing the smile. "How does your letter relate to me, sir—Jason?" she amended hurriedly as he frowned.

"Miss Chistleton writes that Aunt Martha wishes to make her will and has summoned her remaining niece and several great-nephews and nieces to what she believes to be her deathbed, though I trust this is not the case," he said briskly. "Naturally she desires to make the acquaintance of my bride."

"No," Amy said decisively, having seen at last where this tale was heading. "You have no right to ask this of me and you would be ill advised to insist on taking me to your aunt's estate against my will."

"Ill-advised?" he repeated with soft menace, but Amy was not to be cowed.

"You told your servants a cock-and-bull story about my having amnesia so they would watch my every movement, but that strategy will not serve you at your aunt's house where no one knows what your wife looks like." She stood up and looked him in the eye. "I trust I make myself clear?"

"Very clear, but you disappoint me, my dear Désirée." He rose also and placed himself squarely in her path to the door. "I would have thought you would be delighted at the chance to acquire Aunt Martha's vast riches—a very good chance actually, since I am widely held to be her favorite relative. I am willing to make over half of anything I should inherit to you legally, even if we dissolve the marriage. How can you resist such an advantageous proposition?"

"Because I am not Désirée," Amy said, examining his satiric countenance sadly. "I am very tired, so I will bid you good night, Jason."

She walked out of the room with unhurried steps, though her nerves were as tense as violin strings and her dread that he might stop her physically had her heart hammering in her chest.

When she reached the stairs unhindered, she abandoned all pretense of courage and flew up them at a rate that had her panting when she reached the dubious haven of her bed-chamber.

Amy would have been hard-pressed to say whether it was fear or relief that caused the trembling in her limbs, but it took the best part of a half hour before she could stop pacing and sit quietly in a chair, and even longer to summon her faculties to her aid.

It was vital that she execute every stage of the plan she had evolved during the hours she'd spent in this room if she was to get safely away tonight. The first stage was to ensure that Elsie should find nothing to arouse her curiosity or doubt when she came in less than an hour to get her mistress ready for bed.

As Amy sat, mentally going through the plan a step at a time, her courage gradually rebounded to equal her resolve and her breathing returned to normal. She would be ready when the time came.

Chapter Seven

Jason's eyes and his thoughts were on the young woman walking away. The irony of this repeated act was not lost on him. From the fiasco that was their wedding night she had begun turning away from him. What was the matter with his brain that he still refused to accept this simple reality?

At the time when he had set out to find his runaway bride his intellect had accepted that Désirée was not the girl he had believed her to be. She was neither innocent nor in love with him, as she had convincingly demonstrated by eloping with another man. His pursuit of her had been driven not by love but by a need to satisfy his honor and find a way to end the wretched business with as little scandal as possible.

Well, he had found her, and clarity had become chaos; simplicity and truth had ceased to exist for him, replaced by confusion and doubt. During the lonely weeks of searching for Désirée he'd had oceans of time to wonder what he would find when he found her again. Would she be defiant, flaunting her lover in his face? Perhaps she would be penitent, realizing that she had embarked on a rash and disastrous course.

In none of his imaginings had he pictured her flatly denying her identity! When she had done so at their accidental meeting in Rye, threatening to cause a public scene, he had drawn back, conceding the efficacy of her spur-of-the-moment tactic. His retreat had been temporary while he planned his next move in the contest, allowing no moral qualms to prevent his carrying out a swift and efficient abduction.

Jason's eyes shifted involuntarily to his mother's portrait as he sat down again. Would she sympathize with the son she loved or remonstrate with him for his continued intimidation—implied intimidation at the very least—of his errant wife? Probably both, he decided, indulging in a futile wish to be able to talk with her for just fifteen minutes. His gentle mother had been a strong believer in the power of remorse to improve one's character.

His character should be approaching beatification by now, he concluded glumly, remorse having become his constant companion from the moment in the hired carriage when Désirée had looked up at him with her beautiful eyes full of appeal and protested that she could not drink any more of the tea he had drugged. He had withstood her defiance and temper unmoved, but her distress left wounds in his heart—or perhaps his conscience.

Nothing had gone according to plan from the moment he had awakened yesterday to find her going through his pockets looking for the key to her bedchamber. It had not occurred to him that she would persist in denying her identity once he had made sure that she could not run away again.

Over their short but eventful acquaintance he had learned that she could be charming, wily and untruthful in the pursuit of her own ends, but he would have said that she was *au fond* a realist. He would have expected her to try to negotiate an advantageous settlement if she was determined to end their marriage, but she had refused to talk about her lover at all and continued to deny her identity in the face of unanimous recognition from the staff at Oakhill.

He would have to hand her the palm for being a convincing actress, as her ability to maintain a fictitious persona of sweet adoring vulnerability during their courtship had amply proved. He could not see how this present pose could further her ambitions, however, for if she succeeded in convincing him that she was not his wife there would be no inducement for him to enrich her by a penny. Of course he would then let her go, and she would be rid of him. But she could have achieved that end in Rye by sitting down and talking seriously with him, unless her pretense of being someone else had arisen out of fear for her lover's continued health should her irate husband confront him.

And that was another unaccountable factor. Where was this Martin? He'd had ample time to follow Désirée to Oakhill by now. Could they perhaps have quarreled? Did that account for her refusal to mention him? Did she feel trapped in her current posture? The lines in Jason's forehead deepened as he pursued this line of thought.

So fierce was his concentration that he failed to hear Hatcherd's entrance and started violently at the butler's voice wishing to know if he had any further requests.

"No, thank you—no, wait, Hatcherd," he said, surging up from his chair. "Bring a bottle of the best brandy to the library; then you may lock up and go to bed."

"Very good, sir."

Jason, busy stretching cramped muscles in his back and shoulders, did not see the quick look Hatcherd shot him before removing himself silently. After a couple of minutes he extinguished the candles in the saloon and ambled down the hall toward the library. If his mind, teeming with contradictory theories and observations, was not going to permit his body to sleep, he might as well spend the time in the solid comfort of the big old leather chair his father had cherished.

An hour later, Jason was no closer to solving the enigma that was his wife, and the level in the brandy bottle had sunk by several inches. He had to admit, though, that the brandy level might be higher if Désirée's character were the only mystery engaging his mind. In truth, he was finding his own recent behavior equally troubling. Why when his wife so clearly wished to be quit of him did he not simply announce that he would make arrangements for her to reside in a place of her choice while he set about dissolving the marriage?

Surely that would elicit the necessary information about her lover and put a period to the whole distasteful episode. And what idiocy had prompted him to put his great-aunt's invitation before her?

Knowing there were no answers—no sensible answers, at any rate—to these questions, Jason pushed himself out of the old leather chair and wandered over to the French doors. He unlocked and opened them on an impulse, grateful for the crisp night air that greeted him. Hopefully that would clear the brandy fumes from his befuddled brain.

Different! This Désirée insisted she was different from the former Désirée and begged him to admit the differences. Of course he had perceived differences, and not just the ones she pointed out, such as her ability to ride. He had noted the absence of the playful charm of manner that had captivated him initially. She was not treating him to any displays of feminine charm these days, as was perfectly understandable under the circumstances. On the other hand, she had surprised him by the way she listened with all her attention to what he had to say, something she had not been in the habit of doing before she ran away. He had also seen the pity in her eyes when he had detailed some of her betrayals. Compassion for his feelings had never been evident in the days of their marriage. Certainly she had changed of late, but change had been the one constant of his enigmatic wife. As with a chameleon, change defined her nature.

Jason stepped out into the shrubbery, inhaling the scents of earth and vegetation as he looked up to the canopy of stars. The moon was getting higher in the sky, its cold white light revealing the shapes of the trees and bushes set about like pieces on a chessboard. The only sounds were unidentifiable rustlings of tiny creatures that shared the night with him. He stood motionless, his eyes on the stars, and suddenly heard an alien sound, one he could identify—the closing of a door.

Instantly alert, Jason moved nothing but his head, glancing back over his shoulder to ascertain that the library door remained open. That being so, the sound must have come from the door to the kitchen area. He remained still for another few seconds without hearing any other unnatural night noises. About to return to the library, Jason decided to err on the side of caution since no valid reason for the opening and closing of outer doors had occurred to him. Moving like a cat, he headed through the opening in the shrubbery that led to the kitchen garden, pausing against the greenery while he scanned the area thoroughly. Nothing moved and the kitchen door appeared closed.

A moment later he frowned as he found the door closed but not locked. If a house servant had returned late and been let in by someone, the door should now be locked. Likewise, one of the outdoor servants would have had someone lock the door behind him as he left unless his presence had not been known to anyone.

Jason was turning possibilities over in his mind when his ears caught another isolated sound—pebbles being dislodged by a hasty footstep perhaps. He set off swiftly toward the stable block, cursing silently when his own shoe crunched against the gravel. All was quiet as he rounded the side of the barn, but he saw immediately that the tack room door was ajar. He was about to enter a few seconds later when a soft whicker brought him to a standstill with his hand on the latch. *Solomon!* Puzzlement vanished in a blaze of certainty as he quietly relatched the door.

As he sprinted for the field where the bay grazed, Jason's thoughts defied description, but not least among them was a grudging admiration for her resourcefulness and courage. This did not preclude raging fear and fury at the foolhardiness of the endeavor. He refused to admit into his thought processes any feelings of chagrin at how much she must detest him to resort to such an action. Time enough for that when he had scotched this adventure.

A cloud passed over the moon as Jason reached the paddock and vaulted over the fence. She had left the gate unlatched, he noted in passing, but he doubted she'd had enough time to remove a saddle and bridle from the tack room before hearing his own steps approaching. He was

aware of soft noises that must be coming from Solomon,
though he could not see them while the moon was hidden.
Ah, now the cloud was drifting past. He spotted girl and
horse over in a corner by the back of the fence. She must be
trying to mount by climbing up the stile.

"Were you planning a midnight ride, my dear?" he asked
sotto voce as he strode forward.

There was a gasp from the girl and a soft whicker from
the bay as the moon slid behind another scrap of cloud, blot-
ting out everything farther away than a few yards. Jason
heard Solomon coming toward him and increased his pace
to a near run when there was no further sound from his wife.
"Where is she, boy?" he asked, running his hands over the
animal who had found him. As he suspected, Solomon wore
neither saddle nor bridle. What was she thinking to attempt
a stunt like that? And where was she at this moment? There
were no alien sounds in the paddock, and he could see nothing as the moon glided free once more. She must have gone
over the fence and headed for the stand of trees that bordered the next field and ended at the lane leading to the village a half mile away. It would behoove him to catch her
before she reached other habitations if he wished to keep
this episode from becoming known in the neighborhood.

"Stand still, boy," he commanded before taking a few
running steps and vaulting up onto Solomon's back as he
had often done in his youth. His amiable steed needed little
guiding as Jason walked him quietly out of the field and into
the trees before increasing the pace to a trot. He trusted
Solomon's instincts to weave his way between the trees to
the lane. Jason's anxiety increased as they came within a
few hundred yards of the village without spying Désirée, but
he gave her credit for knowing her only chance of escape
without a horse was to remain out of sight. Consequently, he
left the lane and entered a copse that straggled behind the
village and paralleled the road to Petersfield for a time. He
signalled Solomon to stop while he listened in utter stillness
to the whispering noises of the night.

After what seemed like a small eternity, his patience was

rewarded as a twig snapped some way ahead of them. He urged Solomon forward with his knees and bent over his neck to avoid hanging branches. Whatever was ahead of them could not fail to hear the noise they were making, but there was no help for that. Jason scanned the darkness from side to side until he saw a shadow separate from the darker shadow that was a tree and dart to the right. Horse and rider pursued the shadow, which moved with a speed that made Jason question whether his quarry was not a woodland creature after all.

A moment later he realized the shadow had vanished. Jason whispered to Solomon and they stopped once more to listen, but there were no unusual sounds to be heard now. Anxiety for her safety prompted Jason to call out, "Please, Désirée, do not do this. It is too dangerous. You could injure yourself seriously. You must see that I cannot leave you to wander about unknown country alone and on foot. Come home and we will talk this situation through to a solution."

Silence greeted this behest, and he urged Solomon forward again, more cautiously now since the trees were closer together and the moon's assistance less pronounced. Nor were there any sounds to aid their progress at present. Jason's jaw clenched more tightly as he pressed on, driven by fear.

Suddenly from close at hand came a cacaphony of breaking branches, followed by a thud and a cry of pain that was bitten off instantly.

"Are you hurt, Désirée? Where are you?"

Jason's anxious cries brought no vocal response, but Solomon solved his problem by turning left undirected and stopping after a few yards.

She was on the ground struggling to rise when Jason saw her in the small clearing. "Good boy." He patted Solomon's neck and jumped down. "What happened? Where are you hurt?" he asked, putting an arm around her shaking shoulders.

"My—my foot," she said on a sobbing breath. "It . . . caught in a . . . tree root."

"Fortunately, your noble steed is at hand and will carry you back home. Put your arms around my neck and I'll put you up on his back."

"It is my right foot. If you will just help me stand and make a step for the left, I'll be able to mount by myself."

"I assume you have no objection to riding astride," he murmured while doing her bidding.

"I prefer it actually." She ignored his dry tone and landed neatly atop Solomon with minimal assistance.

"Ah, ought I to mention perhaps that Solomon and I have been close companions since our shared youth and he will obey my spoken commands?"

He could not see her face distinctly, but her sigh was audible. "I will not try to get away tonight."

He received the unspoken message that this promise applied only to tonight without comment, and they set off to retrace their steps with Jason walking beside the mounted girl.

The trip home was accomplished in nearly total silence. Jason, experiencing the draining fatigue that often follows a fraught period of sustained physical activity, was attempting to evaluate the aborted escape. He was shocked and shaken by the degree of desperation she must have felt to embark on such a reckless and foolhardy feat.

"Where were you heading, if you had succeeded in saddling Solomon, I mean?" he asked at last, just as they came out of the trees near the bay's field.

"Home, of course."

Jason put a hand on Solomon's neck. "This way, boy," he said, heading toward the back of the house. "Home? Do you mean Portsmouth?"

"I mean Marshland, of course—Kent."

He said nothing until they reached the lighted library where the open door beckoned. "Come." He raised his arms and she came down off Solomon's back, stiffening when his arms tightened around her. "Go home, boy," he added, walking into the house and carrying his protesting wife.

"I can walk."

"In due course." He set her down in the big chair and went over to the desk where he poured more brandy into his glass. He glanced at the clock on the mantel, mildly surprised to discover that scarcely an hour had elapsed since he'd left this room.

Désirée was slumped in the enveloping chair in a posture of total exhaustion. "Here, take this," he said, holding out the glass.

She looked up briefly then, making a gesture of refusal when she saw the glass.

"This is medicine; you need it." He heard the roughness in his voice and took care to keep the hand that wrapped her fingers around the glass from tightening as he raised her hand with the glass to her mouth until she pushed his hand away and took a sip.

"That's a good girl," he said, gentling his voice. "Here, I will hold it while you remove that hat that has gone sadly awry."

She obeyed him mechanically and accepted the glass back after placing the hat in her lap. He kept one eye on her while he went over to close and lock the French doors.

"Should you not see to Solomon?"

"He'll go straight back to his pasture," he replied, taking the question as a sign that the brandy was already having a restorative effect on her mental powers.

"He is a wonderful horse." She turned her face away from him, pretending interest in the brandy in her hand as he returned, but he had already noted the silent tears sliding over her cheekbones.

"Is your foot very painful?" he asked, kneeling in front of her to remove the black half boot. He was as careful as he could be, but she winced as he pulled it off. "I'm sorry to have to hurt you. Is the pain very bad? I'll send for the doctor."

"No, no," she protested quickly. "It is really just a little sore, that's all, truly. It will be fine by tomorrow."

"But you are still crying," he pointed out softly, producing a handkerchief from the inside pocket of his coat.

She wiped her cheeks and blew her nose unself-consciously; then she straightened her shoulders and lowered the handkerchief, looking him straight in the eye. "I beg your pardon," she said with dignity. "I know your opinion of females who use tears to manipulate men."

"But you do not know my opinion of females who suppress tears they need to shed," he rebutted with a smile. Her eyes, still showing the effects of tears, flickered with sudden alarm, and he pulled back quickly, rising from his knees.

"Désirée," he began, giving voice to an idea that had occurred to him on the walk home when he had realized how close he had come to losing her again, "I have a proposal to put before you." He dropped into an armless chair near the desk and tried to discipline his expression to a friendly neutrality to combat the fear she could not disguise.

"What sort of proposal?" she asked in a husky little voice when he waited for a response before proceeding.

"Do you recall that you had urged me to write to this Marshland to check on your identity?"

She nodded, hope flaring in her face.

"Well, I propose to do better than that: I will take you into Kent . . . if you will first accompany me to my great-aunt's estate for two or three days."

He watched as hope gave way to doubt and she gnawed on her bottom lip. Huge jeweled eyes between damp lashes questioned him while she twisted his handkerchief between nervous fingers. "What do you mean precisely by desiring me to accompany you?" she asked finally.

"Well," he replied with a twisted grin, "it would scarcely do my credit with my aunt any good to present to her a bride who plans to run away during our visit. All I ask is that you refrain from proclaiming yourself someone other than my wife while we are her guests. If you could manage to enjoy yourself during your stay, that would be a bonus," he finished.

Her lips twisted into an equally rueful smile. "I fear you must not expect a bonus, Jason. I could never enjoy pretending to be someone else, but I will promise not to run away or deny that I am your wife while we are at Glendale—on one condition."

"Yes?"

"I cannot *bear* to be called by that name," she said with a revulsion that startled him by its vehemence.

"I fear I have already told my aunt that your given name is Désirée," he said slowly.

"Then tell her Amy is my second name and I prefer it, or make up some other tale. What is one more lie among so many?" To his rising concern, her eyes filled with tears once more and she had recourse to the mutilated handkerchief again, sniffing inelegantly.

"You are totally spent," he declared, rising and scooping her out of the leather chair in one determined motion. "It is time you were in bed."

"What are you doing? Put me down this instant! I am perfectly capable of walking up the stairs."

"Unless you wish to be kissed and kissed hard, you will stop this childish struggling right now," he declared, near the end of his own tether at this point. Gray eyes compelled green ones that glared back furiously, but her struggles ceased.

"Take one of the candles," he instructed her, blowing out the rest as she did so.

She held herself rigid, not relaxing against his chest as Jason toiled up the staircase. She might be small but she was a worthy adversary, he conceded, admiring the fiery red glints that the candle coaxed from her chestnut tresses.

Arriving at her bedchamber, he tried to open the door, only to find it locked. His eyebrows shot upward. "I sincerely hope you did not throw away the key," he said, setting her on her feet.

"No, I—I have it here," she said, thrusting the candle at him while she unbuttoned the top of the riding habit. Her cheeks were crimson as she withdrew the key from somewhere beyond his view.

Suddenly lighthearted for no readily apparent cause, Jason laughed.

She looked up, startled and questioning, her luscious mouth rounding in a circle, the key poised between her fingers.

Jason tried but failed to resist an impulse to kiss that inviting mouth. He swooped down and seized her lips with his, not as he had threatened earlier, but lightly. And such was the advantage of surprise that he was able to enjoy an extra second of sweet contact before her reflexes, dulled perhaps by brandy, were able to coordinate in a strong shove that pushed him back.

"You are not to do that!" she sputtered. "Not again, not if you wish me to go with you to Glendale!"

Reading the rising hysteria in her face, Jason stiffled the words crowding on his tongue as he took the key from her limp grasp and unlocked and opened the door. He handed the key back to her with the candle and bowed. "Good night, my dear Dés— Amy."

"Wait! I will light a candle inside; then you may take this one."

"No need. I can navigate around this house blindfolded," he said over his shoulder. He had his door open before she withdrew into her room, her expression troubled in the light of the candle.

Moonlight was streaming through a window in his bed-chamber, rendering it unnecessary to prove his boastful claim. He ambled over to the window, staring absently out at the myriad pinpricks in a black velvet sky while he drew off his cravat that felt more like a noose at this hour. The untimely elation that had bubbled up, most likely from having Désirée safely back and prepared to play her part at Glendale, had ebbed as quickly as it arose, leaving his spirits totally depleted. This in addition to the ordinary fatigue one could reasonably expect from a midnight adventure. In truth, he could no more explain the second than the first emotion, he told himself as he went about preparing for bed in the neat, methodical fashion that was a legacy from his years of military living.

Even when he had stretched out gratefully in his bed his

tired brain refused to leave the subject, however diligently he tried to focus on the practical preparations necessary before their temporary removal to Glendale. He was sliding close to sleep when a reason for his rapid descent into the dismals became as distinct as if it were written on his eyelids: at almost the same moment when he had realized the depth of Désirée's desperation to escape him, he had finally comprehended his own desperate desire to keep her with him.

Protest suffused his whole being. Knowing her to be a conniving fortune hunter with no moral compass, he could see it would be the height of madness to fall in love with her again. Not that it had ever been love, of course. Even before she eloped with Martin, he had come to see his attachment for the infatuation it most certainly was. Her face and figure were all he really found to admire save perhaps a grudging respect for the single-mindedness with which she pursued her ambitions.

Jason threw off the bedcovers and wiped his sleeve across his damp forehead. How could he still desire to protect and guard someone who had demonstrated that she was eminently capable of taking care of herself? If not misguided chivalry, then what? Surely not that impulsive excuse for a kiss just now! He must have deluded himself that she displayed a sweetness of nature at present that he had not seen before—as well as an integrity of spirit.

He must remember that he had been wrong about her character before. Most of all, he must keep in mind that Désirée was a chameleon if he was not to make a fool of himself a second time.

Chapter Eight

Thanks to the combined efforts of Mrs. Natwick and Elsie, an elegantly attired and beautifully coiffured Amy presented herself at the entrance door at the precise moment appointed by Sir Jason.

She had been partaking of a hearty breakfast in her room on the morning after her abortive escape when his message was delivered. Embarrassed by her panicky reaction to her supposed husband's casual kiss and disquieted by nebulous fears about future interactions, she had taken the prudent decision to delay their next encounter. This had only added self-disgust at her cowardice to the emotions churning inside her. As her eyes had deciphered the message written in bold, slanting script, sheer shock that he proposed to set out for Glendale before noon on this very day drove every concern clean out of her mind except the practical problems of getting herself and her borrowed finery ready by the stated hour.

Pushing the tray aside, Amy had leapt out of bed, startling Elsie into spilling some of the water she was pouring into the basin. After sending the maid posthaste for the housekeeper, she flung open the armoire and assessed the garments therein for their suitability for a visit to an elderly invalid. The result had been a marathon session of sewing by all three women as they proceeded to sacrifice fashion for increased modesty by altering the necklines of the remaining gowns. Mrs. Natwick, again raiding an attic trunk containing possessions of the baronet's late mother, had unearthed several pairs of gloves, a charming spencer of white pique and, most welcome of all, a pair of light shoes that, though a trifle large, could be worn with all the daytime dresses.

For traveling, Amy had elected to wear the plainest of Désirée Archer's gowns, made of polished cotton in a soft shade of mauve with a slightly wider skirt than the others. She slipped her arms into the crisp spencer and watched in the mirror as Elsie tenderly placed the new straw hat with its crown of lavender rosebuds atop her gleaming tresses arranged in a complicated knot at the nape. She tied the matching lavender ribbons under one ear before pulling on the gloves.

"You do look a picture in that hat, ma'am," said Mrs. Natwick, handing her a lace-edged handkerchief she had thoughtfully removed from the trunk they had packed before the footman could take it away.

Amy tucked the handkerchief into the sleeve of the spencer. "Thank you both for all your help this morning," she said, fighting back silly tears at the sudden realization that she would not be seeing them again, "and please convey my gratitude to Cook for sending up that delightful early nuncheon after I let my breakfast get cold."

"It is time to go, ma'am," Elsie said, with a pointed glance at the clock.

"I . . . yes, goodbye." Amy dashed out of the room and ran toward the stairs, flicking away a tear from the corner of each eye with her gloved finger as she did so, aware of their "Godspeeds" caroling behind her.

By the time she descended to the entrance hall, she had regained command of her emotions, but her smile for Hatcherd was a bit tremulous.

"Ah, punctual to the moment, my dear," said Sir Jason, turning from the open door where he had been watching the loading of their baggage. "And looking particularly charming too, I might add. I like the new hat."

"Th-thank you." Amy heard the formality behind his complimentary remarks and decided they had been made for the benefit of the servants. On her mettle once more, she was able to reply appropriately to Hatcherd's expressed wish for a pleasant journey and visit as she offered him her hand in farewell.

Amy was more than a little unsettled by this strange sense of actual sorrow at leaving Oakhill, so she was grateful when, having handed her into the carriage and taken his seat opposite her, Jason placed a travel desk on his lap and proceeded to read some papers he took from it. She stared resolutely out the window, trying to make sense of this perverse reluctance to leave a place that had been no more than a prison to her, however lovely the architecture and landscape. It must be simply the knowledge that under other circumstances she would have adored to visit this estate, she assured herself as they rolled between green fields and past the occasional solidly built farmhouse.

"What do you find so riveting in the landscape?"

He must not have been so absorbed in his reading as he had seemed, she thought, turning to meet his dark gaze. "I was just thinking that your land appears to be in good heart and the farms well built and prosperous, and recalling that you said the estate was encumbered," she replied with more truth than diplomacy. "Not that it is any of my affair," she added hastily, as he looked surprised.

"Of course it is your affair," he said shortly, and when she would have spoken, cut across her protests. "My father was devoted to my mother, and her death two years ago left him devastated. He lost interest in the property and couldn't bear to be in the house after she was gone. He went to London when he was not visiting friends during the hunting season, but wherever he was, it seems that he gambled—race meetings, sports, cards—anything and everything. I blame myself for not suspecting how depressed he really was. Perhaps if I had sold out then and come home to Oakhill he would not have started down that path. We were better friends than most fathers and sons, but I was far away and oblivious to anything beyond the war. Eventually he lost more than he could cover by selling off the good paintings and the London house. He died of pneumonia shortly after taking a mortgage on the estate. He was only two-and-sixty."

"I am so very sorry. Did he ever ask you to sell out?"

"No. Nor was he one to put his thoughts down on paper. He wrote infrequently, and his letters gave no hint of how matters stood with him."

Amy had to press her lips tightly together to keep from relating her father's somewhat similar story, but Jason's impatience at her reticence about his affairs just now had been palpable. Every previous reference to her own life or family had provoked annoyance or outright anger. The prospect of riding for hours in close proximity to an irritable man kept her silent on the subject. He had lost so much these past two years, she thought, eyeing his set features in troubled sympathy.

"Tell me about Glendale," she said quickly when his eyes that had been sombre when recounting his father's last days warmed slowly as they roved over her face, bringing a rush of color to her cheeks. She turned hers away on a pretext of retying the ribbons on her hat.

There was a good deal of understanding in his smiling eyes, but he launched obligingly into a description of his great-aunt's estate near Cuckfield, going on to recount stories of his childhood visits, including adventures with cousins who stayed less frequently at Glendale. His easy manner in this reminiscent vein had a calming effect on her jumpy nerves.

When he was not directing sarcastic comments or accusations at her in the mistaken belief that she was his faithless wife, Amy found Jason's voice much to her liking. It had a pleasant tonal quality with hints of a deeper timbre that had her idly speculating about his ability to sing. She could picture him singing ballads, or even lullabies, his voice was so smooth and soothing. Her qualms and concerns about the awkwardness necessarily attendant on the upcoming visit faded into the background under the spell of his words.

A sudden jolt sent the carriage swaying and Amy with it. Her head hit some part of the coach frame and her eyes flew open, confusion overcoming her as she could only see out of one eye. A little gasp escaped her lips just as strong hands steadied her.

"Easy, my dear," said a soothing voice, and she gazed into pewter eyes inches away from her own, hazily aware that his hands were straightening her hat that had descended over one eye. "The carriage wheel went into a rut and jolted you awake."

"Awake!" The confusion cleared from her face, replaced by consternation. "Do you mean that I fell asleep?" Naked disbelief in her voice had his lips twitching as she sat up straighter, pushing his hands away and taking over the task of retying the ribbons of her hat.

He settled back into his side of the carriage and nodded. "I am afraid so, and without any adulterated tea this time. You have been sleeping for four hours. I must beg your pardon. I really had no idea my company was so . . . soporific, and I promise to take care not to tell boring stories again."

His tone was light, but Amy rushed to dispel this impression. "Of course you were not boring me. It is just that I did not sleep well last night and—and the motion of the carriage was soothing." Her voice trailed off and hot color suffused her face as she heard her own words and regretted the impulsive admission. "How close are we to Glendale now?" she asked quickly, to divert his thoughts.

"We'll be there in less than fifteen minutes. We have already passed through Cuckfield."

"Is this the same route we traveled the—the last time?"

"Pretty much. We are roughly halfway to Rye."

"And I still have seen nothing of the countryside," she said with a rueful shake of her head.

"Désirée, I—"

"Please, Jason, can you not call me Amy?" she pleaded.

"I know it is idiotish of me, but I—I *cringe* when I am addressed by that name!"

Amy's voice must have sounded ragged because Jason's features softened. "I won't forget again," he promised. "I know I am asking a lot of you, but you must not think I should be ruined without Aunt Martha's fortune, nothing of the sort. I can still command some of the luxuries of life while I repay the mortgage loan. My mother's fortune came to me upon her death, you know. I am not on my last legs, nothing like."

Something caught his eye outside the window and he leaned forward, looking over his shoulder. "We are coming up to the Glendale gates now, just ahead of you on the left."

"Oh my, aren't they impressive! I assume the gold emblem in the black iron is some sort of crest?"

"Yes. A peacock figures prominently in the Glenallan crest, and you will see them in the flesh, so to speak, roaming freely on the grounds."

"How delightful." Amy's eyes sparkled with anticipation. "Are the Glenallans an old Sussex family?"

"I don't believe so. My aunt's husband was the last of his family and was nearly fifty when he married and acquired this estate. He had died before I was born, leaving everything to his wife."

They were driving along an avenue of beeches now, and Amy caught glints of water off to the left before the carriage drive swept around a small lake in front of a magificent house.

Like Oakhill, Glendale was built of brick, but there the resemblance ended. Where Oakhill rambled, having been added to haphazardly over the centuries, Glendale had clearly been designed and erected in its entirety at one period, and it radiated a self-satisfied but friendly presence. The central block was all under one roof, hipped and surmounted by a white balustrade, with a charming cupola centered on the roof line. The projecting wings at either end were duplicates, with dormers inserted in their hipped roof fronts.

"I take it the design is a true H-shape?" Amy inquired after expressing her admiration for the handsome ediface.

"Yes. It dates from the late Stuart period, built in the 1690s, I believe."

By now the coach was pulling up in front of the broad flight of steps leading up to the center entrance doors, which opened within seconds, emitting a stream of bewigged footmen.

The next few minutes passed in a blur of activity, though Amy scarcely took it in since she was descending rapidly into a state of frozen terror at the untimely realization that a misstep on her part could have ruinous consequences for Jason. Numbly she allowed him to propel her up the steps and into the house with a hand under her elbow. She lifted dazed eyes at the sound of his voice.

"Dearest, I am pleased to present Cantley, who has superbly managed this household for Lady Glenallan these thirty years and more. This is Lady Archer, Cantley."

Amy said all that was proper in a shy little voice to the tall, silver-haired butler whose aristocratic features and dignified bearing would have done justice to an archbishop.

"We have arrived at an awkward hour, I fear," said Jason when Cantley had welcomed his bride to Glendale.

"Not at all, sir. Most of the guests are dressing for dinner at present, but I expect you would like to pay your respects to her ladyship before Mrs. Halesby shows you and Lady Archer to your quarters."

Upon Jason's assuring him that they did indeed wish to see his aunt before meeting in company in the saloon before dinner, Cantley turned and led the way to the main staircase. Amy was aware that Jason asked after their fellow guests and was alarmed anew by the list of names rattled off by the butler as they ascended. When Jason, seeming to divine her internal state, took her hand in a warm clasp, she made no effort to assert her independence but clung to it for comfort.

On the first floor Cantley paused before a pair of glorious boiserie doors that drew Amy's admiring gaze like a magnet and turned to the couple. "A slight indisposition has kept

Lady Glenallan from leaving her apartment these past two days, but two hours ago Miss Totten told the chef that the mistress was planning to go down to dinner tonight."

"Totten has been my aunt's dresser since before I was born," Jason told Amy with a smile, "and I cannot imagine Glendale without her. The two bicker like children, but each would be miserable without the other. Has my aunt been unwell lately, Cantley?"

"Her arthritic complaint grows worse with the passing years, sir, and causes her much discomfort, especially in damp weather." The butler hesitated before adding in lowered tones, "so if you should find her a trifle . . . out of sorts at times, I am persuaded you will understand."

"Of course, Cantley." As the butler opened the doors and stepped forward to announce them, Jason said in a whispered aside to Amy, "Brace yourself. If Cantley admits that my aunt is 'out of sorts' you may depend upon it that she is rampaging about the place snapping off heads."

Amy scarcely heard his words as her eyes went winging across the large room to a blue velvet chaise longue where a white-haired figure reclined. A cane leaning against the chaise was the only visible sign of ill health, for the woman occupying it, though clearly advanced in years, appeared strongly made with good color and an alert air about her. Dark eyes darted to Amy, then shifted at once to her nephew as she said in ringing accents, "Take yourself off, Totten; I'll ring when I want you. You too, Cantley."

The stout, fresh-faced woman who had been brushing her mistress's hair beamed a smile at Jason and slid a friendly glance at the young woman before effacing herself, hurrying through a door at the side of the fireplace, still carrying the brush. Amy heard the door behind them close as Cantley retreated smartly.

"So, you have had the effrontery to show your face, have you, after not coming next nor nigh this place for over four years?"

Amy froze at this unwelcoming speech, but Jason replied mildy, "Good afternoon, Aunt. I am delighted to find you in

such fine fettle. I have been acting under the impression—
perhaps mistaken?—that I was actually bidden, one might
almost say commanded to appear at Glendale." He gave his
aged relative a teasing smile that Amy privately found irresistible.

Lady Glenallan, however, seemed impervious to its
charm. "And I suppose it is the fault of the mail service that
I received no reply to my invitation," she charged, still on
the attack.

"Not at all, ma'am. I am happy to be able to reassure you
on that point. It was simply a case of being away from home
when Miss Chistleton's epistle arrived. When we returned to
Oakhill yesterday, we acted immediately on your request,
and here we are, more quickly than any letter could reach
you." Jason had been moving Amy forward with a guiding
hand during this conciliatory but mendacious speech, saying
now with a note of pride, "Aunt Martha, may I at last present to you my wife, Amy?"

"How d'ye do," Lady Glenallan said in response to
Amy's deep curtsy, "And not before time, I might add." She
turned penetrating dark eyes that put Amy forcibly in mind
of Jason's from the girl back to her nephew. "If you had the
slightest sense of propriety or decency, you'd have brought
her to meet me *before* that hole-in-corner marriage that has
set the gossips in the family abuzz."

"There was nothing hole-in-corner about our marriage,"
retorted Jason. "My father was recently dead; I had little
close family and Amy even less, so there was no reason for
an elaborate wedding, and certainly no cause for gossip."

"Hah, when did that crew ever require a reason for gossip?" Lady Glenallan said with a cackle, doing an unconscious about-face. "Come closer, girl, and let me get a look
at you in the light."

"Here, take this chair, Amy."

As Jason brought an armless chair alongside the chaise,
Lady Glenallan drew still-dark brows together suddenly.
"What is all this Amy business? You wrote me that your
bride had some outlandish name—foreign, as I recall."

"She is actually Désirée Amy but prefers to be called Amy."

"Let her speak for herself," snapped his aunt. "I presume she has a tongue in her head!"

"Yes, ma'am, I have." Amy smiled at the old woman. "In fact, my father was wont to say I was a prattlebox at times. He always called me Amy, and I do prefer it."

Lady Glenallan nodded. "Sensible sort of name, Amy. I don't hold with burdening helpless children with fantastical names. Miss Chistleton's sister, who has more hair than wit, has just christened her latest 'Primrose' if you please." She emitted a sound that might have been described as a ladylike snort by the charitably inclined, and Amy's eyes twinkled in appreciation.

"I expected a beauty, of course, after that hasty courtship," Lady Glenallan went on, transferring her gaze to her nephew again and speaking as though Amy were absent. "Most men can't see past a female's good looks, but at least she doesn't try to ape an air of *à la modalité* like that little peagoose your cousin Calver married. Dresses just as she should, with becoming modesty. And she don't fidget or twitch—praise be—but sits quietly like a lady."

Amy tried not to look as self-conscious as she felt at being thus discussed, but worse was yet to come as Jason's aged relative turned back to her and pounced. "It is easy to see what captivated my nephew, but what about you? What did you see in him at first glance? How did you meet?"

"We—we met in Rye."

"Where a mutual friend introduced us," Jason added, coming to her rescue.

"Let her answer for herself!" commanded his aunt. "Did you think you had found a wealthy man—an eligible *parti*?"

"I—I knew nothing of Jason's background at first, ma'am," Amy said, meeting her antagonist's gaze straightly, "but within four-and-twenty hours of our meeting I had discovered that there is a basic kindness to his nature and that, although he might be provoked to anger on occasion, his response will be governed by reason, not by reckless emotion. He has been a soldier, but violence is foreign to his nature. He is a man of solid integrity, and I would trust my life to him."

"Well, you have done just that, have you not?" Lady Glenallan observed, but her tone had softened, and Amy thought she detected a lurking twinkle in the dark eyes examining her as she continued to probe. "So you would have me believe it was not my nephew's position or his *beaux yeux,* manly physique or polished address that drew you in, but his sterling character?"

"Please, Aunt, spare my blushes."

"Quiet!" Lady Glenallan took no notice of her squirming nephew as she waited for his bride's reply.

A responsive gleam dwelled in Amy's eyes as she said demurely, "I was not unappreciative of the appeal of a pair of fine dark eyes, which I now see are quite similar to your own, ma'am, but I must confess that I failed to detect any particular charm or polish in Jason's address initially."

Lady Glenallan looked intrigued, but any comment she might have been tempted to utter was forestalled by the entrance just then of a tall thin woman of middle years, dressed in the sober garb of a housekeeper.

"Ah, Mrs. Halesby, it is good to see you again."

Amy heard the relief in Jason's voice as he met the woman in the middle of the room and shook hands with her. Modesty could now be added to his other attributes, she thought, disciplining an incipient smile. Or perhaps he simply feared dangerous revelations on her part. This thought erased any desire to smile. For a moment while parrying Lady Glenallan's impertinent questions, she had allowed the dangers of this horrible farce to fade into the background in the wake of a minor and meaningless triumph over her questioner. No, worse than meaningless—it was shameful, even sinful to be scheming against an old woman who, whatever her faults might be, had the right to expect simple honesty from her great-nephew even without all the years of affectionate relations between them to command it.

Of course Jason was not the primary offender in this situation. He believed her to be his wife and still hoped to forge a true marriage. His lies in the present circumstances were in the interest of gaining time to achieve this desirable end. She, on the other hand, possessed knowledge that would ultimately prevent the fulfillment of his hopes, which made her complicity all the more despicable. Her defense that she had a captive's right to do whatever might attain her freedom seemed specious when she looked into Lady Glenallan's eyes.

Amy's unhappy musing was terminated when Jason called her to be introduced to Glendale's housekeeper. Back in her role again, she produced a smiling greeting, aware that she was being thoroughly measured by Mrs. Halesby as that lady gave her a civil welcome.

"Your old rooms have been kept ready for you, of course, Sir Jason," said Mrs. Halesby, her gaunt face warming into what a surprised Amy could only describe as an adoring look directed at her supposed husband.

"There's no 'of course' about it," declared Lady Glenallan with another crack of laughter. "You may thank Mrs. Halesby that the green suite didn't go to my nephew Geoffrey Selthorpe who is first in consequence, as that wife of his will be eager to tell you."

Jason grinned. "I take it then that you and Lady Hortense are still on your usual terms of frigid formality?"

"I cannot abide a snob," his aunt said shortly, "but that is neither here nor there. You had best be off with Mrs. Halesby and leave me to Totten's ministrations if I am to preside over tonight's mawkish affair with any credit. But come back here before you go downstairs and we'll make an entrance together. That should give the vultures something to chew over," she added with that malicious cackle.

A bemused Amy dipped a curtsy and joined Jason in following the housekeeper from Lady Glenallan's boudoir.

While Mrs. Halesby offered Sir Jason condolences on his father's recent death, Amy was still mulling over the conversational inquest just conducted by his redoubtable relative. She was, therefore, unprepared for the reality of the green suite.

Her first impressions were certainly favorable when Mrs. Halesby stepped back from the door she had opened and gestured to the couple to precede her inside. The apartment they entered was a beautifully proportioned sitting room of modest dimensions, whose walls and ceiling were painted a pale green, the latter adorned with delicate white plaster designs typical of the Adam brothers' style. A green, gold and cream carpet echoed the motifs in the plaster work. Amy noted that the furnishings were graceful: a settee and several chairs covered in a gold and white-striped fabric that was also used to dress the windows. Satinwood tables and a glass-fronted cabinet were on a small scale, bearing the sheen of loving care down through the years.

"What a perfectly lovely room," Amy said to an expectant Mrs. Halesby who permitted a brief smile to lighten her austere aspect.

"My aunt had this suite redone for my mother who came to stay with her after she was widowed," Jason explained. "That was before she met my father, of course."

"Cantley tells me you did not bring your maid with you, Lady Archer," said the housekeeper, "so Ellen, who has some experience as a lady's maid, will wait on you during your stay. She is unpacking your trunk in the bedchamber now. It is through that door." She gestured toward a door in the short wall to their left. "If there is anything you require, tell Ellen and it will be brought to you." She turned toward the hall door before saying, "With your permission I will leave you now to attend to some pressing tasks elsewhere."

Amy was too stunned to do more than nod, but she found her voice the instant the housekeeper closed the door behind her. "Did she say bedchamber in the singular?" she demanded in a strangled whisper, darting a glance at the door behind which she could now distinguish the sound of closing drawers.

"Take a deep breath and exhale slowly," Jason advised the agitated girl in cold tones that matched the bitter line of his mouth. "The bedchamber I used as a boy is on the other side of the sitting room." His eyes never left her face as the panic subsided and she took in a shaky breath. "My compliments on your accomplished performance for my aunt's benefit just now. From the look of it, you have persuaded her that this might be a love match after all."

"I—I did not say anything that was not essentially true," Amy replied, keeping her voice low as he had done, "but of course I said what I did in the hope that she would read more into it than was true—in short, that she would receive a false impression of your connubial bliss. Essentially, I lied with the truth." She gave him a troubled look.

Jason laughed out suddenly, a teasing glint in his eyes. "Lying with the truth! Now there is a concept that could spark a philosophical discussion." He glanced at the French enamel clock on a side table, adding, "But this is not the time to delve into that fascinating subject. Can you be ready in twenty minutes?"

"Yes," said Amy. Then, as he turned toward the far end of the room, "Jason?"

He looked over his shoulder. "Yes?"

"Do not *you* read too much into what I said to your great-aunt. I am not your Désirée." She turned after issuing the soft warning and walked to the near door.

But, oh how I wish I were!

The forbidden thought hit her like a lightning bolt, and her step faltered for a second before she scrambled her defenses together and, pulling her shoulders back, opened the door to her bedchamber, which she entered with her head held high.

Chapter Nine

"Oh, ma'am, you look positively regal tonight," Amy exclaimed when she and Jason entered his great-aunt's boudoir a scant half hour after leaving it.

"Nonsense," Lady Glenallan said briskly, but she looked pleased at the girl's spontaneous admiration. "I was never pretty even in my salad days, but I've held up better in my old age than most of the beauties of my day, and I trust I am not quite a mean bit yet."

"No indeed," Amy agreed, chuckling. "That burgundy satin is handsome and a marvelous complement to your beautifully dressed white hair. Totten is an artist."

"Now don't, I beg of you, pander to her conceit of herself," Lady Glenallan warned, casting a disparaging glance at her beaming dresser who paused in her task of neatening an array of bottles and jars on her mistress's dressing table to smile at Amy. "She will be even more impossible to live with if she takes it into her head that she is indispensable around here."

"Which we both know she is," Jason chimed in with a wink at the dresser. "I see you are hung with the Selthorpe diamonds tonight, Aunt Martha. Is this a state occasion or are you merely flaunting them to annoy Lady Hortense?"

"The latter of course, but I'll have none of your impertinence in this house just the same. My father gave me the diamonds outright when my older brother married to disoblige him," Lady Glenallan explained to Amy, motioning her to come closer. "Henry couldn't get them back for his wife, and Geoffrey won't get them for Hortense either, no matter how much he fawns over me. I intended them for your mother," she added, turning to Jason. Amy saw the look of pain that flashed into her eyes as Lady Glenallan pressed her lips together and inhaled deeply before continuing, "So they will go to your wife eventually."

"Oh, but ma'am," Amy cried, "surely there are those closer to you with more claim—"

"No one has a claim on anything of mine unless I say so," Lady Glenallan snapped, "including you two, but it is my present intention to leave the diamonds to Jason's wife."

"I—I don't know what to say, ma'am; I am over-whelmed," Amy replied at last, prompted by an expectant air from her hostess and her supposed husband's unreadable countenance to end the short silence that followed this announcement.

"You have no need to say anything at present because I am not planning to shuffle off this mortal coil anytime soon, despite anything that fool medical practitioner might say to the contrary. While I live, the diamonds stay with me."

"I cannot imagine anyone who could carry off their magnificence with equal credit," Amy said sunnily, relieved to be past this stumbling block and undaunted by her hostess's astringent tones. "Such beautiful craftsmanship," she added, taking the liberty of studying the intricate designs of the necklace glittering above the bodice of the satin gown.

"When I was a child I loved watching my mother, who was tall and elegant in all her movements, dressing for an evening party. She used to let me fasten the necklace about her throat. It was a little ritual that we both cherished." For a moment Lady Glenallan seemed lost in memories, then she raised her eyes and called "Totten!" in a peremptory voice.

The abigail, evidently reading her mistress's mind, picked up a box reposing on the dressing table and presented it to her before bustling back to her duties. Lady Glenallan's gaze roved over Amy's person briefly; then she said, "What a fortunate coincidence that you elected to wear emerald green tonight because I have selected this for your wedding present." She extended the case to Amy who accepted it after an imploring look at Sir Jason that told her nothing of his wishes in the matter.

"Go ahead, open it, girl; time is passing."

Amy obeyed the old woman's command and, with an exclamation of delight, took a delicate necklace of filigree work embedded with numerous small emeralds from the case. "Oh, Lady Glenallan, this is absolutely exquisite. I have never owned anything so lovely before. How can I thank you sufficiently? It is much too good of you, but I adore it!"

"There, there, it is nothing of great value really, but quite unusual and more suitable for a young woman than most of my jewelry. Put it on for her, Jason."

As her nephew accepted the necklace from Amy's hand he added his thanks to hers, smiling at his aunt.

Lady Glenallan, watching him place it around the girl's throat, remarked suddenly, "My niece had some lovely pieces. I must say I am astonished to see you wearing no jewelry at all, not even a wedding ring."

"The blame for that oversight rests with me," Jason put in smoothly, addressing himself to the disapprobation in his aunt's voice as Amy grew very still beneath his hands. "I had the whole house in an uproar this morning trying to get everything ready for us to get off at a decent hour, and I fear Amy's jewel case was a casualty of the mad rush. By the time we realized the omission it was too late to turn back for it, but you have remedied that situation, Aunt, in great style. There, it is fastened." He straightened up and held out an imperative hand to Amy. "Come over to the dressing table mirror and see the effect of the necklace against your skin."

Amy obeyed him, her pulses settling down again as his aunt seemed to accept his explanation. She was actually relieved at the criticism and advice when the old woman said, "It looks very well on you, my child, and it disguises the line of demarcation at your throat too. You have been most unwise to allow your skin to become burnt. You should never go out in the sun without a parasol unless you wish to ruin your complexion."

"I am persuaded you are quite right, ma'am," she replied meekly. "Unfortunately I do not have a parasol with me either, but the brim of my hat is fairly wide." She curbed the impulse to babble on, hoping her nervous dread of the evening to come was not as apparent as she feared. They had narrowly avoided one pitfall just now, but any number of unknown hazards still awaited someone with her total lack of knowledge about Jason's family. Short of sitting completely mute the entire time, there was no guarantee of avoiding all embarrassment or the possibility of committing some terrible blunder, but surely the less she said the better, even if Jason's relatives rightly judged her to be a total nonentity. That would be his wife's problem to deal with in the future, assuming she ever returned, she decided with a perverse satisfaction.

"Would you hand me my cane, please, Amy," Lady Glenallan said to derail her previous speculations.

Amy jumped up and proffered the gold-topped cane while Jason helped his aunt to rise. Lady Glenallan was an impressive figure, even taller than the girl had expected, and with only the slightest hitch in her gait as she set a good pace once they were in the corridor.

The threesome was proceeding toward what Lady Glenallan referred to as the new great room when she asked Amy if her husband had explained the relationships existing among the guests at present enjoying Glendale's hospitality.

"No, not at all, ma'am."

Lady Glenallan nodded sapiently. "I am not at all surprised; for the most part men are quite useless in the social sphere. Never mind, I'll give you a quick lesson in Selthorpe history. I had two brothers: Henry, who inherited the barony, and Matthew, who was Jason's grandfather. Henry's son Geoffrey and his wife and son, Martin, are here. My brother Matthew, had three daughters, Lydia, Sophia and Nell, who was Jason's mother. Only Sophia survives. She is Mrs. George Damien, a widow, and she is here with her son, Charles, and his wife and child. Lydia's son, Mr. Edmund Calver, and his new bride, Sylvie, complete the party except for Miss Chistleton, who has been my companion for five-and-twenty years. Does that give you a picture of your husband's family?"

"Well, I apprehend that there are two—no, three generations represented since one of Jason's cousins has a child. It will take me a little time to put names and faces together correctly, ma'am, but thank you for giving me a head start on learning the branches of the family."

"Good girl. And here we are," Lady Glenallan said as a footman opened a pair of doors. "Let me take your arm, Amy," she hissed before they stepped into the room.

Any doubts Amy might have harbored about Lady Glenallan's mischievous desire to discompose her relatives were put to rest by the entrance their hostess now orchestrated, leaning on the arm of the newest family member while her reputed favorite trailed behind them like a page.

"Good evening, everyone," the grand lady said blandly, pausing long enough to make sure that the eyes of all present were fixed on the tableau before she indicated the chair she preferred and allowed Amy to assist her into it. "I don't believe any of you have had the privilege of meeting Jason's wife, Amy, as yet," she went on once she had settled into the chair with a soft grunt of relief that revealed what that stately parade had cost her physically. "If you will just introduce yourselves to her, we'll be able to get the preliminaries behind us before going in to dinner."

The next few minutes, though admittedly a strain on her memory, were not as trying as they might have been. Amy was open and friendly by nature and thus did not suffer the agonies of shyness that could render such occasions an ordeal. What had initially seemed like a sea of staring eyes reformed into fewer than ten individuals who came forward to express civil pleasure at making her acquaintance. As she smiled, curtsied and mouthed polite phrases in response,

Amy was thinking that on the whole Jason's relatives were a pleasant inoffensive-seeming set of persons with two possible exceptions, the wife and son of the present head of the Selthorpe family. Lord Selthorpe was tall with thinning gray hair and what Amy was beginning to recognize as the Selthorpe dark eyes. He had a pleasant voice and a somewhat hesitant manner of speaking. In contrast, Lady Hortense, also slender and attractive, projected an air of haughty condescension that detracted from the appeal of regular features and a fine clear skin. A disinterested glance at the new bride turned into an intent examination of the emerald necklace, then passed onto the magnificent diamond parure worn by her husband's aunt. The baroness's greeting was uttered in a chilly voice that matched her icy blue eyes. Martin Selthorpe had inherited his father's height and his mother's light eyes. Their expression when they roamed deliberately over Amy's person was a good deal warmer, however, and sent a tingle up her spine even before he spoke to her. Having absorbed the early warning, she was able to receive the excessive gallantry of his initial remarks with no loss of composure.

Thankfully, Mr. Charles Damien and Mr. Edmund Calver, while perfectly amiable in expressing their delight in her acquaintance and offering felicitations on her marriage, reserved their real enthusiasm for their cousin whom they greeted with what Amy considered pummels on his shoulders as they wrung his hand in turn. Their wives, pretty girls both, appeared well disposed toward the new arrivals and made Amy feel welcome. On being presented to Mrs. George Damien, Amy said in pleased recognition, "Oh, ma'am, you seem familiar to me already from your resemblance to the portrait of Jason's mother at Oakhill."

Mrs. Damien smiled but demurred, "We three sisters looked much alike as children, but Nell was the one people always remembered. She was so vital she seemed to light up any room she was in. You must miss her terribly, Jason," she said to her nephew who gathered her into an affectionate embrace.

"Yes, but not so much when I see you, Aunt Sophie," he assured the faded but still pretty little woman.

Miss Chistleton, who completed the party in the great room that evening, could never have been pretty even in her youth. In her middle years she was a tall gaunt woman whose most salient feature was a Roman nose that lent an aura of austereness to a thin-lipped countenance, partially redeemed by a pair of lovely hazel eyes full of intelligence and humor. They would have to be, Amy thought in amusement, shaking hands with the companion, if Miss Chistleton had remained with Lady Glenallan for a quarter of a century without having her spirit crushed.

Dinner was announced shortly after the introductions had been performed, leaving little time for Amy to do more than register the fact that the room where they had assembled was truer to the spirit of the house's period than the more modern bedroom suites she had seen so far. Here the plaster ceiling was more ornate and the wooden overmantel bore exuberantly carved, naturalistic designs that she would be pleased to study at her leisure if the occasion permitted.

The dining room they entered was large and paneled in oak with bolection mouldings bordering the panels. The table in the center could easily have accommodated twice the number of persons enjoying Glendale's bounty tonight.

And bountiful was the *mot juste* for the feast that Lady Glenallan, who obviously kept greater state than at Oakhill, set before her guests that evening. Amy's eyes widened at what seemed to be a regiment of footmen assisting Cantley to serve the most lavish array of dishes she had ever seen in her admittedly limited social career. A beautiful soup made of fresh new peas was removed with semelles of carp and a trout in a tomato and garlic sauce. There was an elegant salmon with cucumbers in a dill sauce and buttered lobsters among the foods she recognized. Though very hungry after a day of traveling and quite adventurous in her tastes, Amy was careful to accept only a spoonful of several new dishes, rightly judging that the second course would be equally tempting to the eyes and palate. She enjoyed duckling with oranges, tender asparagus and a small portion of a raised pie later, leaving the spit-roasted ham, sauteed sweetbreads and heavier dishes to the gentlemen's heartier appetites.

The conversation during dinner was lively, moving from the doings of Parliament to the bright hopes for this summer's campaign in Spain in the light of the recent Russian debacle that had weakened Napoleon's ability to replace the troops he'd lost in last year's Peninsula fighting. The conversation proceeded from there to the current books and plays enjoying a vogue in the capital.

For her part, Amy tried initially to follow the prudent course of listening rather than speaking that she had set for herself. Finding Mr. Martin Selthorpe on her left at the table, she gritted her teeth and lent one ear to his unsubtle attempts to flatter and charm her while she did her best to savor what might well be the best dinner it would ever be her good fortune to have set before her. He bemoaned the unkind fates that had kept her from crossing his path in town, thus permitting his absent cousin to discover her on his untimely return to his native shores and thereby steal a march on more worthy men. In response she produced a faint smile and replied kindly that she had never been to London, so he must not feel that the fates had personally conspired against him. When he claimed that her eyes were so unique there was nothing for it but that he must compose a poem in their honor, she thanked him civilly but regretted that such creative effort should be wasted on someone with no taste for poetry. She then suggested that perhaps he might find inspiration in Mrs. Calver's bright golden curls or Mrs. Damien's pearly teeth to arouse his sleeping muse.

With increasing relief she turned periodically to Miss Chistleton who was seated on her right. This good lady welcomed her kindly to Glendale and offered to serve as a guide if Amy should find herself with time on her hands during her stay. An idle question about the gardens proved to be inspired. Amy was treated to a fascinating description of the grounds and gardens from one who obviously knew and loved every inch of the estate that had been her home for so long.

Living a retired life in one location among familiar persons was a poor training ground for cultivating a social persona. Amy was unaware that her countenance faithfully recorded her moods when she was not on her guard, as now, listening with avid interest to Miss Chistleton's word pictures. At one point, drawn by the sound of laughter, she glanced down the table and, meeting the intent dark eyes of her supposed husband, experienced a jolt of electricity sizzling along her nerve ends. It was the only time this had happened during dinner; her occasional glances had discovered an entirely unknown Jason from the brooding, tormented man who had abducted her. Here he appeared carefree and charming, if the expressions on Lady Glenallan's and Lady Hortense's faces were to be believed. That his avoidance of her had been deliberate was now confirmed as he quickly looked away.

She did not have far to seek an answer to this sudden reversal of his previous attitude. She had been alarmed at their first meeting with his great-aunt by her reference to a hole-in-corner wedding and her quizzing about how the pair had met. While the maid Ellen had helped her to remove the travel stains and scramble into a dress for this fateful dinner, she had turned the matter over in her mind and arrived at the distasteful decision that it was necessary to learn as much as possible about the courtship between Jason and Désirée if she was to play her role the way he wished. She had greeted him with a spate of determined questions when he arrived to walk her back to his aunt's suite, noting his surprise and subsequent reluctance to really be forthcoming. She had persisted however, so nervous about the possibility of disaster that she had abandoned her usual placatory posture and avoidance of topics that tended to arouse his ire.

The result had been a discernible—but only to herself so far, she trusted—removal from her on an emotional level, just when they should be trying to present a picture of wedded bliss to his family. She had noticed the effort it had cost him to act the proud bridegroom while fastening his aunt's gift for her and swelling her chorus of gratitude. It had been the same during the prolonged introductions and greetings before dinner. No doubt that was why she had been so struck by the spontaneity and pleasure he had exhibited while chatting with his relatives just now.

Could it be that her determined probing for information about his courtship had finally caused him to doubt that she was really his wife? All external noises and movement vanished suddenly, and Amy was conscious only of her own chaotic thoughts until a touch on her arm brought her head around to see Miss Chistleton looking at her oddly.

"I—I beg your pardon, ma'am. I fear I have been woolgathering. Did you speak to me?"

"I just mentioned that Lady Glenallan is about to lead the ladies out of the room," Miss Chistleton said in a low tone.

Amy mustered a smile for the older woman and rose with the others, sliding toward Jason a glance that caught him directing a remark to his cousin Calver across the table from him. He did not meet her eyes.

By the time the gentlemen rejoined the ladies, Amy felt vindicated in her decision to press Jason for details of his wedding. Both the younger Mrs. Damien and Mrs. Calver had displayed friendly curiosity about the circumstances of her meeting with Jason. Amy had done her best to seem open and confiding while turning the questions back to her interrogators at the first possible opportunity as when she commented on the prevalence of distinctive dark eyes in the Selthorpe family.

Mrs. Damien, whose given name, Henrietta, was ignored by all in favor of Hetty, laughed and exclaimed, "Now that you mention it, it was exactly the same with me. I found Charles's eyes most compelling and when I met Mama-in-law I saw the similarity immediately. It was not until we came to Glendale, though, that I realized just how widespread this trait really is. I believe all the Selthorpes except Martin have inherited the eyes, even my little daughter."

"How old is your little girl? I hope I shall get to meet her while we are at Glendale," Amy said with unfeigned pleasure at the prospective treat.

During Mrs. Damien's detailed description of the small Elizabeth that included her amusing attempts to acquire proficiency in her mother tongue, the wry thought came into Amy's head that her safest course in avoiding detection as the fraud she was would be to spend all her time while at Glendale with the only non-speaking member of the family.

The three young women were still chatting about domestic matters with emphasis on the adjustments required of a new bride in assuming the responsibility of directing her husband's household when the gentlemen came in and music became the program of choice for the evening.

All in all, this was probably the safest option, Amy silently agreed, once she got past the issue of performing. When the inevitable invitation came she pasted a smile on her lips and declared with rueful candor, "I am so sorry to seem disobliging, but I faithfully promised my grandmother that I would never under any circumstances subject unsuspecting persons to the trial of listening to my attempts to sing. I might manage to play for those who wish to sing in groups," she added in an effort at atonement.

Lady Glenallan chuckled. "I can sympathize with you, my dear, because it has always been the same case with me, but we ungifted ones make a desirable, noncritical audience. I can assure you there are some fine performers among us tonight. Charles, would you and Hetty favor us with a duet or two?"

As the attractive couple made their way over to the pianoforte, Amy exhaled gently in relief at having dealt with the familiar preliminaries. She was not quite the attentive audience Lady Glenallan had expected for the opening bars of the ballad the Damiens were singing, however. When the gentlemen had returned from the dining room, she had been seated next to Hetty Damien on a settee, and Jason and Charles had pulled up chairs near the three young ladies. Her eyes had swept around the room in making her apology just now and she had noted in passing that Jason was looking at her strangely, his lips parting and then closing again as he evidently decided against giving voice to the thought that had come into his head. Her seeking glance now went unanswered, for he had shifted his eyes to the performers. She followed suit but could not help wondering if a good singing voice was yet another difference between herself and Désirée Archer. She made a mental note to challenge Jason on this point tomorrow even if she had to tie him to a chair in order to demonstrate her woeful ineptitude at singing.

There was enough musical talent in Jason's extended family to entertain those with a much more critical ear than Amy could boast. During the next hour she was disarmed and delighted by a succession of lovely interludes of playing and singing. The tension that accompanied being always on one's guard seeped slowly away, leaving her in a state of mindless contentment. Her eyes drifted idly around the circle of attractive, amiable-looking people in the saloon. They were a nice family. She was most fortunate—*Oh no!* Amy went rigid in her chair, not altogether certain that the voices clamoring in her head were inaudible to the others in the room.

Fortunate! She was fortunate? Amy closed her eyes in an agony of self-loathing. What was the matter with her? Where was that organ she had considered her brain? How could it have let her sit here like a dreamy child hearing a fairy tale, imagining that this was her family—no, she must admit the whole truth—*wishing* Jason's family was her family too! How could she be so stupid? Becoming aware that she was crushing the emerald silk of her skirt in her palms, she imposed control over her hands, relaxing the clenched fingers and releasing the fabric. The notes of Beethoven's Ninth Symphony played by Miss Chistleton washed over her taut form like a soothing benediction while she fought to reestablish her own identity. She had been correct to dread being thrown into the midst of Jason's family, but her fears had not gone far enough. She had worried about committing a blunder that would humiliate Jason before his relatives. It had not even occurred to her that there would be pain and desolation in the knowledge that she did not and could never belong here. Should she have known that being treated so kindly by Lady Glenallan would hurt because the kindness belonged rightfully to another?

Amy, suddenly submerged in a tidal wave of nameless longing, was slow to realize that Lady Glenallan had requested a song that was a special favorite of her niece Nell until Jason took Miss Chistleton's place at the pianoforte and began to sing to his own accompaniment. Within a few seconds she experienced the mental satisfaction of having her suppositions about his singing ability confirmed. In the next moment academic interest gave way to pure esthetic and emotional reactions as the unintelligible but stunningly lovely sounds washed over her in a gentle shower. He was singing in Italian and about love—that much was obvious. Beyond that the imagination took over the task of comprehension. The poignancy in his tones suggested the realm of love and loss, and a shudder of empathetic unity produced gooseflesh on her arms as her eyes devoured the musician creating the spell.

There was no danger that Jason would discover her staring at him, for he was seated at the instrument with his profile presented to her and his eyes on the keyboard. With the slightly aquiline modeling of his nose and a square jawline, this was the most intimidating aspect of his countenance, but the proportions and sculpting of his head were artistically fine. His broad brow, lean cheeks and well-shaped ears lent him an air of distinction. By any standards Jason Archer was a compelling figure of a man, without even taking into account attributes such as his beautifully shaped, long-fingered hands now moving authoritatively over the keys, and the sensitive mouth that sometimes betrayed his disciplined, stoic facade. Any inventory of his attractions must include this melifluous voice that would play havoc with any woman's emotions. If he had sung this song to Désirée, how could she have run away?

As before when she reached this point in her ruminations

on the motives of the woman Jason had married, the knowledge that *she* could never have acted thusly swept over her, but this time it was contradicted by the frightening certainty that she *must* do the same. For the sake of her sanity and even more for her moral salvation it was crucial that she put an unbridgeable canyon between herself and this man who had burst into her life and filled all the corners of her mind in just four short days. Surely she possessed enough of a basic instinct for survival to bar him admittance to her heart! As the notes of the song wound down, Amy concentrated on reaffirming this position.

She was ready to add her enthusiastic applause to all the rest when Jason rose from the pianoforte. Her proud smile slipped a little, however, when she encountered his burning regard. Indignation ousted confusion in her mind. After practically ignoring her all evening, how dare he look at her like that! This little spurt of temper died back to lingering doubt once more as she wondered whether she had presumed too much earlier in speculating that he had begun to seriously question her identity. He could not have gazed at her in that seductive fashion if he doubted she was his wife.

Fortunately for Amy's whirling senses, the arrival of Cantley with the tea table at that moment put an end to her disturbed reflection as everyone indulged in a general shifting around and spontaneous conversations broke out. Obeying a summons from Lady Glenallan, she took her tea in hand and joined her hostess and Miss Chistleton on a sofa where the former surprised her yet again by declaring, "If I were fifty years younger and not his aunt, I believe Jason could reduce me to a quivering jelly with that Bonancini song. I suppose you are used to it by now?"

"No indeed, ma'am, I am still quivering," Amy admitted with perfect truth as she smiled at Lady Glenallan who gave her a shrewd look before changing the subject.

"Miss Chistleton tells me you expressed a deal of interest in the gardens at dinner. In past years I'd have been delighted to show them to you myself because they have been the joyous occupation of my half century at Glendale, but this dratted arthritis has made walking on uneven surfaces a penance of late. So if you should like it, Miss Chistleton will be free at ten tomorrow to be your guide."

"I should like it above all things, ma'am. Thank you, and you, Miss Chistleton, for making time to conduct me around the estate."

"It will be my pleasure, my dear," the companion said warmly. "I have only been here for a quarter of a century but I believe I feel almost as Lady Glenallan does about their beauty."

Amy enjoyed the next few moments as Lady Glenallan gave instructions and reminders to Miss Chistleton about finding the perfect spots from which to best appreciate some of her favorite vistas, but she was more than a little grateful when her hostess suddenly declared herself ready to retire. As she rose with the rest of the ladies, she was dimly aware that the constant strain of the unnatural circumstances surrounding this visit had taken a toll on her usual vitality. There were things to be said between herself and Jason, but she was more than willing to put off the telling until a night's repose had recruited her energy and restored her confidence.

Chapter Ten

As a pair of gateposts came into view in the distance, the heartbeat of the man on the white horse speeded up at the same time that he slowed the pace of his mount, torn between eagerness and dread. Was he a fool to hope that the property ahead represented the end of his search? Would this be just another in a string of disappointments? He was a man who knew how to exercise patience, but the fact was that a trail grew cold after a time, and so much time had crawled by—nearly four days—hour by weary hour.

He had set her down in Mermaid Street in Rye near midday on Tuesday, and it was now getting toward sunset on Friday. He had not been worried when she was not waiting for him at the appointed hour. Miss Amy was not one to mince words, and she had left him in no doubt about how much she resented having a keeper, as she called it, while her brother was away. He'd had a feeling she was up to something more than buying a dress, and he'd expected that, like himself, she hoped to search around Rye for any news about Mr. Rob or his boat. When she had not put in an appearance after nearly an hour, he'd told a youth to hold the horse while he inquired at Clothilde's. The dressmaker had sent him to a milliner who told him Miss Cole had left her establishment well over an hour before with a new hat. Even after driving the gig all over town for another hour without spotting her he had not been overly concerned, thinking she had maybe met up with an acquaintance and was either having something to eat in town or had accepted a ride home. He did check the most likely places before returning to Marshland in the expectation of seeing her there before him.

The real uneasiness began when the Fentons reported that no word of her whereabouts had reached them. Mrs. Fenton had raked him over the coals for losing the young mistress, but he hadn't minded that, knowing the poor lady's rage was driven by fear that something terrible had befallen her chick. After inquiring at the house of every acquaintance in the area and making another search of Rye without coming across anyone who had seen her, he had begun driving down every road out of the area, checking at the inns within a few miles until nearly midnight when exhaustion had driven him home.

It had been the worst night of his life, with the Fentons near-crazed with anxiety and looking to him for a solution, and he, woolly crown that he was, with no idea under the sun occurring to him except to search all of England for her rather than fail Mr. Robert.

The next morning the woman had come to the door just as he was about to set out again. The woman—Mrs. Greyson, she called herself, though Mrs. Fenton had declared darkly that *she* knew what to call her—had offered the first clue as to how Miss Amy could have disappeared into thin air without anybody seeing her go. Her story had been full of protests of her innocence and pure intentions and no doubt downright lies, but she was the only person who claimed to have seen Miss Amy after she left the milliner's. When he demanded to know why she had not come to Marshland yesterday with her information, the woman had stuck to it that she had believed the man's story until she learned in a tavern last night that someone was searching all over Rye for a young lady by the same name that the girl had given her. More than likely she was afraid the returning postilions would peach on her when they came to hear about the missing girl, but no matter her reasons, he was grateful. Over Mrs. Fenton's strenuous objections, he had given the woman some money to mollify her and eventually had coaxed out of her a description of the man who had abducted Miss Amy, including a mention of his saddle horse.

Recalling the events of Wednesday morning now, Tom Watkins acknowledged soberly that if he found Miss Amy here it would be thanks entirely to the existence of the chestnut stallion. He had started off on Pegasus with high hopes and all the money he and the Fentons could find in the house, including what Mr. Rob had given him when he left. He'd lost count of the posting inns and tollgates he inquired at and the false trails he'd followed in coming clear across Sussex into Hampshire over the past three days. At first he'd asked about a man and young woman traveling together, but it was only when he described the chestnut tied to the post chaise that the trail did not peter out. He'd been worried at no mention of a dark-haired girl in a black dress anywhere until it had gradually become clear that the kidnapper had driven all day and night on Tuesday. Always westward. It wasn't until this last sighting at a post house, however, that a destination other than a posting house had been mentioned. And now he was approaching an estate called Oakhill that was owned by Sir Jason Archer who was last seen riding his chestnut stallion at dawn on Wednesday, accompanying the hired chaise in which his wife was traveling.

Pegasus shifted beneath his motionless rider, and Tom wiped a none-too-clean handkerchief over his sweaty face and cast a glum eye over his dusty person. It would not be lying to say that Pegasus had been better accommodated these past two nights than he, but not knowing precisely what the cost might be in getting Miss Amy back home from wherever he found her had made him wary of depleting his meager resources. He'd felt like a blindman trying to find his way out of a forest these past days, retracing his path each time a trail ended. Pray God this was the final destination, not that he had the least idea what to expect when he did catch up with this man who had coolly made off with a respectable girl in broad daylight. He laid a hand briefly on the saddlebag containing a pair of Mr. Rob's pistols and rode between the gateposts.

Bracing himself as always for the reactions of strangers to his appearance, Tom Watkins avoided the house he glimpsed through a grove of mature trees to his right. He kept to a path he hoped would lead to the stables, thinking it would be easier to deal with outdoor servants than niffy-naffy butlers and such, especially when he was riding Pegasus, as fine an animal as was ever owned by any lord in England. Despite the ever present fears for his master's young sister that had led him farther away from home than he'd ever been before, he could not but help notice the beauty of the rolling land hereabouts. For himself, he could never be happy away from the sound and smell of the sea, but it could not be denied that this was a fine green country. It queered him to figure how a man who owned all this land and a big mansion could do what he had done. By heaven though, if this was the man, he would make him pay even if it meant jail.

Tom's senses quickened when he spotted two horses in a field near the stables. His glance passed over the bay and fixed on the big chestnut cropping grass near the fence. He patted the neck of his own mount absently, stopping to cast a knowledgeable eye over the chestnut's points. "Yes, sir, Pegasus, you are in fine company with that there stallion."

"Hey there! What do you want?"

Tom turned at the hail, sitting unmoving as a thin, wiry lad of no more than twenty summers approached from a door that must have led to a tack room. He knew the exact moment when the youth's eyes passed over the white horse and took in his ruined face. His step faltered and stopped, his eyes started, and bravado colored the thin voice that demanded, "Who are you? What do yer want here?"

"I am a courier with a message for Sir Jason Archer."

"He ain't here. Yer can give it in at the house."

"I must give it into Sir Jason's hands personally. When will he be back?"

"I dunno; they went this morning."

Tom's scarred face grimaced. "If Sir Jason is away from home, I will see Lady Archer."

"Yer can't; she's gone too."

"Are you sure? I saw a lady reading in the garden just now—a tall lady with blond hair. Is that Lady Archer?"

"I dunno who that may be. Lady Archer is smallish and 'er 'air is sort of brown and red together."

"Then I shall have to go after them," Tom said with a gusty sigh. "I hope they did not set off for Scotland or foreign parts?"

"No, no, just into Sussex a ways."

"That's a help. Do you know where in Sussex?" Tom waited wtih baited breath, hoping he would not have to tackle the butler or steward after all.

"To Glendale, just past Cuckfield. His auld auntie lives there," replied the youth, eager to show off his knowledge of the family's affairs.

"I am much obliged to you. Good day," Tom said, raising a hand and wheeling Pegasus around to retrace their path.

The confident mien he'd assumed fell away from him and he fought disappointment and fatigue at the realization that his quest was not over, nor could he even be certain he was on the proper trail. The stable lad's description of his master's wife could fit Amy Cole, but he'd not dared to come right out and ask if her eyes were green lest he arouse suspicions among Archer's servants that could lead to warning messages being sent ahead to this Glendale place this evening. It was necessary that he and Pegasus rest tonight before setting out again. Thank heavens they would be traveling eastward tomorrow. For that much, at least, he must be grateful.

"Just two more steps this way. That's fine. Now you may look," said Miss Chistleton, releasing the girl's hand.

Obediently, Amy opened her eyes and gazed before her

in silent delight for a long moment before she let out a soft breath and turned shining eyes to her guide. "What a lovely prospect down the long straight waterway—almost like a canal, is it not? What is that little building at the end?"

"It was designed by Thomas Archer many years ago. I believe such purely decorative structures were called follies in the last century."

"Well, I call it perfectly charming, and so unexpected after that grove of trees to suddenly come upon this vista in its entirety. Shall we walk along the path toward the pavilion, ma'am, if it will not be tiring for you?"

Miss Chistleton laughed. "Until Lady Glenallan's knees became so painful these past few years, she would walk me regularly over the property and over the surrounding landscape too for hours on end. I still enjoy walking myself on occasion, but I miss her stimulating company on my walks," she added, heading for the gravel path bordering the water.

The women strolled along the water's edge, stopping midway at an inviting stone bench to absorb the peaceful scene. Gazing at the baroque pavilion with its domed roof, Amy asked if Lord Glenallan had commissioned it.

"No, most of the structures on the grounds, including the gazebo near the bowling green and this summerhouse, were built nearly a century ago when gardens were much more formal. They have been kept in good repair, and the knot garden and topiary in the parterre, as well as the hornbeam allée near the house, have been maintained in their original formation. The Glenallans have established the more naturalistic landscape around the lake and the profusion of flowers. Lady Glenallan has made a study of plants and has introduced many new bloomers to the country. It was she who built the succession houses after Lord Glenallan died, which is why we enjoy the best citrus fruits and other out-of-season treats. Ask Jason to take you there this afternoon if you are interested. He is the only one who can wheedle fruit out of old Derwent who is Lady Glenallan's head grower and an absolute tyrant in his domain.

"Jason's mother could charm him too," Miss Chistleton

said softly after a pause. "She was a very special person, and her death was a great blow to Lady Glenallan."

"Yes, I had apprehended that from our first conversation. Judging by the portrait at Oakhill, her niece looks to have been of a kind and sympathetic nature."

The pair had begun walking toward the pavilion again, when Miss Chistleton signified her agreement with this assessment. "Yes, I have seen that portrait and was struck by how well the artist caught the essential Nell—her gentle spirit and forgiving nature. That was done about the time I first met her, when Jason was just a little boy—a little imp, I should say," she amended with a smile, "but immensely likeable for all his mischievous ways. He was very like his mother even then—not in looks particularly, except for the eyes and coloring; and he has his father's more impulsive and passionate nature, but the warm and and forgiving heart he inherited from Nell. I hope you will not think me presumptuous if I say that I think you have been wise in your choice of a husband."

"Of course not," Amy said promptly, summoning up a smile. "A forgiving heart must be near the top of any list of qualities to look for in a husband unless one is a saint and never in need of forgiveness."

"Oh, especially then, I would imagine," Miss Chistleton rebutted with mock solemnity. "All that piety and goodness would be bound to irritate most mortals after a time."

The younger woman laughed, and the pair approached the domed pavilion in perfect amity. After a brief visit inside to look at the murals of scenes from Greek myths, which Amy pronounced charming, they wended their way slowly toward the house, enjoying small detours to admire another view of the lake and a walled courtyard dominated by a large fountain with a statue of Neptune at its center.

The hours she had spent with Miss Chistleton this morning had been a wonderful restorative, Amy realized later as she glanced in the mirror in her bedchamber and brushed some escaping tendrils of hair back into the neat knot at the back of her head in preparation for joining her fellow guests for lunch. In the older woman's undemanding and incurious company she had actually forgotten her invidious position for a time; unclouded enjoyment of a pleasant interlude in beautiful surroundings was something she would not have believed possible when she had opened her eyes before dawn on her fifth day of captivity.

After a close examination of the skin under her eyes, she decided that she looked more rested now than when she'd arisen after the most disturbed night of the whole ordeal. The first night had been spent in a carriage in a drugged sleep; during the second her natural fears had been leavened by hope as she plotted and dreamed of her escape from Oakhill. On the night following her frustrated bid for freedom, exhaustion had claimed her body and Jason's promise to take her to Marshland had eased her mind of much of its burden.

Last night had been entirely different, however. Amy turned away from the mirror, unable to bear the shame she read in her eyes. She had been waging an inner battle from the moment before changing for dinner yesterday when a little voice in her head had whispered that she would like to be Jason's wife in reality. The sensible part of her brain had instantly slapped the abhorrent thought away, but even with all the demands on her intellect necessary to maintain the fiction of a newly wedded couple before a houseful of his relatives, she had been unable to eradicate the insistent little voice that popped up at regular intervals during the musical evening.

She had spent the better part of the evening denying its truth, summoning all the rationalizations at her brain's service to argue against such an irrational and wicked desire. In the wake of the tumultuous feelings aroused in her breast by Jason's singing, however, denial became impossible, at least if she still wished to claim a respect for the truth.

Amy wandered over to a window that looked down on a garden rioting with roses, but she was blind to their beauty at present. All the evils of her situation, ignored for a time while she was with Miss Chistleton, rushed in to torment her now as they had last night. She had tossed and turned in the big tester bed and railed against a malevolent fate that had plucked her from her peaceful obscurity and flung her into a maelstrom that required a degree of courage and honor that she feared she might not possess. She had pummeled her pillow in impotent rage and then soaked it with despairing tears at the pain of desiring a man she could never love without abandoning honor and decency. She who had not experienced the slightest flutter of her pulses at the overtures of three respectable and attractive young men in the past few years now had to struggle to subdue a wild and wanton response to the mere presence of a married man. The fact that he thought her his wife excused his conduct, but it made her own situation the more unendurable.

She had known Jason Archer less than a sennight. Even in circumstances that promoted a false intimacy, it was too brief an acquaintance to result in love, she told herself reasonably. This tumult of the senses must be only infatuation, but she could recognize the danger of prolonged contact with a man who could exercise such frightening power over her being. She must prevail upon him to bring this visit to a quick conclusion. She needed the comfort and security of her own home and the people she loved around her, she acknowledged, as she squared her shoulders and walked out of her bedchamber. Only a stiff pride kept her head high and her expression composed.

Miss Chistleton presided over the luncheon party in a small, ground-level dining room that looked out on a velvety lawn enclosed within a brick wall covered with espaliered fruit trees.

"Lady Glenallan was hoping to join us here, but she had a rather disturbed night," Miss Chistleton explained, "so I persuaded her to curtail her activities today to conserve her energy for the evening." She acknowledged the sympathetic murmurs that wafted around the table with a nod and passed along Lady Glenallan's hopes that her guests would find ways to pass their time enjoyably during the afternoon hours.

Amy, who until she had entered the dining room had not set eyes on a single guest all morning, including her supposed husband, assumed what she trusted was an interested expression and listened as various family members mentioned their own activities in passing. It seemed that all the gentlemen had gone riding together and bore on their faces the stamp of satisfaction brought on by beneficial exercise in good company. The ladies' activities had been less communal. Mrs. Calver confessed that she had spent the morning closeted with her maid in order to make some adjustments to her wardrobe. The younger Mrs. Damien had supervised her child's regimen with a new nursery attendant while her mother-in-law visited with Lady Glenallan for an hour before joining Lady Hortense in the morning room. There they employed their fingers with needlework until meeting with the rest of the party for lunch.

Amy allowed Miss Chistleton to recount their perambulations, making appropriate comments at suitable intervals while the company partook of another excellent repast.

"By the way, Jason," Lady Glenallan's companion added at the end of her narrative, "I told Amy to ask you to conduct her through the succession houses this afternoon."

Jason winked at Amy, explaining with mock sobriety, "Miss Chistleton has not dared face up to old Derwent, the head gardener, since he caught her stealing his prized cherries when I was a youngster."

"I shall not dignify that ridiculous calumny with a denial," Miss Chistleton said with a lofty air, continuing to satisfy her appetite in the face of chuckles from all the young men who then vied with each other in producing gruesome accounts of running afoul of the testy gardener during boyhood visits to Glendale.

Amy's face sparkled with appreciation at their ludicrous exaggerations put forth in a spirit of competition.

"You should always wear green, especially this willow shade, to enhance your marvelous eyes," said Martin

Selthorpe, again seated beside her at the table, gazing at her with fatuous admiration.

"But Mr. Selthorpe, how boring and predictable that would be," she chided, widening the eyes in question. "I daresay people would think I was a piece of furniture after a while and not notice me at all."

Suppressing a smile at his earnest protests, she returned her attention to her plate, but not before spotting the amusement in Jason's dark eyes—more evidence that he had gotten over his slight pique of last evening. Suddenly she was on tiptoe with anticipation at the prospect of visiting the greenhouses with this new, cheerful version of her generally brooding abductor.

A half hour later Jason put a staying hand on Amy's wrist as they were about to go out through the garden doors. "Just a moment, my dear. Haven't you forgotten something?"

She raised questioning eyes to his, noting the quirk at the corners of his well-cut mouth. "Wh-what?" she asked, conscious of heat in her cheeks and an annoying breathless quality to her voice.

"Did I or did I not hear you promise my great-aunt that you would wear a hat out of doors?"

A smile broke over her face and her eyes danced as she said with pursed mouth, "Strictly speaking, no you did not." As his eyebrows elevated, she clarified hastily, "I admitted I had no parasol and humbly pointed out that my hat has a largish brim. I did not actually promise to wear it however."

"Hair splitting of the most shameless sort. You show alarming signs of possessing the slippery mentality of a lawyer, my girl, not a trait that one would choose to live with."

"I—I'll get my hat now." Amy spun on her heels and set off at a fast clip, affecting not to hear Jason's protests that he'd been joking. At least she had not yielded to an impulse to retort that he would not have to live with this unamiable trait, which would only have set up his back again.

Or perhaps she should have done just that, she reflected with an unhappy droop to her lips as she tied the ribbons of her hat under one ear. She was always on her guard when Jason was annoyed with her: there was more danger of succumbing to the lighthearted, charming side that he'd revealed in the midst of his family. And it was of the first importance that she guard against this newly discovered desire to respond joyfully to his teasing manner. Taking this caution to heart, she set her mouth in a grim line as she turned from the mirror.

Amy permitted neither grimness nor joy to surface a few minutes later when she greeted Jason with a cool smile and a mock salute. "Ready as ordered, sir."

"It was an observation, not an order," he corrected smilingly, "but let it be said that I find you absolutely delectable in this charming hat." He opened the door, and she passed through with a light laugh to disguise her pleasure in the compliment.

The pair ambled toward the succession houses under a strong afternoon sun. The air was soft and still. The birds and insects must be napping, Amy decided whimsically. Turning to her silent companion, she said, "I apprehend that you all had an enjoyable ride this morning."

"Yes, most pleasant. I would have asked you to join us, but since my aunt gave up riding a few years ago and Miss Chistleton does not really care for the activity, there are only carriage and work horses in the stables nowadays. I rode my aunt Selthorpe's hack this morning."

"That is kind of you, but I enjoyed myself immensely with Miss Chistleton. The grounds of Glendale are simply spectacular and so well maintained," Amy said warmly.

"They are that," Jason agreed. "It costs a fortune to run this place what with a small army of gardeners and outdoor servants required to keep the grounds manicured in this style. Fortunately, my aunt possesses a large fortune. It is much more impressive than Oakhill, of course," he added, eyeing her with a curiously blank expression.

"Yes, but not as intrinsically beautiful," she said matter-of-factly. "Oakhill has grown and changed through the centuries, and its setting near the Downs is singularly lovely. It is not—not *imposed* on nature, but part *of* it morelike. I don't know how to explain it," she confessed with a little shake of her head.

"I think you've done rather well. And here we are," he said in cheerful tones as the path through the kitchen garden turned around a brick wall, exposing a series of three structures that were built primarily of glass.

During the next hour or so, Amy felt as if she had wandered into another world. The fragrance of citrus blossoms greeted them as they stepped into the first greenhouse. "Absolutely heavenly," she declared, delighting in the dark glossy foliage of trees that seemed too delicate to support the weight of their bounteous fruiting. "Imagine, flowers and fruit at one and the same time—it's almost too much to wish for—or perhaps I mean to expect or—or take for granted."

Jason chuckled at her happy incoherence, remaining at her side as she wandered from one specimen to another, peering minutely at buds and fruit and leaf formations. She peppered him with questions, most of which he couldn't answer. "What we need is old Derwent," he admitted, apologizing for his general ignorance of matters horticultural.

It wasn't until they entered the next succession house that they encountered the gardener. Amy, stepping into a steamy atmosphere where exotic, unknown plants in riotous colors competed for space, gasped, "This is my idea of what a tropical jungle must be like!" She was gazing in astonishment at plants with striped red foliage and others with blossoms unlike anything she'd ever seen in a garden when Jason's voice, answering a hail above her ear, caused her to start.

The hailer, wearing gloves and carrying pruning shears, came into view around a spreading bush. She estimated his age at around three score, but he exuded an impression of controlled power. Though only of middle height, his compact body and sinewy arms below rolled-up sleeves presented a vigorous picture. His face, the color and texture of old leather beneath a full head of tightly curling gray hair, was rendered doubly forbidding by a deeply furrowed brow and a straight mouth set in a rocky jaw. His eyes at first appeared to be mere slits in his seamed countenance, but they widened as he recognized her companion. He laid down the shears and stripped off one glove, coming forward with hand outstretched to meet Jason.

Amy marveled at the difference a change of aspect could make as the two men shook hands warmly. "I collect I'm to call you 'sir' these days, but I'd wager my best loping shears you'd rather your governor was still answering to the title," the gardener said, fixing a pair of bright blue eyes full of affection on Jason.

"And you'd win," Jason replied. "It's good to see you, Derwent. It has been a long time since you used to chase me out of these houses brandishing those shears."

"You were a horde of vandals, the lot of you—ignorant as Paddy's pig, they were," Derwent retorted, shifting his gaze to Amy who smiled shyly.

Jason performed the introduction, and Amy found her hand engulfed in a strong callused grip as she expressed her admiration for the variety and quality of Glendale's plantings.

"Aye, her la'ship is a great one for improving and breeding new species here. Do ye ever get your own hands dirty in the earth, my lady?"

Amy laughed, withstanding a fierce blue-eyed stare with equanimity. "Oh yes, I love grubbing in the garden, but we have nothing to equal this magnificence at my home, although our roses are really quite lovely."

"Which ones d'ye prefer?"

Amy's laugh trilled again. "All of them—the *gallicas,* especially *Rosa Mundi.* We have *Rosa Alba,* the Austrian yellow and *foetida bicolor,* and I love the cabbage roses, especially *centifolia muscosa,* and *damascena versicolor,* of course. Ours are mostly the old varieties, but my father brought me back an *eglanteria* from a trip a few years ago that seems to prosper in the salty air."

"Ah, Manning's Blush, yes."

Amy, nodding at Derwent's observations on this species,

failed to note Jason's sudden frown at her mention of her father.

"Shall I show ye a new rose then if ye like?"

"Oh yes," Amy said, her eyes sparkling.

"This way then."

She followed the quick-footed horticulturist out of the tropical garden into the third succession house while Jason trailed along, forgotten by both enthusiasts. He listened with an air of benign ignorance to the animated discussion of rose culture that ensued.

After Amy had exclaimed over the new rose variety promised by Derwent, she touched a velvety petal and bent to sniff appreciatively of its heady scent. "It is exquisite. What is it called?"

"Empress Josephine," he replied with an air of expectancy.

Jason watched as surprise was succeeded by mischief on Amy's expressive countenance. "Does growing the rose cast a shadow on your patriotism, Derwent?"

"I haven't heard tell that the lady has led any armies against us as yet, ma'am."

"No, of course not." Amy looked as though she regretted her levity in the face of his dignified response. "I would certainly not object to giving this lovely lady a place in my garden," she said in placatory tones.

"And so ye shall, ma'am, if Lady Glenallan agrees," the grower said, bending to cut a tumescent bud. He snipped the thorns off and presented it to her with a gallant flourish. "Meanwhile, ye can put this in ye room and watch it open."

Amy glowed with pleasure as she accepted the gift. "Thank you so much, Derwent. I am honored."

"It's nothing," the old gardener protested gruffly. "I must get back to my work now, but you're welcome to come by anytime."

"Thank you. I should love to." Amy beamed a smile at him as he retreated to the jungle house.

"I should say you have made a conquest," Jason remarked, but not until Derwent was out of hearing.

"Pooh, nonsense. He was just being kind." Amy inhaled her rose again, her face serene. "I am persuaded he would welcome anyone who was truly interested in gardening."

"Are you?" Jason smiled and indicated the flower. "Had you not better get that into water? You would not like Derwent to think you did not value his gift as you ought."

"No, of course not." Amy cast a wistful eye over the other specimens in the succession house before heading obediently for the entrance.

They were walking toward the kitchen garden when Jason turned to her and said with some urgency, "Amy, I must ask you not to—"

His next words were stillborn as a small pink and white whirlwind sailed around the brick wall, calling over her shoulder, "You can't catch me, Mama!"

"But I can," said Jason, swooping on the tot who had come to a surprised halt at sight of them. He hoisted the little girl up into his arms. "And who might you be, Miss Mischief?"

"I'm Lizbet, of course. Who are you?"

"I believe I am your cousin Jason."

Amy stared in fascination as two pairs of dark gray eyes just inches apart examined each other solemnly before the child's mop of golden-brown curls shook as she retorted, "No, you're not. My cousin's name is Henry and he is a baby. Will you put me down, please."

"Cousins come in all sizes," Jason said, setting her on her feet again with a smile before straightening up.

"That's right, sweetheart. You have several grown-up cousins at Glendale." Hetty Damien, an unseen audience at the recent tableau, left the wall and came up to the others.

Elizabeth ran up to her mother. "Is the pretty lady my cousin too?"

"Not exactly. She is Jason's wife, and her name is Amy."

"I am happy to meet you, Elizabeth."

The little girl, who had commenced swinging from side to side while holding her mother's hands, stopped and addressed Amy. "I have learned a new song. Would you like to hear it?"

"I would indeed."

When the tot had finished chirping her tune and had been lavishly praised, she asked Amy, "Can you sing it with me?"

"I'm afraid I don't sing, Elizabeth, but if you like, I can whistle it while you sing."

This offer was accepted by the young singer who repeated her song, accompanied by flutelike trills from Amy.

"My word, I should say you can whistle," Mrs. Damien said in startled admiration.

"I would like to do that," the little girl cried. "Will you teach me how to whistle?"

"I will show you how, Elizabeth, but it takes a little while to learn to do it correctly. My brother taught me to whistle when I was a child, but I was much older than you are," she added, knowing the tot's first attempts would be discouraging. "Put you lips together like this and blow," she said, squatting down to the child's level while she demonstrated.

The whistling lesson was proceeding amid much laughter when Mr. Calver came around the wall looking for Jason to join the men in a game of billiards. It seemed to Amy that Jason hesitated briefly before he went off with his cousin, splitting the party along gender lines for the rest of the afternoon.

Chapter Eleven

His years in the military may have increased his knowledge of the world but they'd had a deleterious effect on his skill at billiards, Jason concluded ruefully as he made his way back to his room to change for dinner. Unless his memory deceived him, he had been the best player in the family in his youth, but all his cousins had beaten him today, including Martin who cherished no pretensions to skill at games or athletics. He'd played better in the last game though; he had sensed the necessary precision of eye returning gradually.

Jason whistled a snatch of a march tune as he ran up the stairs, stopping suddenly as images of his wife, forgotten for a time during the raucous session with his cousins, came flooding back into his mind.

Following the pleasant interlude with old Derwent earlier, he'd been on the point of warning Amy not to mention a father again when they had come upon Hetty Damien and little Elizabeth. She'd surprised him anew by demonstrating an unsuspected talent for whistling; then she had alarmed him by telling the child that she had learned the art from her brother. In exchange for his promise to take her to this Marshland place, she had agreed not to deny being his wife during the visit to Glendale. He had been satisfied that the first evening had gone quite well. Despite Aunt Martha's annoyance at the rapidity and style of his nuptials, it was obvious that she had taken an instant liking to his wife, a rare event from his knowledge of his opinionated relative.

Amy's artless revelations this afternoon, however, could bring the house of cards that was their travesty of a marriage down about their ears if they got back to his great-aunt. He could not at this distance call to mind the precise wording of his letter to her announcing his marriage, but it was more than possible that he had mentioned that his bride was mourning the recent passing of her mother. Of a certainty there had been no mention of a father or brother. *Were* today's disclosures artless, though, or a deliberate attempt on her part to sabotage their charade?

Jason's mouth thinned to a grim line, and a sense of urgency prompted him to reverse his steps. He strode back through the sitting room to the door to his wife's bedchamber. He entered after a cursory knock but didn't see her immediately. A strangled sound spun his head around to the fireplace wall, and he froze in his tracks at the sight of his wife, one shapely leg out of a bath, reaching for a large towel on a nearby chair.

"Get out! Get out!" she cried, her expression frantic in the split second before she redoubled her fumbling efforts to unfold the towel and wrap it around her wet, glistening body.

Jason's shoulders and legs automatically aligned themselves in the direction his head faced, unaided by his brain which remained inert. Only his eyes functioned normally as they roved over his wife's beautiful naked form as she struggled to cover herself, while long damp strands of chestnut hair cascaded from a careless topknot over her eyes and further impeded her progress. It was the note of rising hysteria in her voice as she repeated her shrill demands that he vacate the premises that finally jolted his other senses into action.

"Calm yourself, my dear. I merely wish to tell you something important before we go down to dinner."

"Later! Go away!" she insisted, glaring at him as she retreated a step.

"Now you are being ridiculous. Stop acting like an outraged virgin."

"I *am* an outraged virgin," she declared, eyes snapping and breasts heaving beneath their scanty covering as she retreated yet again.

When she caught her foot in a dragging loop of the towel and lurched backward, Jason pounced swiftly to avert an ignominious dunking, towel and all. He sprang forward and grabbed both her arms, hauling her back from the bath and steadying her as she tried to plant both feet securely once more. The initial purity of his intentions was not proof against the tantalizing nearness of such a delectable creature however. He was studying the inviting curves of her lips while unconsciously kneading alabaster shoulders with his thumbs when she tried to pull away. Shakily she demanded, "What did you wish to tell me?"

"Tell you? Oh—" He relaxed his grip somewhat as he scurried mentally to retrieve his thoughts. "It is important that you not mention a father or brother anymore. I am nearly certain that I wrote to Aunt Martha that you were mourning your mother."

Jeweled green eyes pleaded with him. "But I am not, Jason. I am mourning my father's death. I do have a brother and I cannot sing. You must know by now that I am not Désirée."

"What are you trying to do to me?" he cried, aware of perspiration on his upper lip and heat coursing through his body.

"N-nothing. I—I am—"

It was the distress on her face and the shimmer of unshed tears that impelled Jason's next response. "Ah, love, don't," he begged, enfolding her, towel and all, in a one-armed embrace and cupping her chin in his other hand. As his mouth descended to cover hers he was treated to a view of silky black lashes. She wouldn't look at him but she hadn't pulled away, he thought exultantly before abandoning thought for sensual pleasure. The desire to kiss her had been growing more insistent from the moment this afternoon when she had demonstrated the technique of whistling for a rapt little girl and an equally enchanted husband.

At first she remained utterly still, almost unbreathing, but then as he took that luscious lower lip between his and pressed tiny kisses at the corners of her mouth, moving with deliberation, she exhaled gently, melting into his embrace. Flames licked along his nerve endings as her lips warmed and clung to his, seeking and giving pleasure. He released her chin in order to wrap his other arm around her with an inarticulate growl of satisfaction.

His elation was short-lived, however, for she began to struggle in his arms, making little whimpering sounds. He put her a little away from him, his fingers splayed on her bare shoulders. "What is it, love?" he inquired, dismayed by the tears coursing silently over her cheekbones.

Her attempts at explanation, if such, were incoherent at best as his fingers moved caressingly over the silky skin of her shoulders while he stared helplessly at the beautiful forlorn face before him. In the midst of his concern over her distress he became aware suddenly of something marring the smooth perfection of one shoulder. For the space of a heartbeat his fingers stilled, then resumed their movement despite anguished protests from his brain. He felt it again and his hand tightened, drawing a murmur of pain from her. He was only dimly aware of her continued attempts to free herself while he turned her shoulder and angled his head, enabling his eyes to confirm that there was a small raised mole behind her left shoulder.

Sweat was running down his forehead now as he thrust her away, staring at the lovely, beloved visage in dawning horror. "You—you are not—"

"I am sorry to have been so long, ma'am," called a feminine voice from the door he had left open.

The rest of the maid's explanation was lost on Jason. He heard the relief in Amy's voice as she bade the woman to come in, but he had no recollection of what he might have said while making his escape.

Jason's state was pitiable indeed in the time remaining before he must again take up the role of happy bridegroom in his great-aunt's drawing room, watched by a bevy of his relatives. The small part of his brain that was not reeling with shock was grateful that at least there was no valet to witness his wild appearance as he stumbled over the threshold of his bedchamber and threw himself into a chair, tugging to remove a cravat that was choking off his air supply with fingers that shook and fumbled the task.

What had he done? How could such a thing have happened? It was impossible, absolutely impossible, but it must be true!

He leapt out of the chair, tossing aside the cravat. He tore off his coat, wiping his streaming face with his shirtsleeves while he paced like a caged tiger, arguing with himself, rejecting the knowledge that he could not face—that he *must* face. It was impossible that two unrelated persons could be identical; it could not happen! Yet he had seen the mole with his own eyes just now. Désirée's shoulders were free from any blemish; that he knew. There had been little physical intimacy between them during their short and stormy marriage, but he could not have missed the mole; it was as obvious as a beauty patch on a belle of his mother's era. If only he had noticed it before this!

But that was nonsense of course. The mole would always be covered by the sleeve of whatever garment she was wearing. It could have played no role in what he had done, which was to kidnap an innocent stranger. There was no easing his guilt from that source, especially since the original crime had occurred five days ago! To be sure, the act itself had been committed in good faith, but he had kept her a prisoner subsequently and scoffed at her attempts to prove her identity.

Jason's exhausting pacing ceased, and he dropped into the chair once more, sinking his chin into his hand. There had been differences, of course there had, and not just the obvious ones that she had pointed out, such as her ability to ride. He had ignored them or found explanations that suited him—even for the fact that she had tried to run away from him. Désirée had run away too, but not in the middle of the night, penniless and alone. With every excuse for surliness, Amy had endeared herself to his servants in the two days she was in his house. He had noticed a sweetness in his wife's demeanor recently that had not been apparent before and an absence of the coyness that had. He had blithely, wrongheadedly attributed such basic differences to Désirée's changeable nature.

As he sat morosely staring at a piece of lint on the rug, it hit Jason with the effect of a lightning flash that the biggest changes were in him! And these he had not noticed. He'd set out in a black mood in pursuit of his runaway bride, disillusioned with her character and furious with his own gullibility, but she was his wife and matters could not be left in limbo. They would reach a mutual agreement to live together or the marriage would be dissolved. He had not realized until now how greatly his intended plan had altered in a few short days. Trying to be ruthlessly honest, he could see *now* that he had actually been courting his wife all over again, but he had not really considered his behavior or motives until today. He had realized that he loved her before he kissed her, however, the quiet joy he'd experienced in her company in the gardens this afternoon had brought that home to him like a benediction.

Amy's ardent participation in that kiss should have been enlightening, he realized now with self-disgust. Désirée had suffered rather than responded to his lovemaking. When he should have been questioning Amy's identity he'd been glorying in her nearness, the softness of her skin and his general good fortune. *Sic transit gloria mundi*. He'd been given a glimpse of heaven before it was snatched away.

Jason, wallowing in his own pain, groaned aloud as he considered Amy's response to his kiss. He would take his oath that she felt something for him. Despite everything that had gone before, all the compounded wrongs he had done her, she had clung to him and melted into his arms as though she belonged there. The thought pierced his selfish preoccupation with his own wretchedness like a poisoned arrow spreading remorse through his system.

His revengeful, ill-considered action may have ruined an innocent girl because there was nothing he could do to repair the damage done to her reputation if this episode should become known. *If?* There was no if about it, he realized instantly. She had vanished from a public street! Her people must be frantically searching the area, very likely aided by neighbors and friends. Jason wiped his arm across his brow again, increasingly shaken and appalled as the enormity of the impending disaster was borne in on him. He had not used his own name when making the posting arrangements, but it would not be impossible to trace the movements of the chaise from posting house to posting house across Sussex in time, especially if that woman in Rye—he frowned in an effort to recall her name—Greyson, that was it—told her story to the authorities. In his favor was the fact that no one along the route had actually seen Amy face to face; on the other hand, Samson had accompanied them and he would be a memorable creature at tollgates and inns.

Jason found himself pacing again as he tried to recreate his flight. They knew him at the last change in Rogate of course, but anyone inquiring at Oakhill would hear a truthful account of the expected return home of the master and mistress from any servant questioned. That should convince any searchers that they were on the wrong trail, but on the off chance that one of his people might have revealed his present whereabouts, it would be prudent to leave Glendale as soon as humanly possible.

Jason glanced at the mantel clock and saw that it wanted only ten minutes until the predinner gathering in the saloon. He speedily divested himself of his boots and put his military training to good service in getting himself ready for what felt like the night before his execution. By censoring any thought of his future beyond tonight he managed to present a fair imitation of his customary neat appearance when he knocked at the door to Amy's bedchamber barely five minutes later than usual, only to be told by the same maid who had interrupted their tryst that Lady Archer had already gone downstairs.

Amy turned her back on Jason's exit and the maid's entrance, concentrating on wiping away the foolish tears that had betrayed her with a fold of the towel and trying to bring a sudden attack of shivering under control. As it turned out, the idiotic shivering served her well because it brought the maid's motherly instincts rushing to the fore.

"Goodness, ma'am, you'll catch your death of cold!" she declared, rushing up to her mistress, unfolding one of the extra towels in her arms. "Here, just drop that wet one," she ordered, pulling it from Amy's slackened grasp and substituting the other, which she wrapped around the shivering girl as she urged her into an upholstered chair. "There now, you'll soon be warm," she promised, rubbing at the damp hair with a smaller towel that she then wrapped around Amy's head.

Over the next half hour Amy regained her composure. She accepted the abigail's skilled ministrations and donned the gown selected for her with the unknowing placidity of a sleepwalker while she scrambled mentally to review the scene just played in this room. Her intention was to assess and undo any damage to her self-respect. The lowering conclusion to this cogitation, as she allowed herself to be seated at the dressing table in the white evening gown a few minutes later, was that the damage was considerable, all of it self-inflicted and most likely irreversible. It had been her fault entirely from start to finish, she acknowledged with a stab of self-loathing. Jason had acted throughout on the premise that she was his wife, while she, poor fool, had been at first mortified by the assault on her modesty that was his untimely entrance just as she was getting out of the bath. Then she had crowned her missish reactions that had led directly to a near-dunking by committing the fatal folly of responding to his lovemaking. As though falling in love with a married man was not enough to ensure her misery, she had added to her wretchedness by revealing her sin to the one person who should never have learned of it. If she had only kept the resolution she had made last night she would have been able to return home with her pride and self-respect intact even if her heart was broken. She cringed internally at the idea of meeting him again.

"Is something wrong, ma'am?"

Amy blinked at the maid, hairbrush in hand, peering at her in concern in the looking glass. "No—no, nothing, Ellen," she denied hurriedly.

"I shouldn't be surprised if you have stayed out of doors too long in the heat today," the maid continued. "You do look a trifle pale, but we can fix that with a little rouge, just the merest touch, if you will allow me, ma'am?"

Amy did not recall her reply, if any, but she must have agreed to every suggestion the abigail made for that good soul eventually stood back with an air of prideful accomplishment, saying, "There now, you do look a treat in that dress with your necklace shining all golden and your hair all arranged on top of your head like that, if I do say so myself."

Had Amy, startled out of her unhappy musing into glancing at her reflection, realized that the elaborate arrangement of curls enhanced her likeness to the detested Désirée, she would probably have demanded that the abigail restore her hair to its simple knot. Fortunately for the servant's obvious pride in her work, she barely took in her appearance before thanking the woman for her efforts as she rose from the chair and accepted the fan and reticule being held out to her. Since she could scarcely claim an indisposition and cry off dinner at this point, it occurred to her that she could gain some time and delay a private meeting with Jason if she could get downstairs before he had finished changing. Acting on this inspiration, she refused the maid's offer to tap on Sir Jason's door, adding mendaciously that he had had one or two things to do before getting ready and had told her to go ahead without him.

In the time it took to reach the saloon, Amy assumed con-

trol of her emotions and reasserted her resolution to conceal
her feelings for Jason and treat him with just enough friend-
liness to pass muster with his family. Needless to say, she intended to avoid any tête-à-tête during the remainder of this
visit. He had said they would stay only two or three days.
Surely she could get through this, if not with her pride quite
intact, at least with her integrity reinstated. With her chin up
and courage bolstering her smile, she entered the saloon and
headed for the sofa where Lady Glenallan was holding
court.

The evening began pleasantly. Lady Glenallan made
room for Amy on the sofa and launched into a friendly cat-
echism regarding her impressions of the gardening scheme
at Glendale. They were deep in a discussion of the growth
habits of certain perennials when Jason arrived. Though
every cell and nerve in her body was alert to his proximity,
she managed to appear unaware of his approach, unless
someone happened to be studying her closely enough to
note the slow relaxation of her muscles when his cousin
Calver seized his arm and drew him into conversation. She
was not seated next or across from him at dinner, which
blessing enabled her to do justice to the chef's marvelous
and varied dishes. The delicious meal enlivened her spirits
to the point where she dared to hope that she might be able
to keep out of his path for the rest of the evening. By tomorrow she would have put that fraught embrace behind
her, she predicted with a precarious but valiant assumption
of control.

Alas, her feeble plans were thwarted almost immediately
after the gentlemen joined the ladies in the drawing room.

"Ah, now that we are all here, shall we have some
music?" suggested Lady Glenallan with a smile at the company.

"Would you begin without us, please, Aunt Martha?"
Jason said, reaching for Amy's hand where she sat next to
Hetty Damien.

"Old Derwent told me there has been a nightingale down

near the gazebo recently, and I thought to bring Amy to hear it sing."

"You can do that tomorrow evening just as well, can you not?" his great-aunt replied on a note of protest as he pulled a surprised Amy to her feet.

"I'm afraid we won't be here tomorrow evening, Aunt. You see, we had already made plans to visit Amy's brother, who was out of the country at the time of our wedding, and we delayed our arrival in order to stop here first."

"You are leaving tomorrow?"

Amy heard the disappointment in Lady Glenallan's voice, and she quickly dropped her eyes to conceal her own shock at Jason's announcement.

"I am sorry to have to make this visit such a short one," Jason replied in a warm, affectionate tone as he smiled at his aged relative, "but perhaps we might stop in on our way back to Oakhill if you will have us."

"Of course," Lady Glenallan said, recovering her countenance quickly. "Go along then and leave us to our music." She made little shooing motions with her beringed hands before turning to Miss Chistleton with a request for a Vivaldi concerto.

Amazed disbelief kept Amy silent as Jason, with a hand on her arm, propelled her out of the room, down the stairs and out through the French doors in the small dining room. The door closing behind them released her tongue, however, and she shook off his hand, stopping short. "I do not understand, Jason. Why did you announce that we are visiting my brother after warning me so fiercely against mentioning my family?"

"Not here near the house," he said, taking her hand firmly in his. "Let's walk toward the stream and the gazebo."

After an unsuccessful attempt to free her hand, Amy surrendered to force majeure and allowed herself to be led away from the safety of numbers, though with many misgivings. Her head was awhirl with questions that she was strangely unwilling to ask as the beauty of the grounds at dusk and the evocative presence of the man beside her worked their magic on her anguished spirit.

Neither spoke as they made their way silently through gardens exuding a faint whiff of roses and lavender as her skirts whispered past. Her body became suffused with a quiet, dreamy contentment. Fortunately for her resolutions, her mind still functioned sufficiently to recognize this dangerous elixir. When they stepped up into the small shelter at the end of the bowling green near the stream, Amy gently dislodged her hand and watched with grave eyes as Jason dusted off a portion of the encircling bench with his handkerchief. His face was shadowed under the roof, but she could sense the tension in the line of his jaw and knew he was exercising a tight control over his demeanor.

She sat down and said quietly, "What is it, Jason? Why did you bring me out here on a transparent excuse?"

She knew he exhaled a sigh as he sat beside her, keeping a few inches of space between them. His voice was even as he replied, "Because suddenly I could not stomach the idea of sitting around the saloon all evening in a crowd, pretending that everything was fine; but it wasn't a lie, you know, even if it was transparent. This is a favorite spot to hear a nightingale sing on a summer evening. I haven't lied to you, Amy, only to myself. I hope you will believe that at least." There was a pause that she did not attempt to fill, and presently he went on.

"I needed to speak to you, to tell you that I know now that you are not Désirée. I know now what I have done to you by my rash action, and that it is unforgivable and perhaps irreversible. I—I have been cudgelling my brains all evening seeking a way to undo the damage to your reputation without finding any viable solution so far."

Amy had remained completely still during his confession, listening intently as his voice filled with misery and regret while one vital question resounded in her head. Now she asked, "What made you decide so suddenly that I was not Désirée, for it was sudden, was it not?"

"You have a mole on your left shoulder," he answered

readily, "but I should have known days ago had I not been such a blind, self-deceiving idiot! You are everything that she is not!"

She could see his jaw clench and her heart began to race madly, but he said after a second, "No more of that! Even had I discovered the truth on the very next day, the damage to your reputation could not have been averted. You asked why I cited your brother just now—it was simply that he made a convenient excuse to leave here tomorrow. Undoubtedly your people are combing the countryside for you even as we speak, and I would hope to avoid further scandal if possible, at least to spare my aunt the humiliation of your being discovered at Glendale—if you would not object to maintaining the pretense until we leave in the morning?" He rose from the bench as if moving his body were a task almost beyond his strength.

"Of course not," she said, forcing a voice through parched lips, aware of an immeasurable mournfulness in her soul that encompassed her own hopeless love and his regret and self-loathing.

Just as she took his extended hand to leave the gazebo, there came an audible embodiment of her feelings as the sweet, plaintive song of a nightingale was heard in the shrubbery near the stream. The pair stood handfast outside the gazebo near the hedge, listening as the last clear notes sounded. The beauty of the call caught in Amy's throat, and without thinking she pursed her lips and imitated the bird's song. Jason's hand tightened about hers until she winced with discomfort, and then suddenly he uttered a strange sound and her hand was free. She turned toward him instinctively and gasped at the sight of his large form crumpled on the ground. She started to kneel near him when she found herself grabbed from behind and a hand went over her mouth, stifling the scream rising in her throat.

"Shushhh, Miss Amy; it's me, Tom!"

She stopped struggling at the hoarse whisper and her captor released her. "Tom! What are you doing here?" she hissed, whirling to face the young giant. "Never mind." Her attention flew back to the man lying on the ground ominously still. "Oh, God! You—you haven't *killed* him?" she cried in horror.

"No," he replied grimly, "but I will if you say the word."

It was then that she saw the pistol in his hand, gripped by the barrel, and she seized his arm frantically. "Good God, no! Help me turn him over onto his back," she ordered, dropping to the ground beside the injured man.

"Leave him be, Miss Amy. Let's get away from here before he wakes up. I'll get you home safely, I promise."

"I know you would, Tom, and I thank you for finding me, but I am in no danger, I assure you. We are leaving for Marshland tomorrow morning."

The servant was shaking his head as he tucked the pistol into the waist of his breeches. "No, Miss Amy, it's not safe to leave you with him. He kidnapped you. You can't trust his word. Come with me now."

"No, Tom. Even if you have a carriage waiting outside the gates—*do* you have a carriage?"

"No," he admitted, "just Pegasus, but I can hire a carriage for you at the nighest inn. I've been scouting around this place for the past two hours, trying to get the lay of the land before going up to the house and asking for you, and then I heard you whistle like the nightingale."

"Thank heavens you did not do that!" she cried. "Listen to me, Tom. Do not think I am not immensely grateful to you. I prayed that you would find me, but I swear to you that Sir Jason means me no harm. He thought I was his wife who ran away. I must be her exact double because all his servants believe I am his wife too. I tried to escape one night and he stopped me, but he promised to bring me to Marshland to prove my identity if I came to Glendale with him to meet his great-aunt first. His relatives are good people, and I will not embarrass him by running away like his wife did since they do not know about that here. We will leave tomorrow. You may follow us on Pegasus if it will make you feel better, but he will keep his promise. Now, help me turn him over."

When he did not budge, continuing to stare at her unhappily, she added, "I will scream my head off if you try to take me away, Tom, which will bring a score of servants down on your neck in seconds."

Recognizing from old the determination to follow her own course in the face of opposition, Tom did her bidding reluctantly, his brain busy assessing ways to make sure that Archer could not disappear with her again.

Jason groaned a little but did not waken immediately. Amy, satisfied that he would revive shortly, looked up at her faithful servant. "Before you go, Tom, have you any word of Robert?"

He shook his head. "I've been gone from Marshfield since Wednesday when that Mrs. Greyson came to tell us what had happened to you."

"Perhaps there will be news when we reach home tomorrow," she said, sighing. The unconscious man stirred again, and she turned back to him. "Go now, Tom, quickly."

After a long look at the pair on the ground, Tom Watkins withdrew as silently as he had approached.

Chapter Twelve

The effort required was prodigious, but Jason opened his eyes and was rewarded by the sight of the loveliest face in the world gazing down at him from the shadows.

"Why are you so sad, my love?"

"Oh, you are really awake this time, thank goodness!"

Something shifted beneath him as she bent closer. Jason realized that he was lying on the ground with his head in Amy's lap; his head ached abominably. "What happened?" he asked, more because it seemed appropriate to the occasion than from any urgent desire to know anything beyond the fact that he was alone in the gathering dusk of a summer evening with the girl he loved.

"You were hit on the head."

"Hit? By what . . . why?" He lifted a hand to the back of his head, discovering a lump the size of his fist.

She sighed before she said, "By my servant, I'm afraid. He has been tracking us since Wednesday. He planned to take me away with him before there could be any hue and cry, so he . . ."

"But you did not go," he prompted when her voice trailed off.

"Of course not! That would have produced just such a situation at Glendale as you would most wish to avoid. Besides, I did not know how badly you were injured—he hit you with the handle of a pistol," she explained. "I told him we planned to leave in the morning."

"And he went away . . . just like that?" Scepticism rang in his tones.

"Not exactly," she admitted. "It took me some time to persuade him that you would keep your word to me . . . and I expect we may have an escort tomorrow."

"I see. Well, I think the better of him for that at least." Jason bit off a groan as he pushed himself up onto one elbow against every inclination to stay where he was, impelled by the knowledge that he could not in honor be this close to Amy again. Looking back over his shoulder, he noticed the white of her gown against the scraggly lawn where she had knelt to cushion his head for heaven knew how long. "I—I fear you will have ruined your gown with grass and earth stains," he said irrelevantly, swallowing back all the things he really wished to say to her.

"Not to worry," she replied serenely, rising to her feet in one swift motion and extending a hand down to assist him. "It is Désirée's gown and her problem."

He laughed at the little note of feminine satisfaction he detected but protested sharply, "Nonsense, the clothes are indisputably yours, all of them."

"We shan't argue about that," she said, holding onto his arm until he was steady on his feet.

"No, and we shan't change my mind about that either," he warned.

She allowed him the last word as she set about brushing grass from the back of his coat and then went on to shake out her skirts when Jason moved away to straighten his own appearance as best he could.

"Fortunately your head did not bleed, and your hair covers the lump," she assured him as he brushed a smoothing hand back over his hair and tugged at his cravat a bit. "There, that is better."

"Wait, Amy; don't go yet. We must talk about this situation, put our heads together and plan what we shall do to salvage your reputation."

"I doubt anything can do that since everyone in Rye must know about the incident."

"I grant that there must be talk about that, but we will come up with some tale to account for your absence. If invention fails us, I honestly believe Aunt Martha would swear that you were in her company the whole time. I won't accept that there is no solution that will leave your character intact."

"Jason, do not torture yourself over this, I beg you," she said earnestly. "I live very quietly in the country. My friends and neighbors will not shun my acquaintance. It may be a nine-day wonder at first, but my life will be unchanged in the end."

Jason glanced from the delicate, ringless hand on his sleeve to Amy's wide honest eyes gleaming in the fading light and swore a private oath that he would not let her suffer ostracism for this episode if he had to perjure his soul to prevent it—or remove her from the area if her brother were willing. Of course, if *he* were her brother, he'd be intent on killing the man who had wronged his sister. "Tell me about your brother," he said abruptly.

"Robert?" she said in surprise, not resisting as he guided her back to the gazebo. "Like you, Robert has been a soldier these past five years, and he too sold out this spring after our father died."

"Was he in the Peninsula fighting?"

"Yes, he served under General Lowry Cole, who is not, by the way, a relative."

"Ah, 4th Infantry Division?" When she nodded, he said, "I do not believe we ever chanced to cross paths. What was his rank?"

"Captain, but I should think Robert is considerably your junior. He is only two years older than I am."

"And how old are you, if I may be shockingly presumptuous?"

"I am one-and-twenty."

"So is Désirée," he said thoughtfully. "You say that you never knew your mother, but that she was English?"

"Yes, of course. Robert doesn't remember her either. She

died shortly after I was born, and he was only two at the time."

"Were you born at Marshland?"

"No, my parents were visiting my grandmother, who had just been widowed for the second time, in Northumbria. My mother is buried there."

"And her name before she married?"

"Helen Forrest."

"Did she have any sisters?"

"No, she had no immediate family. Robert and I have no maternal relatives that we know of. What are you thinking, Jason?"

"My dear . . . girl, it is simply inconceivable that such a striking resemblance, to put it mildly, could exist without consanguinity. Did your father never refer to his wife's family? Where did she come from?"

"I—I do not know." Amy's answers were coming more slowly now. "I don't believe I ever heard my father speak her name. There was no likeness of her in our house, and when I asked him once if I favored my mother in looks or personality, he said 'no' very brusquely and would not describe her to me. Grand-mère never spoke of her either."

"Did you not find this odd?"

She shrugged. "I suppose I did, but that was the way it was."

"Did any of the neighboring families ever refer to your mother or mention having known her?"

"Not that I can recall. My father eschewed society entirely. Grand-mère, though respected for her philanthropy in the area, never formed any real friendships among the genteel families, though she was certainly on civil terms with a number of those we saw regularly at church."

"How old were you when your grandmother died?"

"Nearly sixteen."

"Did you ever go to school?"

"No. Grand-mère taught me at home. After she died, I kept house for my father."

Each answer added to Jason's escalating pity and wonder

that such a sterile existence could have produced such a strong and valiant and basically optimistic character. He cleared his throat of a lump that was threatening to choke him. "Did you take part in any of the local social activities?"

"Not often, due to my father's reclusive habits, but occasionally he permitted me to attend informal gatherings at the homes of our nearest neighbors, and I was well acquainted with all the villagers, of course. I did have one particular friend who married two years ago and left the area. She now lives near Midhurst, which is where I was heading the night I tried to—to leave Oakhill. So you see, I wasn't being as foolish as you imagined, and I would have sent Solomon back as soon as arrangements had been made for my return to Marshland."

The hint of challenge in her voice nearly undid Jason's resolve to keep a prudent distance from the temptation her sweetness and vulnerability always represented. He rose abruptly from the bench. "You must be getting chilled sitting here. I believe we may return now with no worse consequence than a mild teasing at the well-known preference of newlyweds for privacy. It will only remain to get through the rest of the evening and say our good-byes at breakfast."

"Yes, of course," she murmured, rising obediently, but he noticed that she kept her eyes downcast as they headed back to the family gathering. Neither seemed able to introduce an innocuous topic to break the silence that had grown between them like a wall by the time they arrived at the drawing room. The sounds of Mozart being played by an artist beckoned them.

The westering sun, distorted by old window glass, caught one corner of a scarred desk and shafted narrowly across the worn rug without delineating the original colors of the faded pattern. The apartment's furnishings were scant, consisting of a carved settee with a cracked leather seat and a round table flanked by two armless chairs in addition to the desk. A tray containing a teapot and a couple of dishes stood on the table; a clock on the mantel and a mirror over the fireplace with a broken pediment frame of mahogany constituted the only quasi-ornamental features in the otherwise utilitarian space, except, that is, for the room's sole occupant.

The young woman sitting nearly motionless at the desk was decorative enough to grace the fabled halls of Versailles. She possessed a porcelain complexion enhanced by a wealth of chestnut-hued curls framing a heart-shaped face of riveting beauty. Her green gown, though simple in style, was made of a fine supple silk that matched the color of her eyes and showed to advantage her delicate but decidedly feminine contours. At present, her loveliness owed everything to nature's beneficence and nothing to expression, for hers alternated between annoyance and anxiety as she sat in the only upholstered chair; her stillness was imposed by will, not by serenity.

A sheet of paper lay on the desk in front of her, and from time to time the silence in the room was broken by the tiny scratching sounds of a pen, but never for long. Once she picked up a cup near her right hand and sipped absently, grimacing at the cold contents before setting it down again. Her eyes kept straying to the window that looked down on the busy street. At one point she found herself gripping the pen so tightly that her knuckles whitened. She flung it down, flexing her fingers while she read the few lines on the paper.

On completing this unnecessary exercise, she uttered an impatient exclamation and crushed the paper in her hands in a burst of ill temper. Turning to toss it into the fireplace, she pulled up short in belated recognition that no fire had been needed on such a warm day. Gnawing on her bottom lip, she eyed the wadded paper dubiously for a moment and then meticulously smoothed out the creases before tearing the paper into small pieces that she pushed into a pile with her fingertips.

Rising from the chair, she headed for the adjacent bedchamber where she retrieved a tinderbox and a candlestick. Returning with these items, she detoured by the tea tray and picked up the smallest dish, in which over the next few minutes she proceeded to burn the scraps of paper with the flame from her candle. She waited, motionless until the ashes had cooled, whereupon she brushed them into the fireplace. Leaving nothing undone, she then washed the dish and her fingers with water from the pitcher in the bedchamber, drying them on a napkin from the tray.

With the same mechanical precision, the lady seated herself at the desk again and withdrew another sheet of paper from a drawer. Its blank surface consumed her frowning concentration for several minutes. At last she inhaled deeply and straightened her back, a look of purpose replacing her former indecision.

Before she could take up her pen, however, footsteps sounded outside the entrance door, barely giving her time to cap the ink bottle and fold the paper, which she slipped between the pages of a book on the desk, before the door opened and a man entered the spartan room.

"Where have you been? You've been gone for ages!" she cried, rushing over to cast herself against his chest.

The recipient of these attentions accepted them willingly, kissing her with an enthusiastic thoroughness before unwinding her arms from around his neck and putting her away from him.

"What is this *crise des nerfs, mon coeur,* that you must strangle me?" He surveyed her calmly, a little smile playing about his lips, while he removed first his gloves of York tan and then his hat. These the young woman took into her possession, freeing him to make a minor adjustment to his cravat with the slender fingers of a well-shaped hand.

The gentleman's neat modest raiment may have been designed to assist him in blending into the scene in a seaside town on the southern coast of England, but everything essential about his appearance would ensure that he stood out in a crowd. Indeed, he was the lady's counterpart, for if she was the epitome of feminine beauty, he could be described as the beau ideal of masculine perfection without fear of contradiction. A bit above the average in height, he was beautifully balanced, slim but with a promise of sinewy strength in his wide shoulders, and he moved with the lithe economy of a natural athlete. His lineaments bore a patrician stamp, forcibly putting an observer in mind of heroic Greek statues. The static perfection of sculpture told only half the story in this case, however. Fine-grained skin was alive with rich olive tones, and large, black-lashed hazel eyes that gleamed with amber lights radiated a sharp intelligence. Even his thick black locks bespoke vitality as they sprang back into waves after he passed a hand through his hair upon removing his hat.

Had the gentleman's appearance been totally unexceptionable, he would still have attracted notice the moment he uttered his first words. His English was fluent and idiomatic, the tonal quality pleasant, but there was a faintly foreign inflection in his speech that was alien to British ears.

He said now, his eyes following the young woman's progress as she turned away to place his hat and gloves on the desk, "What is it, *ma belle?* I told you I would be away at least two or three hours."

"It seemed much longer," she said with a pout. "You know I detest being cooped up in this horrid little room with nothing to do and no one to talk to. In Dover I was able to walk around the town and go into the shops."

"Dover is bigger than Newhaven and much farther from Oakhill," the man said patiently. "We agreed that it was vital that you not be seen with me. He will be looking for a couple."

"Then it should be perfectly safe for me to leave this wretched place as long as I am not with you," she argued, turning toward him as he sank into the upholstered chair with a sigh of weariness.

His light eyes surveyed her from head to toe, a lengthy process that deepened the color in her cheeks, before he shook his head. "Not with those eyes and not in that dress," he said flatly.

"I cannot help my eyes," she said with a provocative flicker of long curling lashes, "and I wore this dress for you."

He reached out an arm and tumbled her into his lap. "Believe me, *ma belle,* I am most appreciative of your eyes," he said, kissing first one and then the other, smiling at her little shiver, "and of this delectable gown, but it would not do to attract attention to ourselves. Our position is too precarious."

"Do you seriously believe Archer is searching for us?" she asked, settling herself more comfortably and winding her arms around his neck. "It has been more than a fortnight since I left and there has been no sign of pursuit."

He looked at her incredulously. "How can you doubt it? The man believes you are his wife! Of course he is searching for you! We have been fortunate thus far in avoiding him."

"It is my belief that he considers himself well rid of me; all we ever did was quarrel."

The man administered a shake to one shapely shoulder of the girl nestled against his chest. "I have explained to you, Désirée, that what we have done is a terrible affront to his honor. If he is half the man I expect he is, then he will not rest until he calls me to account for the insult."

Her eyes widened in fear during this speech. "You must not fight a duel with Archer, Etienne! We can simply tell him the truth as I wanted to do in my note when you came for me. He must understand and accept the situation then."

The man she called Etienne gave a mirthless laugh. "Your fear for my safety at the hands of your second choice is heart-warming though scarcely flattering, *mon coeur*. I yield to no man in my respect for the primacy of truth, but I must remind you that I am a Frenchman in an enemy country at present. I would therefore prefer to have a large body of water between us and the reach of your government when I tell this particular truth."

"But I am persuaded Archer will be happy and relieved to help us when he learns that his marriage was not legal."

Etienne cast his eyes up to heaven as if asking guidance before saying carefully, "I fear we again are left with that concept you find so so difficult to comprehend—honor. It would violate my honor to accept assistance from the man who has been, in a sense, wronged by me or mine."

Désirée pulled back like a scalded cat, her magnificent eyes flashing. "I did *not* wrong Jason Archer—not intentionally. You left for the continent almost immediately after our wedding, and I heard nothing from you for ten months— ten long months! I was wild with anxiety about you, and my mother was dying. Then that ugly little man came to the house one night with a letter you had written to me months before and a report that you had been killed in Spain. I was in agonies of grief over you when my mother died the next month, and then I was all alone with almost no money—certainly no income since her annuity ended with her death. What would you have had me do? I could not stay with my friend Lucy indefinitely. Do you have any idea of what it means to be a female all alone in the world with no means of support? The constant fear that eats away one's confidence, one's generosity and goodness, one's very soul!" She burst into sobs, burying her face in her hands.

The man held her tighter. "There, there, *ma p'tite,* do not weep so. It was ungentlemanly of me to bring this up again. I am well aware that everything that has happened is my fault, starting with the secrecy of our marriage. I had no right to marry you in the first place, situated as I was with no power to provide for you in this country and every likelihood of being killed in circumstances where no one would ever identify me. If I'd had any inkling that your mother's health was so poor—but there is nothing to be gained in regretting one's choices. You would have been better off if the bullet that left me for dead had finished its work," he declared in bitter accents. "Eventually you would have been happy with your stuffy English—"

"Do not say that!" she cried, putting her fingers over his mouth and staring into his eyes in sudden fear through wet-clumped lashes. "Do you regret marrying me, Etienne?" Tears still coursed down her cheeks.

"Not a bit," he replied promptly. "I knew from the start that you were a vain little baggage who would be very expensive. I went into this with my eyes open."

"Well, that is comforting, I must say!" She pulled back from his embrace. "I wonder you should have wished to marry me at all if that is your opinion of me!"

"I beg your pardon. I should have said a *beautiful*, vain little baggage; you do have other redeeming qualities. I'll be able to afford you once we are in France."

She boxed his ears and scrambled off his lap, shaking out her skirts and jumping away with a squeal when he gave her a playful swat on her derriere. "And when will that be, my lord? In your perambulations from tavern to tavern today, did you meet the person who will sail us to France?"

"No, my love, but I told you not to expect that it would happen this quickly. The agent I hope to contact is a fisherman who returns here periodically."

"So we must wait in this terrible place? This would not have happened if your captain in Dover had not left us in the lurch."

"Again, it was a matter of timing. He could not wait around Dover indefinitely without arousing suspicion. He agreed to remain in the area long enough for me to go to Portsmouth to collect my wife and return with her. We did not allow for the circumstances of a deceased mother-in-law and a missing wife that took an extra three days to unravel and rectify."

"Is there no other place where you may hire a boat?"

"Possibly, but only if one has unlimited funds and good intelligence about whom to approach. Asking the wrong person could prove disastrous. Our best chance is to stay here and not draw attention to our presence until my contact returns. I know this confinement is hard on you, but it should not be more than a few days, three or four at most, before he returns. Perhaps I might purchase some sketching supplies or embroidery materials to help you pass the time more pleasantly. Have you finished your book?"

"No, I cannot concentrate when you are out there in danger, but, Etienne, I have a black dress and veil with me. I am persuaded no one would notice me, especially in shops that are mostly patronized by women."

"No, *ma belle,* it isn't safe. I had hoped not to worry you, but I learned today that someone was asking about a Mr. Armand Martin traveling with a green-eyed brunette. This was eight or ten days ago when we were in Dover. The interested person was described as a big, dark-haired chap with black eyes."

"So, Archer *is* looking for us, but surely he has passed on to another place by now."

"Most assuredly, but he will have paid someone or promised someone money to send him word if this Armand Martin and his companion should appear in Newhaven."

A knock on the door at that moment caused Désirée to freeze in the middle of the room, her imploring gaze on her husband, who said calmly, "I ordered us a meal. Go into the bedchamber."

She swallowed her fear and obeyed him at once, closing the door silently behind her. When she returned to the sitting room presently at his beckoning, she was once more in full command of her emotions. She chatted away smilingly while they ate, questioning him about his estate in Burgundy and encouraging his accounts of his remaining family members. She also was assiduous in keeping his glass filled during their meal.

In all likelihood the heat in the cramped room and the accumulated effect of libations taken in the course of an afternoon spent searching the taverns for his contact contributed as much as his dinner wine to his succumbing shortly thereafter to a pre-bedtime nap.

Désirée eyed her husband's relaxed form in the armchair for a long thoughtful moment. She shifted her gaze to the desktop then and quietly gathered up her writing materials before settling herself at the dining table. This time when she began to write there was no hesitation or indecision in her manner. Within ten minutes she had completed her task and restored the ink and pen to the desk where her letter now reposed between the pages of her book.

Chapter Thirteen

"Good Lord, is that misbegotten cur on the white horse the one who hit me?"

"Tom Watkins is neither misbegotten nor a cur," Amy replied hotly to the man standing at the open carriage door. "He suffered horrible burns in a childhood accident, the effects of which continue to make daily living a heroic struggle for him, but he is highly intelligent and a rock of integrity, as well as being kind and intensely loyal."

"I see he has one good friend in you," Sir Jason said on a calmer note, a bit taken aback by her fierce defense of the servant. "You said Watkins—Tom Watkins?"

"Yes. His speech is a bit difficult to understand at first. Just ask him to repeat or write anything you are not sure of."

Sir Jason gave her a searching look before nodding and turning away. Amy took a deep breath and closed her eyes, uninterested in the bustle attendant on the business of the inn yard. This was the first stop to change horses enroute to Marshland, and she was finding the goal she had set herself—to preserve a calm friendly facade on the last day with Jason—nearly impossible to achieve. A second sleepless night had left her physically and mentally out of tune. Her jaw ached from the effort required to keep a smile plastered on her face, and her muscles and nerves seemed bent on acting without authorization from her brain. If she looked as twitchy as she felt, she must resemble someone with St. Vitus's dance, she thought, clenching her teeth in impotent disgust.

From the revealing moment when she had comprehended the forbidden nature of her feelings for Jason, she'd felt her sane and sensible persona slipping away from her grasp. The possibility of losing any degree of control over her de-meanor sent waves of cold panic coursing through her. Try-ing to project a comfortable air that suggested a temporary interruption in what would be a permanent relationship with Lady Glenallan and Miss Chistleton when she had said her good-byes this morning had cost her agonies of regret and self-reproach. Nor could she permit herself to dwell on her personal sense of loss at knowing it would not be her privi-lege to enjoy a permanent bond with these wise and inter-esting ladies. She had snatched a measure of comfort from the warmth of the farewells she'd received from Jason's ex-tended family, but she would not dwell on that either.

For this one last day she must keep all thoughts of her barren future at bay. The only thing she could salvage from what Jason had referred to as "the episode" was her dignity. As long as she preserved this he would not be able to look at her with pity; she would avert that final knife thrust. Pride might be one of the deadly sins, but she must cloak her wounds in its protective mantle—just this once, she begged of a benevolent Creator.

Meanwhile, Amy took deep relaxing breaths and stretched her neck muscles. Best not to think about how she loathed being confined in a moving vehicle either. At least on this return trip she would be able to walk about a little and partake of a meal during one of the changes en route. Jason's traveling carriage, though its interior padding was beginning to show its age, was well built and more comfort-ably sprung than the public conveyance he'd hired in Rye. These petty considerations flitted into her consciousness as she wracked her brain for indifferent topics to offer to keep the conversation from lapsing into seething silences and, even more importantly, to prevent straying into any areas that verged on the personal.

Jason's curiosity about Tom Watkins when they started on their second leg of the journey dissolved the constraint between them and provided innocuous material for discussion. Amy obligingly related the story of how her brother had repeatedly come to the aid of the damaged boy during their childhood, fighting the village bullies who made his life a prolonged inferno of another sort. She confessed to her own initial shrinking from the scarred youth until she had witnessed his gentleness and authority with small animals. "He taught me to recognize all the marsh plants and birds, and he carved marvelous replicas of them for me. I still keep them on the top of a bureau in my room."

"Do I understand that he can read and write?"

"Yes, Robert taught him when he found out that Tom stayed away from school because the children were so cruel to him there. Despite the difference in station they are truly friends, not just master and servant, though Tom refers to my brother as Mister Rob when speaking to others, and I am always Miss Amy. He would do anything for Robert. The hardest thing for him is approaching strangers and seeing their reaction to his face, so it is a measure of his devotion to us that he found me, with all the meeting and questioning of people that must have entailed."

"I must agree with you, judging from my own reaction to his scars, not to mention the lump on my head. Does he own the white horse?"

"No, Pegasus belongs to Robert. Tom's mount cut his fetlock last week, and my mare is not up to his weight."

"Your brother did not take his horse with him to London then?"

"N-no, he drove his phaeton," Amy said, hoping her delayed response to his sudden question did not sound like the blatant lie it was. She looked out the window, making an observation on the scenery and avoiding Jason's keen look. He did not challenge her, but the constraint between them was palpable once more.

It was with heartfelt relief that Amy exited the carriage at the inn where they were to break their fast before resuming the final stages of the journey. A cursory glance around the inn yard showed no sign of Tom Watkins, but merely stepping out into the fresh air was enough to expand her spirits marginally. She took advantage of a brief spell of privacy in the dining room Jason had hired to remove her hat and spencer and do a few vigorous stretches.

The interval in the inn proved unexpectedly pleasant. Jason, entering the dining room a few minutes later, cast a keen eye over her slightly flushed cheeks and smiled in some relief. "Ah, you look much better now that you are on your feet. Does the motion of the carriage make you feel unwell?"

"No, just homicidal," Amy answered unthinkingly, looking startled when Jason gave a shout of laughter.

"Then I had best watch my step today, since I appear to be the only potential victim within reach should this impulse gain ascendance over your better nature."

"No, no," she protested, blushing furiously. "It has nothing to do with you. I beg your pardon for forgetting my manners."

"Do not apologize. I have no doubt that Grand-mère would consider you quite sunk beneath reproach, but I have found that our most memorable moments have occurred when you have forgotten your manners."

"Now you are being idiotish," she said with an assumption—rather belated—of stern dignity. "Ah, here is the waiter with our food. I don't know about you, but I am quite hungry."

Amy was aware that she was chattering inanely but, lulled by Jason's easy flow of impersonal conversation, she did justice to the simple, well-prepared food the inn provided. This repaired the omission of the morning when she had been unable to swallow her breakfast while she battled the emotional storm that complicated her departure from Glendale. She responded quite naturally to a quality in Jason's manner that sprang not from facile charm but from what she perceived as genuine liking and respect for the people of whom he spoke. For the duration of their luncheon she was able to forget the difficulties of her personal situation and the bleakness of her future in the quiet contentment of the present.

All too soon she came smack up against reality when they took their places in the carriage once more. The new team of horses had no sooner gotten underway when Jason announced that they must now decide on an explanation for her long absence that would leave her reputation uncompromised. For a disbelieving second Amy experienced a sensation akin to being doused with a pitcher of cold water. Her breath caught in her throat and she shivered, staring blindly at the man across from her until her mental balance and his image steadied. Her voice when it returned surprised her too by its steadiness.

"I believe the simplest story will be best, and you need not figure in it. I was abducted by a dark stranger whom I managed to escape at a posting inn and was rescued shortly thereafter by two respectable ladies who gave me asylum. You see I have borrowed your facetious suggestion about your great-aunt."

"Which respectable ladies? From where?"

"Two spinster sisters perhaps. There is no need to identify the ladies because no one will go in search of them."

"And why did these good Samaritans not return you immediately to your anxious family?"

There was a charged pause and then Amy said triumphantly, "Because I had suffered a fall in my flight which left me with amnesia so I could not tell them where my home was. That also was an invention of yours, and quite successful with your staff, as I recall."

His lips twitched briefly but Jason ignored the hint of resentment in her voice. "And why, when you had recovered your memory, did these benevolent ladies not add to their goodness by personally delivering you into the arms of your family?"

"Their health is too poor to permit them to travel long

distances, and by the time I had regained my memory, Tom Watkins had tracked me down. He can hire a carriage for me when we get closer to Marshland, and then you need not go anywhere near Rye."

"I fear my good opinion of your saviors has suffered a reversal at their failure to provide you with an abigail on your journey for appearance's sake," Jason said. "Enough, my dear. You cannot keep me out of your adventure for I must and shall see you safely home." He silenced Amy's incipient protest with an upraised hand. "No matter what story we may decide to tell the rest of the world, I owe your brother the truth."

"But Robert may not have returned from London by now," Amy cried. "You cannot stay camped on my doorstep until his return. That would certainly defeat the purpose of whatever tale we might offer to account for my absence. How are we to explain your appearance with me at Marshland? Oh, I have it! The old ladies asked you to escort me to my home. Perhaps you are a—a beloved nephew or a helpful neighbor or—"

"Or a wandering minstrel? Give over, my child. You cannot turn me into a knight-errant, however inventive your schemes. For one thing, Tom Watkins knows the truth."

"Tom would never breathe a word of this to a soul; he would never do anything to hurt me!"

"Pax!" he said, again raising a hand to stem the flow. A frown appeared between his brows. "Your brother's absence would be a complication since, as you said, I cannot remain in the area. How long did he expect to be in London?"

"I—I don't know . . . a fortnight or so. He—he wasn't entirely certain how long his business would take."

His eyes bored into her mind, and again she could not sustain contact, shifting her gaze out the window.

"There is something you are not telling me about your brother's absence."

"No! How many men ever take their female relatives entirely into their confidence?" she demanded, going on the attack to prevent herself from giving in to the growing desire to tell him about Robert's mission. She knew he could be trusted completely and she longed to enlist his assistance in tracing her brother, but she had vowed to keep silent.

"I would say the degree to which a man takes a woman into his confidence depends on the strength of the bond between them," he said slowly, his eyes never leaving her face.

She gripped her bottom lip between her teeth, fighting an urge to weep. Not yet. She could not know how clearly her green eyes reflected her troubled soul.

Jason's expression softened. "What a brute I am to add to your problems! Never mind, my lo—my dear girl, I can see that you do not mean to confide in me, and of course there is no reason that you should trust me."

"I do trust you," Amy replied between gritted teeth, "but there is nothing to confide. My brother did not give a specific date for his return."

"In that case," said Jason, taking his traveling desk onto his lap, "I am going to write a full account of these past six days and assure him that I shall place myself at his disposal upon his return." He suited his action to the words, focusing all his attention on the task he'd set himself.

Amy resumed her previous occupation of gazing unseeingly out the window, her mood seesawing from relief at not having to produce conversational trivialities to apprehension about what Jason would consider a "full" account of the abduction and its aftermath. Did he intend to describe the circumstances that led to the discovery—and location—of the mole that finally convinced him she was not his wife? Surely he would not mention the passionate kiss they had exchanged! Behind a mask of tranquility, her mind was a seething caldron of forbidden fantasies, regrets and fears of exposure bubbling together. She angled her head slightly and slid a sideways glance at the man frowning over his task. She devoured his face with greedy eyes, committing the planes and angles of brow and cheekbones to memory, admiring his wealth of dark lashes and longing to trace the beautiful curves of his mouth with her finger.

Jason looked up suddenly and caught her staring. "Would

you say your brother was *au fond* a rational being, logical rather than fanciful or imaginative?"

"Robert is eminently practical and logical, not at all fanciful. Why do you ask?"

Jason grimaced. "Because I fear that a logical and rational being is going to find this tale incredible in the extreme. My intrusion into your life was reprehensible and unforgivable. I'll never be able to make it up to you. You have every right to hate me."

"Of course I don't hate you, Jason," she declared, alarmed by the bitterness of his self-reproach. "It was an unfortunate error. I know you never meant to harm me, and I really believe there will be no lasting repercussion in my life. I feel we have both been the victims of a capricious fate."

"Your generosity of spirit simply adds to the burden!" He raked her countenance with a brooding regard, started to say something more and then clamped his mouth shut. He fixed his eyes on the paper under his hand and began to write again.

Amy, shaken by the intensity of the exchange, shrank back into a corner of the carriage and closed her eyes, willing the tumult in her pulses to subside. After a while, overcome by lack of sleep and a tempest of emotion, she sank into a lethargy that gradually became sleep.

He'd be hard-pressed to say when he'd last felt this weary, Jason acknowledged, sinking back against the corduroy squabs in the carriage after the last change before Oakhill. Perhaps not since a forced retreat through the inhospitable mountains of Spain. Now he was similarly weighed down by the knowledge that his plans—make that his purpose, even his life—had ground to a halt against his will.

Parting from Amy would be difficult enough under any circumstances, but muffled and gagged as he had been by commitment and duty to another woman had made the occasion hellish. He supposed his honor was more or less intact technically, but at what cost? At the cost of keeping his arms rigidly at his side when they ached to take Amy into a comforting embrace, and clamping his teeth tight against uttering a promise that there would be a life for them together in the future? Certainly at the cost of allowing a white-faced girl to go through a demeaning charade of taking polite leave of an anonymous humanitarian who had done her supposed rescuers a service by delivering her into the arms of two anxious upper servants at her home. She had asked about her brother immediately on their arrival and had been told that no word had come from him during her absence. He had then given her his letter to Robert Cole. His refusal of her impeccable offer of refreshments had been the only kindness he could have done her at that moment.

His last image of Amy had been of a modishly-garbed girl with her head buried in the bosom of a motherly housekeeper. The butler had been shaking Tom Watkins's hand and patting his shoulder in congratulations as Jason had climbed back into his carriage feeling like the outsider he was. For want of any more credible story, he had been forced to go along with Amy's concocted version of her adventure. Galling though it was to have to accept having his role white-washed as it were, he could see that the only way to save her reputation was to distance himself from her as she had pointed out. With a heart bursting to slay dragons and lay the world at her feet, he'd been permitted to do nothing for her, not even the minor gesture of giving her the clothes she had redesigned and made her own by hours of sewing. She had insisted, inarguably, that her hypothetical rescuers might have scrambled together one outfit to replace whatever items had been ruined during her abduction and escape, but they would never have assembled an entire wardrobe in the latest mode for a chance met female passing through their lives. He was left with the unheroic but necessary task of coming up with an explanation that would satisfy his coachman and household staff when he returned to Oakhill with his wife's wardrobe but no wife.

Until the past few days he would have said that the quality of directness defined his character, but it was diplomacy, even deviousness that had been demanded of him just lately. He'd made it his business to seek out Tom Watkins at the last change to inform him of Amy's wishes in the matter of an explanation for her prolonged absence. The man had listened impassively, his one good eye steady on Jason's face with nothing servile in his manner. He'd indicated his understanding that he was to corroborate his mistress's statements; then he'd added that he intended to tell her brother the true story as he knew it. There was no insolence in the man's utterance, but he projected a certain quiet assurance that Jason found impressive, considering his history and disfigurement. Though inconvenient for his own sake, he was glad that Amy had such stalwart support behind her while her brother was away. He'd tried questioning Watkins about his master's whereabouts, but to no avail. The man had parroted the line about a business trip to London that Amy had held to and disclaimed any current information, offering his own absence from Marshland for the best part of a sennight in evidence of ignorance. Though more than ever persuaded that some mystery surrounded Robert Cole's present activity, he was not such a fool as to expect that further probing would discover the answer to the puzzle. Amy, because of her reluctant attachment to him, was the weakest link in this conspiracy of silence—just where had that word come from, he wondered—and she had held resolute. With his deep loyalty and affection for brother and sister, Tom Watkins had every reason to distrust and despise him. There would be no confidences from this source. With a grudging civility that just escaped disdain, he'd refused the douceur Jason had tried to press on him.

He understood and valued that brand of loyalty enough to mask his resentment beyond a narrowed glance that Watkins had withstood unmoved. His own coachman was of the same stamp. William had sat him on his first pony at the age of three and later taught him to handle the ribbons but he was deep in his sixties now. Once he'd parted from Amy, Jason had been in a fever of impatience to quit the area. If he was recognized and connected with her, her hoaxing tale would come back to bite her even before it had been floated past most of her acquaintances. With the thought of sparing the old coachman, he'd proposed to leave him to a night's rest in a post house down the road a few miles while he pushed on tonight by hired vehicle. William might then bring the carriage back by easy stages. He had reckoned without his host, however. William had been highly affronted by the consideration, and he was in full possession of his powers of expression and argument.

They had argued it out over a tavern meal where the old servant had not scrupled to relate every peccadillo of Jason's youth that had to do with horseflesh or driving, drawing on a memory that bordered on total recall. The upshot of that revealing exercise was a compromise whereby William spurned the proposed rest but agreed to drive alternate stages with his employer. Jason insisted that the coachman abandon the box while he took the reins. By sneakily extending his own driving stints, he contrived to provide some decent rest intervals inside the carriage for the stubborn old man.

As for himself, he had enjoyed the periods of driving, both the physical challenge and being forced to concentrate on an activity that took his mind partly off his personal problems. The night had been mild; the sky was filled with stars, and the moon was still half-full. The carriage lanterns had helped them maintain a good pace over the turnpikes. Anxious though he was to get on with the next phase, there had been something almost soothing in being suspended between the troublesome past and the problematic future. There was a certain solace in riding through the darkness with the stars for company and the rhythms of the clopping hoofbeats and ever-turning wheels in his ears while two tons of horseflesh responded to his commands on the reins.

It was full daylight when they arrived at the house and were greeted by the unshockable Hatcherd who summoned his minions to unload the carriage.

"How is everything at Oakhill, Hatcherd?" Justin asked, handing over hat and gloves.

"Nothing of real moment has occurred during your absence, sir," the butler replied, glancing past his master to the open door. "Lady Archer is not with you?" he asked, his eyes flickering over the trunk being carried upstairs by a footman.

"No," Jason said, rubbing his hand through his hair and yawning. "She received a message that a cousin was ill and went hotfoot to her assistance. She still has clothes at her cousin's house, so she sent the trunk back. I need to sleep for a while. Call me in four hours. Send the post up to my room now, please, Hatcherd."

One bridge crossed, he thought with satisfaction, heading up the stairs. Hopefully, the matter-of-fact fabrication to account for his wife's nonappearance would have circulated to the smallest maid in the scullery by the time he woke up. The Pyrrhic nature of the victory darkened his brow almost instantly, however, while he dragged off his clothing and fell across the bed. He was merely delaying the inevitable disclosures unless he found Désirée soon and resolved the imbroglio.

The moment he closed his eyes, Amy's face appeared behind his lids as she had looked when descending from the carriage at the front entrance to Marshland. "I hope you will find your wife, Jason," she had said simply.

And he, with his insides churning at the sadness in her eyes and even more at the sheer valor in trying to rise above her own pain, had replied, "Have no fear on that head. I am more determined than ever to locate her." He'd wished the hasty words unsaid the next instant as he felt her hand tremble in his as she looked down at her feet rather than meet his eyes while descending the steps. He bit off the explanation on his tongue, afraid to say too much, and the chance was gone in the next second when her servants came hurrying out the door to greet her. Her image had haunted him on the long drive home, and he had resigned himself to having it haunt his sleep; however, somewhat to his surprise he arose refreshed four hours later, with no recollection of dreaming.

Jason tackled the post with the huge breakfast he had ordered upon his arrival. He was hoping to discover a communication from one of the lookouts he had paid in the various ports where he'd sought Désirée and Armand Martin. The tide was turning against Napoleon in the Peninsula after he had squandered so many troops in Russia. If, as Jason suspected, Martin was French, he would be trying to leave the country. His greatest fear was that Désirée would disappear with her lover, leaving him in a kind of limbo. Meeting Amy had made it imperative that he resolve his marital status without delay. He peered at the subscriptions on each item first and, spotting one inscribed in a flowing feminine hand, put his cup down so quickly that coffee splashed onto the sleeve of his dressing gown. Ignoring the mishap, he slit the seal with pulses racing in anticipation and let out a massive breath of relief.

Jason devoured the short message in one gulp, shaking his head in bemusement. Who but Désirée would have the audacity to beg pardon in the first line and money in the next? He scrutinized the missive with the care of a scientist or a solicitor, looking for hidden meaning in each phrase. His eye returned and lingered on her promise to divulge something he would like to learn about their marriage in exchange for a sum of money. He was intrigued as she had meant him to be, but she may simply have underestimated his willingness to give her money. He would never see her in want even if her lover deserted her. He had pursued and married her in haste and was quite prepared, if not to repent, at least to pay at leisure.

The thought came unbidden that if it had been Amy instead of Désirée whom he had met first, there would be no question of repentance, but that was unjust. Désirée may have pretended to be what she was not, but he was solely responsible for the puerile impetuosity that had precluded caution or sense. In his case, infatuation had equaled willful

blindness. He shook his head to derail that useless train of
thought and returned his attention to the letter before him.

Désirée was in Newhaven where Jason had promised a
layabout a sum of money if he reported seeing them to him.
He took the time to go through the rest of the post, but to no
avail. This could mean a number of things, of course. Assuming they were traveling as man and wife, they might be
using a different name. Or his informant might have accepted the small sum of money he'd paid him at the time and
promptly erased the incident from his mind. Désirée's instructions were to send the money to an inn to be held for
Mrs. Smithson, but she could scarcely be naive enough to
expect the transaction to be that simple.

Invigorated by the opportunity to do something positive
to resolve the situation at last, his recent weariness completely forgotten, Jason called for a bath to be readied and
set about devising a plan of attack.

Chapter Fourteen

A knock on the door brought the listless figure in the desk chair bolt upright. At last! It was four days since she'd posted her letter, and she had begun to fear that she might have misjudged Jason Archer. She flew across the room and then stopped short, pausing to compose her countenance before opening the door.

"Yes?" She fought to hold on to a neutral expression while disappointment clutched at her heart. The gangly youth confronting her was empty-handed.

"Please, ma'am, are you Mrs. Smithson?"

"Yes. Do you have a letter for me?"

"No, ma'am. Mr. Gurnley at the inn, he sent me to tell you there's a gen'leman there as wishes to see you."

"To see me?" she said, struggling to subdue the sharpness in her voice. "What man?"

"I dunno. Mr. Gurnley just said to tell you is all. Will you come w' me, ma'am?"

"No—not just yet. Wait," she said, as the youth turned away. She hurried over to the table and returned, holding out a coin. "Here, thank you. Do not tell anyone where I live," she added, and could have bitten out her tongue in the next second for giving him a reason to remember her. As she closed the door she comforted herself with the observation that the boy had looked to be rather dull-witted. She stood perfectly still, but her thoughts were racing around in circles. Foremost was irritation that Jason Archer had come himself instead of sending the money as she had requested. He was the most provoking man in the world, though never less than a perfect gentleman. After their wedding she had seen her power over him slipping steadily away. He was like two different men: the first had been eager and adoring while the second was coolly civil and reproachful, expecting her to care about that moldering old house as his mother had.

Etienne could be reproachful at times too, and he didn't always let her have her own way. The difference was that he *did* adore her. Her eyes went to the clock. He would be returning in an hour or two. The last thing in the world she would wish was a meeting between the two men who believed she belonged to them.

She began pacing, her fingers going to her temples to stop the sudden beating there. She shrank from facing the man she had married and deserted, but better in a public place than here where Etienne might return and create an impossible scene. He would be furious that she had disregarded his wishes, but money in her hand would certainly serve to palliate his anger. She bit her lip fiercely, still undecided, and caught sight of herself in the mirror. She looked as distracted as she felt. There was no time!

As she stood there staring at her reflection, her self-possession streamed back. She was wearing her most becoming dress, a frothy confection in a buttery yellow silk with white bands at the flounced hem. It had been Jason's favorite, she recalled. She moved into the bedchamber where she applied a discreet touch of rouge to cheeks and lips. Tweaking a chestnut curl into place, she then tied the ribbons of a ravishing yellow straw hat adorned with masses of white flowers around the crown. After conducting a search for clean gloves and a reticule, she pulled a white gauze stole from a drawer in the dresser and seized a white lace parasol as she headed out the door.

On the short walk to the inn doubts of the wisdom of her

actions challenged the confidence that generally accompanied the awareness of her charming appearance, but she could see no other solution to the problem of quick, safe transport to France. Every day they were forced to remain in England meant increased danger for Etienne. In any case, it was too late to pull back now. She could not hope to hide from Jason Archer who was obviously determined to see her; he would have no difficulty in finding her direction from the inn's proprietor. The die was cast. Much better to face him on neutral ground, she reassured herself. It was up to her to carry it off with a high hand.

Her head was high as she approached the innkeeper whose stunned reaction disconcerted her until she remembered that she had taken the precaution of wearing her mourning clothes, including a heavy veil, when making her original agreement with him.

"Mrs. Smithson to see Sir Jason Archer," she said, giving him a level look.

"Yes, ma'am, right this way, if you please, ma'am," the man replied, scurrying out from behind his counter.

Her teeth tightened, but she gave no outward sign that she suspected he was shamming the obsequious manner with which he conducted her down a corridor to a closed door that he proceeded to open with a flourish.

"Mrs. Smithson to see you, sir."

"Thank you, Gurnley. We'll have refreshments in five minutes, please," said a well-remembered voice, though she did not see its owner until their host stepped back to allow her to enter the room.

"No!" she cried as the proprietor turned to leave, moderating her voice to add, "Thank you, but I don't care for anything."

"But my dear . . . Mrs. Smithson," Sir Jason demurred in purring tones, "it would be infamous of me not to provide refreshment for my . . . guest. Five minutes, Gurnley."

"Very good, sir." The innkeeper bowed himself out, closing the door behind the exquisite young woman rigid with temper and the elegant gentleman standing at his ease in front of the fireplace, a little smile on his lips.

The two remained fixed in place for a moment regarding each other, the lady's expression wary and the gentleman's unreadable.

She was pleased with the light laugh she achieved as she protested, "You are staring at me as though you'd never seen me before, Jason. Surely I have not changed beyond all recognition in less than a month."

"To the contrary, you are precisely as I remembered you," he replied in a silky voice that she mistrusted. "But I am forgetting my manners to keep you standing. Please sit down."

She glanced from the white linen-draped table set with china and glassware in front of the fireplace to the chair he pulled out for her, saying uneasily, "No, thank you. As I said earlier, I do not care for any refreshments. Why did you come here, today, Jason? You cannot have thought that I would change my mind. I told you in my note that the man I first loved had come back." She looked puzzled as he laughed in what appeared to be genuine amusement.

"So you did, and apologized very prettily also for any pain that your elopement might have caused me. Come, Désirée, you cannot have believed that any man finding himself in that unenviable situation would simply retire from the lists without seeking out the person who had cuckolded him."

"But it was not like that, I tell you! You don't under—"

A knock on the door cut off her voice in midsentence and heralded the entrance of a waiter with an enormous tray containing two bottles, a teapot and various dishes. Neither principal moved nor spoke until he had unloaded his burden onto the table and taken himself out of the room again.

"This interview will not conclude until I am satisfied on a number of points, so you may as well sit down," Jason said.

After a quick look at his resolute jaw, she sat down in the chair he indicated.

"I am going to have a glass of burgundy," he declared, picking up one of the bottles. "Will you join me or take a glass of sherry?"

She declined both and, after watching him pour himself a glass of wine, shrugged and lifted the teapot. She kept her eyes on her task, but her frowning concentration was directed on the argument raging in her mind as she tried to weigh the risks of various actions. How much should she tell him? Would he be more or less inclined to help her if he knew the whole truth? Her movements were slow and deliberate as she debated her best course, though she was aware of his barely controlled impatience.

"Is Martin in Newhaven with you?" he asked abruptly.

"Yes, but I do not wish you to meet him."

"It isn't within your power to prevent a meeting between us. If you desire my help in the form of money or other assistance, you will tell me the truth—all of it—but I promise you that Martin and I will meet soon, whether or not you tell me and with or without your knowledge. Now that we are clear on that, I'll begin. Is Martin French?"

She bit her lip, aware of the uncomfortable pounding of her heart and her own helplessness. She must trust him or run out of this room right now, and if she decided on the second course, she had no doubt that he would catch her before she reached the street. She shivered and capitulated. "Yes," she said, looking him straight in the eye, "but his name isn't Martin. It is Etienne Freneau, and I am his wife."

She thought a light came into his eyes then, but it was too fleeting for her to be sure. They were their usual opaque charcoal color when he barked, "When and where were you married?"

"In Portsmouth thirteen months ago by a Jesuit priest."

"A priest?" he echoed, his eyes narrowing as he muttered, "A marriage between two Catholics is legal. How could you marry me less than a year later?"

"I was told by someone who should have known that he was dead, and I had not heard from him in over eight months."

"Heard from him? Where was he?"

She hesitated. "I don't know. He had to leave England shortly after our marriage."

"Your French bridegroom left you alone shortly after the wedding, which took place in England? Obviously we are talking about a soldier or a spy. Which is it?"

Detestable man, she thought, swallowing her spleen and steeling her nerves. "He is a Frenchman," she replied evenly, "fighting for his country as you fought for yours."

"And yours, I would remind you. I might ask what he is doing in my country, but as I don't wish to hear a pack of lies, I shall refrain," he replied amiably, reaching for a slice of plum cake. "Umm, this is delicious; I can recommend it."

"I am not hungry," she said through gritted teeth.

"Do not say I didn't warn you," he advised, helping himself to another slice of the cake and eyeing her mutinous face with an expression that was not unkind.

"Jason, will you help us? I know I have no right to ask this of you when I have treated you so badly, but I really do feel that we would not have suited in the long run, even if Etienne had not returned for me. What's more, I believe you had already realized I was not the girl you thought you were marrying. I fear we would have led a cat-and-dog existence." She noted a faint twitch at the corner of his mouth and pounced. "I am right, am I not?"

"I would never be so ungallant as to signify agreement with such a theory."

"Touché," she acknowledged with a little smile that faded quickly. "Please, Justin."

"I gather that you and Freneau are eager to leave our fair shores? Take heart; I will help you."

"Thank you, most sincerely."

"You do have your marriage lines as proof of the marriage?"

"Yes, in the place where we are staying."

"Have you been in Newhaven since you left Oakhill?"

"No, Etienne expected we would sail from Dover, but he missed the connection because it took several days to discover what had happened to me and where I was. I really should be going back now, Jason."

"In a few minutes. Drink your tea while I ask you a few questions."

She lowered the cup she had sipped from mechanically, once more on the alert. "What kind of questions?"

"You told me your mother was French." When she nodded, he continued, "What was her name before she married your father?"

"Hélène du Bois."

"Du Bois," he repeated softly. "Helen Forrest."

"What did you say?"

"It doesn't signify. Your father's name was Ryder?"

"Yes, of course."

"Where was he from?"

"I don't know."

"How can you not know where your father was from?"

"He never told me; nor did my mother."

He frowned. "Well, did you ever live anywhere other than Portsmouth?"

"Not that I recall."

"Did your father ever mention his family or any relatives?"

"No, I did not know him very well," she said slowly. "He would go away for months at a time, and he died when I was only seven or eight years old."

"I see. What do you remember about him?"

"Very little actually. He was a big man, or so it seemed to me, very fair coloring, blond hair and blue eyes. When he smiled, his teeth were very white, but he did not have much to do with me. I was mostly in the nursery with the nursemaid when he was at home."

"And when he died, did you and your mother go to stay with his family for a time?"

"No, in fact, I have no memory of his dying at all except that one day my mother told me he had died. And after that I went away to school. Jason, why are you asking me all these questions? What has any of this got to do with my being married to Etienne instead of to you?"

"Probably nothing. I am hoping you will indulge my curiosity as a personal favor," he said, smiling at her in a manner that put her uncomfortably in mind of one reason she had rushed into a second marriage. "Did your mother ever mention knowing anyone, a family perhaps, by the name of Cole?"

"No, I am certain she did not. Jason, I really must not stay away any longer."

"Of course. I beg your pardon for delaying you. I will escort you back since it is important that I see your marriage lines."

She protested, but he brushed aside her arguments in a way she considered unpleasantly familiar, and within a very few minutes she found herself being escorted along the street.

"I know you are determined to meet Etienne," she said after a silence during which each pursued private thoughts, "but I would be grateful if you would postpone it until I have prepared him for the event."

"You did not tell him about contacting me, did you?" he asked with a disaffecting shrewdness that had her tilting up her chin in a haughty pose.

"I did not think to at the time."

"I would even hazard a guess that your Etienne expressed a decided disinclination to seek or accept assistance from your second 'husband.'"

She shot him a look of loathing, than glanced around. "Why have we stopped walking? I told you we turn at the next corner."

"Because the carriage is here," he replied, steering her toward a vehicle waiting by the pavement.

She pulled back but was unable to release her arm. "There is no need of a carriage. It is just a few steps farther."

"I am afraid it is a bit farther than that," he said apologetically, boosting her up the steps and blocking her attempts to turn back. "You see, before I meet your husband, there is someone you must meet." He climbed into the carriage on her heels, ignoring her vociferous protests, and the horses pulled away immediately.

As he walked slowly up the stairs the Frenchman removed his hat and kneaded his forehead briefly with one hand before raking his open fingers back through his hair to his collar. By the time he opened his door the creases in his brow had been smoothed out and there was a smile on his lips.

"Désirée," he called, seeing the parlor was vacant. She must be napping, he thought. The two novels he'd purchased a couple of days ago to help her pass the time were on the desk. Knowing how interminable the days seemed to her, cooped up in the apartment, he could well comprehend a desire to escape into sleep. He drew off his gloves and dropped them into the hat he'd set on the table.

He opened the door to the bedchamber softly and stiffened at the sight of the undisturbed bed. His eyes made a swift survey of the room. Her trunk stood in the corner as usual, and the top of the dresser was littered with her bottles and brushes. Some of his tension drained off, but a frown formed when he noted the absence of the bonnet she'd hung on one of the bedposts for lack of accommodation in the cramped space. A check of the parlor failed to discover the lace parasol she treasured. The sun was quite low in the sky by now, which meant that she had been gone for some considerable time.

The idea of sitting here or, worse, pacing about the restrictive premises until she returned was anathema to one accustomed to making quick decisions and acting on them instantly. He seized his hat and gloves and left the apartment, rapidly considering possibilities. He ruled out a simple walk to stretch her legs and escape the confinement of a stuffy room; she had been gone too long for that to be the answer. Also, familiarity with the workings of his bride's mind told him that, had a need for air and exercise been her motivation, she would have made sure to be back well before his expected return, looking sweet and busily engaged on some innocent occupation when she greeted him. With no clue as to her intentions, he would have to search the whole town blindly, trying not to arouse any interest among the inhabitants. He pulled in the corners of his mouth ruefully. His beautiful bride would get him hanged yet, with her well meant but misguided attempts to save him.

About to leave the lodging house, he paused and knocked on the landlady's door, assuming a smiling civility when a thin woman of middle years opened it a few inches. She had dyed her hair red and resorted to a liberal use of cosmetics in a vain attempt to erase a decade or two, lending an unattractive hardness to her appearance. Once she had identified her caller, the expression of suspicion that was habitual to her underwent a metamorphosis: she eyed him with a keen interest and produced a wide smile that displayed an incomplete set of crooked teeth.

"Ah, good evening, Mrs. Elton," he began, hanging on to his own smile. "I am sorry to trouble you, but I wonder if you can tell me if my wife had a caller this afternoon, someone she might have gone out with later?"

"Well, not to say a caller exactly; it was only Gurnley's boy over to the Dolphin, and she didn't go off w'him, not then at least. She went out a bit later by 'erself, all dressed up to the nines she was, carrying one o' them fancy sun shades to protect 'er complexion."

"Thank you, Mrs. Elton, you have been most helpful. Did you happen to notice the time she left?"

"I have more to do about this place than spy on the comings and goings of the lodgers," she declared with a sniff.

"Of course you do," he agreed, hastily mending his fences. "It must be a huge undertaking to maintain an establishment of this size and keep it so clean and in good order."

"Well, it is," she agreed, mollified by his admission. "Maybe I saw your wife go off around five when I was cleaning the windows in the hall."

"Thank you very much, Mrs. Elton," he said, giving her another smile as he replaced the hat he had doffed. "It sounds as though our friends have arrived in town a day earlier than expected. Good day to you."

His smile vanished the instant he turned away from the speculative gleam in the landlady's sharp little eyes. It had to be Archer of course. Désirée must have written to the man despite his objections. He might think it endearingly naive of her to credit a cuckolded husband—for that was what Archer believed himself to be—with sweet reason if she asked nicely for him to finance her elopement, had she been someone else's wife! As it was, he alternated between a lively desire to wring her lovely neck and a burning fear for her safety as he hurried toward the Dolphin Inn. She had been gone more than two hours, according to Mrs. Elton's report. Why had she not brought Archer back to the apartment for a meeting of all interested parties? She had described Archer as a stuffy, almost prudish sort of fellow, overly concerned with his family's reputation and traditions, but the man had been a colonel in a fine cavalry unit, up to his neck in war and savagery for years. Who knew how he would react to what he saw as a deep personal betrayal?

He had himself well in hand when he entered the Dolphin a few minutes later, thanks to years of self-discipline and pretending to be someone he was not. The tone in which he asked for Sir Jason Archer was that of a man looking forward to greeting an old friend.

"I'm sorry, sir, but Sir Jason Archer is not a guest here at present."

"Do I have the wrong day? I was certain my wife said he was due in Newhaven today."

His pose of bafflement must have been convincing, for the proprietor said helpfully, "Would that be Mrs. Smithson, sir? She had tea with Sir Jason earlier, but they left over an hour ago."

"Ah, then they must be going to my home," he said carelessly. "Thank you." He took a step away, then turned as if recalling something. "They did leave together? In Sir Jason's carriage?"

"They left together, sir, but on foot. I believe Sir Jason insisted on escorting Mrs. Smithson home first, but he had asked earlier about hiring a post chaise and I had sent him to Sloan's in the high street."

"I see. Thank you for your time and trouble." He bestowed a smile and a coin on the accommodating innkeeper and headed off at a leisurely pace.

This speeded up considerably as soon as he reached the street and headed toward Sloan's. He owned to being puzzled that Archer had not come in his own carriage until it dawned on him that the man might prefer to keep his servants in the dark about his intentions at this point, although the news of his bride's desertion must be all over the area by now. He was not in a humor to waste any sympathy on Archer, however, until he discovered what he was up to.

A half hour later a worried but determined Frenchman set off on horseback in the direction of Rye, nursing thoughts of vengeance against the man who had absconded with his wife.

Upon learning that Archer had not given his own home but an estate near Rye as his final destination when renting a postchaise, Etienne had briefly considered whether this might not be a case of trying to throw sand in his eyes to keep him from going into Hampshire again for a personal confrontation. In the end he obeyed a strong instinct to follow his rival's purported trail. There had been no attempt on Archer's part to conceal his destination, a clear invitation to follow him, though for reasons that were not yet evident. Whether it was a ruse or a trap, whatever Archer had planned made no difference to his own decision. He trusted his own powers of speed and deception enough to let himself be led, up to a point.

Stopping only long enough to return to their lodgings to collect a few necessities and pay Mrs. Elton another week's rent to leave the bulk of their belongings intact, he had rented a strongboned chestnut hack from a livery stable and was now committed to another strange detour in his quest to return to his homeland with his bride.

Chapter Fifteen

Jason spied the signpost and sat up straighter, sliding a glance across to his morose companion huddled in the farthest corner of the chaise, her head pointedly turned away from him. "You may come out of the sullens now, my dear Désirée. We shall be there in few minutes," he announced cheerfully.

"I am not in the sullens, as you so elegantly put it," she declared with asperity, "and even if I were, you could scarcely expect elation from me at our arrival since you have steadfastly refused to disclose your destination. For anything I know to the contrary, you could be taking me to a nunnery to separate Etienne and me!" She hunched a shoulder at his shout of laughter and turned her face to the window again.

"You among the good sisters—now that is a concept to invoke tantalizing images," he chuckled before addressing her complaint. "I wish you could have believed me last night when I told you that my reasons for not revealing our destination did not include any wish to annoy or alarm you. It would have made the journey less . . . onerous for you."

"Nothing could have done that," she cried, whirling on him in fury. "You had no right to take me anywhere without my consent!"

"Until I have proof that our marriage is illegal, I have a slew of rights where you are concerned."

"I shall hate you forever if anything happens to Etienne when he comes to find me!"

Jason, hearing the sob in her voice, felt a pang of compunction—not the first since embarking on this high-handed action in Newhaven. She was vain, shallow and selfish, not to mention endlessly tiresome, but he was inclined to believe her love for the Frenchman was genuine, as was her distress. He deserved all the discomfort and bother that she had given him on this trip, but it was too important to his own future to allow the niceties of chivalry to deter him. The knowledge gentled his voice as he replied, "Take heart, my dear girl. I am persuaded that Freneau is hot on our heels as we speak. That is one reason why I could not accede to your repeated requests to stop at an inn so you might sleep last night. Let me allay your fears about our destination at any rate. We are merely going to see a lady whom you need have no reluctance to meet."

"A lady! What lady—that old aunt you were so determined to visit? Are you trying to humiliate me? I have had no sleep and I look a wreck!"

"You are mistaken on two counts. You actually slept in the carriage for nearly five hours—exhausted, no doubt, by a series of hysterics when your persuasion failed to convince me to return you to Newhaven. As for your ruined looks, you must not have checked your mirror after your bath during our breakfast stop this morning. I assure you that you appear quite refreshed despite having had to do without the services of a maid."

"Which you denied me out of sheer revengefulness!" she retorted, her eyes flashing daggers that glanced off their target.

"It seemed prudent to restrict your access to message-carrying maid servants," he replied mildly.

"At least a maid might have ironed the creases out of this crumpled gown and arranged my hair for me. It is on your head if my appearance does you no credit with this 'lady.' "

"May I say that this is not a likely possibility?"

His gallantry earned him a disdainful sniff, but his attention had already shifted as the chaise rolled between the entrance posts of Marshland, coming to a halt in front of the main entrance a few minutes later.

Jason was assisting his reluctant passenger down from the chaise when the door was opened by the Coles' butler. "Ah, good morning, Fenton," he called over his shoulder. "We have come to call on Miss Cole. Do you remember me?"

"Of course, Sir Jason," the man said, stepping back and opening the door more widely, "but I believe Miss Cole is out at the moment. If you would care to wait in the library, I will inquire further."

"Thank you," Jason said, offering his arm to his companion and moving forward. As the pair mounted the shallow steps the event he had been anticipating occurred. The butler's eyes shifted to Désirée and his jaw fell open. "Miss Amy!" he blurted, his eyes bulging, "How did you . . . where did—"

"This is Madame Freneau, Fenton," Jason interposed smoothly. "I see you have noted the resemblance. You did say the library?" he prompted when the shaken butler continued to stare at the young woman on his arm who now turned questioning eyes on him.

Fenton pulled himself together to the extent of moving off, presumably toward the library, without uttering another syllable until he had opened a door and stood back, inviting the couple to enter. "If you will wait in here, please," he said in a voice that wobbled, his eyes returning once more to the girl in yellow before he backed away, closing the door with a jerky motion.

"What was that all about?" Désirée demanded, shaking her escort's arm when he remained staring at the closed door. "What did he mean? Resemblance to whom? Is the man touched in his upper works?"

"No, merely in shock, poor old fellow," Jason replied, his mouth curving in rueful lines. His voice became brisk as he glanced around the well-proportioned room. "Your questions will be answered in due course, I trust. Meanwhile, let us make ourselves comfortable. That velvet wing chair looks most accommodating." He ushered her toward it and selected a larger chair in softly creased leather where she was seated.

"Now what happens?"

"Now we wait," he said, smiling a little at her impatient expression.

A wavelet thrust forward, crested and creamed onto the shore to be followed at brief intervals by its identical successors. Today the regularity of the tidal action, usually comforting and life-affirming, failed to provide solace to the dark-clad girl sitting motionless on the dunes above the beach. In the monotony of the incoming waves Amy glimpsed the dreariness of her own future, and a sudden chill raced through her system, raising gooseflesh on her arms. She rubbed her upper arms vigorously to chase the cold away and averted her gaze from the inexorability of the water's movement in a vain attempt to erase the melancholy image in her brain.

How much better would it have been, how much more settled her spirits had she never experienced the incredible series of events set in motion by her accidental meeting with Jason Archer. She would never have known the tumultuous emotions engendered by that rash abduction, never have discovered that one man embodied everything she could desire in her life.

She had not been unhappy with her personal situation before meeting Jason. Apart from periods of sharp anxiety over Robert's safety and the grieving that was a natural accompaniment to her father's decline and death, she had not found her existence uncongenial. Her days had been filled with the myriad tasks encumbent upon the mistress of a modest establishment like Marshlands, her evenings with reading and sewing. That these activities were solitary employments involving no other society than that of servants had not troubled her. Tending the gardens and rambling about the area in all weathers had provided an unfailing source of pleasure and refreshment to her spirits.

How could one short week change everything, she wondered, staring gloomily at the gray waters. How could the transitory experiences of that aberration in time rob her of her former appreciation of all the small pleasures of her life? She must not allow this maudlin musing. Indeed, it was selfish and cowardly. She should be covered with shame even to be thinking of herself and her own concerns at this moment.

Amy scrambled to her feet, automatically brushing sand from her skirts while her eyes scanned the horizon in a futile search. No masts or sails appeared from the south; indeed, only one small fishing boat approaching Rye from the north disturbed the serenity of the sea at present. She watched blindly as the boat plowed along its course, steadily decreasing the distance to the harbor.

Where was Robert? Was he on a steady course for home at this moment? It was now past the fortnight that he'd given as the maximum duration he anticipated for the accomplishment of his mission, and she could not seem to prevent her uneasy mind from conjuring up direful circumstances that he might not have anticipated. She was tormented by a persistent fear that her brother might have come home unscathed from years of bloody battles and deprivations, only to meet with a solitary death in an enemy country after all. She was no longer childish enough to believe that fate could not be so cruel as to take away the only family she possessed. The tenor of her mind at present—all darkness and desperation—could well conceive of just such a malignant force.

An alien sound in the natural setting intruded on Amy's solitary reverie. Her abstracted gaze swerved toward the south to take in a trio of town children skipping barefooted along the shoreline in noisy camaraderie. She located a watery sun behind a break in the cloud cover and was surprised to see how high it was. She had been gone for hours. For a moment longer she watched the children happily absorbed in their simple game, her expression mournfully wistful, before turning her back on them and setting out with lagging steps for home.

A burning sense of guilt at not wanting to go back to the house where her every action these past two days had been under the scrutiny of her devoted staff prompted her to speed up her pace initially. After about twenty minutes of brisk exercise and high-minded resolve, however, her steps slowed gradually to a dawdling stroll again. There was no doubt in her mind that Mrs. Fenton's hovering over her since her return and questioning her about everything that had happened during her absence sprang from the purest affection and concern, but it was a trial to endure with even a minimal assumption of grace.

For reasons that eluded her understanding at present she was loath to share her experiences with anyone. On the other hand, she could appreciate their concern and desire to comfort her, and she detested telling lies. With no articulated plan in her mind, she had found herself walking a verbal tightrope since her return, trying to satisfy their natural curiosity without creating a tapestry of lies to preserve her privacy. She had refused to talk about her abductor beyond labeling him dark, glum and silent. Driven to the wall by Mrs. Fenton's interest in the fictitious ladies who had succored her after her supposed escape during the abduction, she had found herself describing Lady Glenallan and Miss Chistleton for want of inventiveness until she was alarmed to hear herself praising the gardens at Glendale by name. Determined to avoid any additional slips of the tongue, she had embarked on a frenzy of cleaning and polishing every object in the house in anticipation of her brother's return.

Unfortunately, physical labor had provided no alleviation in the persistent lowness of spirits oppressing her of late. The Fentons and Tom would regret their heroic efforts and fervent prayers to have her returned safely to them if she did not replace her long face with a more cheerful mien. Vowing to redouble her pitiful attempts at normalcy, she curved her lips into a forced smile as she again increased her pace.

Amy's smile became genuine later as she skirted the edge of the marsh when the unmistakable "pump-er-lunk" cry of a bittern reached her ears. She stopped immediately, trying to make herself invisible while her eyes searched the reeds for a glimpse of the bird who would be hiding among them with his long narrow bill pointed upward to blend in with the foliage. She and Robert had spent many fruitless hours in this pursuit over the years, and today's efforts, like the majority in the past, went unrewarded.

The bittern's endlessly repeated cry mocked her when she trudged off a moment later in defeat.

Amy was nearing the lane that bordered the estate on the marsh side when the sound of hoofbeats in the distance caused her to glance over her shoulder. Relieved to see that it was not Tom out in search of her, she proceeded into the lane a step or two before hearing herself hailed from the road.

"Madam, one moment, if you will be so good."

Amy halted, turning with forced civility to assist the rider who, she noted with academic interest, was easily the handsomest man she had ever laid eyes on, despite a day's growth of beard that gave him a piratical air. His profile, while he wrestled to bring his horse's head around and stop, was worthy to adorn a Greek coin.

The next instant their eyes met, and his face was transformed by elation. "Désirée," he cried. "Thank God, you are safe!"

Amy, struck dumb, simply stared. *Another* man mistaking her for Désirée Archer? This could not be happening again! She had no time to indulge disbelief, however. The sight of the stranger dismounting quickly and moving forward with the evident intention of embracing her reversed the paralysis that had gripped her; she jumped back, warding off his advance with both hands.

"My name is not Désirée; you are mistaken, sir!"

The man, looking as flabbergasted as she must have done a moment since, stopped inches away, eyeing her with alarm. "What has happened, *ma belle?* What has that black-guard done to you?"

Amy's stunned fascination at the stranger's words, cul-minating in the conviction that this must be the notorious Armand Martin, robbed her of the advantage of surprise. She jumped back but was too late. With the swiftness of a cat he lunged forward and caught her in his arms, pulling her into a close embrace, all the time murmuring fragments of French and English that were meant to be comforting.

"Don't be afraid, my love. You are safe now. I promise nothing shall hurt you. Do not tremble so."

"I am not trembling," Amy rebutted tartly, pushing strongly against his chest while turning her head from side to side to evade his attempts to kiss her. "I am trying to con-vince a dullwitted Frenchman that he is accosting the wrong female!"

"Accosting!" He thrust her away from him in order to search her face with eyes of a changeable brown and amber, keeping a firm grip on her shoulders as he did so. Amy stared back at him straightly, her initial fears swamped in re-luctant compassion, even when his expression solidified into cold anger. "What black arts has that scoundrel used to make you like this? Has he drugged you? Do not try to keep us apart any longer for I intend to have it out with him today. Where is he?"

Without flinching Amy withstood the shake he adminis-tered. "No one has employed arts of any description on me," she began, striving for a reasonable tone to keep the volatil-ity she sensed in him at bay. "I apprehend that I must bear a striking resemblance to Désirée Archer, for you are the sec-ond person to mistake me for her, but my name is Amy Cole and I can prove my own identity. You are on my family property at the moment. The house is about a half mile ahead if you would care to accompany me there."

"If I would care to—" He laughed with what sounded like genuine amusement, displaying brilliant white teeth, and made her a mocking bow. "I assure you that I have no intention of letting you out of my sight ever again, madame. Lead on."

Amy resumed her progress without another word, though her mind seethed with questions and conjecture. She could feel his eyes raking her profile as he walked beside her, leading his mount with negligent ease, but she refused to look at him. It was difficult enough trying to sort out her thoughts without the distraction of this simmering volcano a foot away. Unless Désirée Archer was as promiscuous as Catherine the Great, this must be the man with whom she had eloped. His dusty and unshaved state was evidence of long hours in the saddle, and it did not require much of a leap of the imagination to deduce that he had come here in search of her. But why here of all places, and why was she not still with him?

Amy's heart was stampeding in tandem with her mental activity. The only explanation that made any sense in conjunction with the presence of this smoldering man with a slight French accent was that he must believe that Jason had brought his wife to Marshland. But again, why? Had Désirée gone with Jason willingly? Despite the heavy warmth of the cloudy day, Amy shivered, her mind beset by a roiling combination of dread and anticipation and her limbs strangely heavy and uncoordinated. She stumbled suddenly on a pebble, and the man's hand shot out and grabbed her arm, steadying her.

"Thank you," she said, breaking the throbbing silence that had hung between them since they had entered the lane. "Why have you come here?"

"I believe that is my question. You know why I am here. I expected to have to rescue you from constraints; instead I find you free as the breeze and jauntering about the countryside calling yourself—what?"

"My name is Amy Cole and I have lived all my life on this estate, Marshfield." She saw the hurt beneath the bitterness of his expression before the name of her home brought him to full alertness once more.

"Marshfield! That is where I have been heading all
night!"

"In pursuit of Sir Jason Archer and his wife?" As his eyes
hardened again, she added, "You missed the main entrance.
This lane leads around to the back of the house just ahead.
Oh my, something must have happened. What is it, Mrs.
Fenton?" she called, quickening her steps to a near run toward the buxom woman who had nearly burst out of a door
in a tearfully agitated state.

"Oh, Miss Amy," the woman half-moaned, half-cried as
the girl reached her. "That man what brought you home
t'other day is here with a girl that looks so much like you it
gave my heart a queer turn just looking at her—and Fenton
too! He came into the kitchen as white as a sheet and fell
into a chair, saying you was in the library with that man, all
got up like a fancy London lady, so of course I went right up
there, and it's true! Though I knew it wasn't you, she's the
spittin' image of you and that's a fact!"

"There, there, Mrs. Fenton, calm down and get your
breath," Amy soothed, wrapping a strong arm around the
distraught housekeeper's shoulders and leading her back
inside. "How did you know it wasn't I?"

"By the way she looked at me like I was beneath her notice. Who is she, Miss Amy?" The housekeeper was wringing her hands and looking piteously up at her mistress.

"I . . . don't know, Mrs. Fenton. Rosie," she said to the
young kitchen maid hovering near the central work table,
"get Mrs. Fenton a strong cup of tea and see that she drinks
it right away. How long have our guests been here, Mrs.
Fenton?"

"A half hour or so, I reckon. I sent coffee up to them."

"Wonderful. You can send up some more in a while, but
not, mind you, until after you've drunk that tea."

Amy patted the housekeeper's hands and turned away,
nearly bumping into the dark, silent Frenchman who had
followed them inside after tying up his horse.

"I'm coming with you."

Amy shot a worried look at his grim face, tempted to

warn him that she would not tolerate fighting in her house, but she thought better of the idea in the next instant and moved off with a mental shrug. When had a woman's words ever dissuaded a man bent on an unreasonable action? She hurried directly to the library, pausing only long enough to tear off her ancient straw hat and toss it onto a hall table in passing; she did not even notice that several strands of hair had escaped from her neat chignon to curl about her ears and neck in charming disarray. She was equally blind to the thoughtful frown that furrowed the Frenchman's brow at her action.

When Amy paused to take a calming breath outside the library, the man opened the door, stepping back to allow her to precede him. At first her anxious eyes saw only Jason rising from Robert's favorite chair just before a feminine voice cried, "Etienne! I knew you'd find me!" A young woman flew past her to hurl herself into the man's arms that reached out and enclosed her, leaving only a profusion of chestnut curls visible beneath a glorious, flower-bedecked bonnet.

Amy averted her eyes from the fervent embrace being exchanged, her pitying glance involuntarily seeking Jason who seemed in no need of pity as he watched the reunion with a faint smile. All this she took in during the first second or two before her eyes were drawn inexorably back to the young woman who had figured so largely in her thoughts since she'd first heard her name on Jason's lips.

The Frenchman was speaking as he gently turned his beloved toward Amy, but the latter heard nothing. For her, sound and time had vanished, leaving only vision as Désirée's eyes met hers for the first time. It was not like looking into a mirror, she decided, but more a sensation of being in two places or two bodies at the same time. These rationalizations came later, however, when she'd had leisure to try to fix the moment in memory. At first she merely experienced the other girl's shock. Désirée gasped and swayed, but was held upright in her lover's arms. Amy felt no faintness, but she had been prepared to meet someone

who resembled her closely. Could it be that Désirée had had
no inkling of what she would find at Marshfield?

Amy's eyes, winging to Jason, must have held accusation
because there was a rueful twist to his mouth as he made the
tiniest negative motion of his head.

"Who are you?"

Désirée's strained question brought Amy's attention back
to her, but Jason now assumed command of this dramatic
meeting of strangers that he had obviously orchestrated.
"Our hostess is Miss Amy Cole, but that is obviously an inadequate reply to the question in all our minds, which is the
reason for this little gathering today. I am getting ahead of
the story, however. General introductions should be the first
order of business. Shall we all sit down, if you will pardon
me for usurping your prerogative, Amy?"

The intimate nature of the smile Jason directed at her
covered Amy in confusion, but his words served to remind
her of her hostess duties. "Yes, please do sit down everyone," she said hastily, watching until the Frenchman led
Désirée to a sofa in the center of the room where he joined
her before she perched on the edge of the wing chair Désirée
had previously occupied.

Jason, who remained standing, continued to address
Amy. "You have no doubt surmised that the lovely lady I escorted here is she whom I had assumed to be my wife." *Assumed!* Amy's eyes widened as he continued after an
infinitesimal pause, "It turns out, however, that she is more
likely the wife of Monsieur Freneau, seated beside her."

"Freneau! But what of Armand Martin?" Amy blurted, all
at sea.

"Martin appears to have been merely a . . . *nom de
guerre,* shall we say?"

The Frenchman made him an ironic bow before bestowing a charming smile on Amy who returned it shyly.

"By the way, my compliments on the speed with which
you joined us, Freneau," Jason added smoothly.

"Your directions were most helpful, Archer," his rival riposted, "but I must apologize to our hostess for my disrep-

utable appearance. Had I known we were to be a party at Marshfield, I would have stopped to make myself more presentable."

Désirée, who had listened in gathering impatience to this masculine fencing, now burst into speech. "This is all very well, but none of it explains how Miss Cole came to be acquainted with you and why she—we are . . ."

Her voice trailed off as she fixed her eyes on Amy again, and Sir Jason reassumed control of the encounter. "As alike as two peas in a pod? Why do you suppose that is?"

"I haven't the slightest idea!" Pique colored her tones as she demanded of Amy, "Have you?" Amy shook her head wordlessly.

"You do not feel you might be cousins—even sisters perhaps?"

"Of course not!" Madame Freneau declared.

"It isn't possible!" said Miss Cole.

"Your mother was English and she died when you were born. Have I this correct?" Sir Jason asked Amy, who nodded.

"And your mother was French, and she died a few months ago?"

"You know that; you saw her grave!" Désirée confirmed.

"What was her maiden name?"

"I told you, Hélène duBois."

"And *your* mother's name?"

Amy hesitated an instant before saying faintly, "Helen Forrest."

"*Bois* means wood in English, does it not, which could be comprehended as forest?"

"Possibly, but it is a mild coincidence at most," Désirée shrugged.

"You are one-and-twenty as I recall," he said to Désirée. "When is your birthday?"

"February tenth."

All eyes turned expectantly to Amy who swallowed and said weakly, "So is mine."

"Ah, another coincidence?"

"It is impossible," Amy insisted. "I have an elder brother, my grandmother lived here until I was sixteen and my father died just this spring. In all those years, no one has ever mentioned the existence of a twin sister."

"And my name was Ryder before my marriage. I never even heard of anyone named Cole."

"Nevertheless, it is true that you are our sister."

None of the absorbed company had noted the quiet entrance of a man through the French doors until he spoke. Then Amy cried, "Robert!" and raced across the room to embrace him. "Thank God you are safe!"

"I told you not to worry," the burly young man with a sandy beard and bright green eyes in a sunburned countenance chided her gently. Then he took her hand and headed toward the sofa where his eyes roamed between the two girls for a pregnant moment. "My word," he said, breaking the silence that had gripped the room's occupants. "The resemblance is uncanny, considering that you have never seen each other."

"You knew, Robert?" Amy whispered, almost as pale as Désirée. "And you never told me?"

"Now, love, don't turn on the waterworks. I found some correspondence of Father's the day before I went away that just about rocked me off my feet. I was going to tell you about it that evening, but you remember I had to leave quickly."

"I do not understand any of this!" Désirée said plaintively, gripping the Frenchman's hand.

"I see that," Robert replied, "and I know only what I have gleaned from my father's few papers; but before we go into the matter more fully, I must become acquainted with these gentlemen. Are either of you Sir Jason Archer?"

"I am Archer, at your service, Captain Cole," Jason replied, bowing.

"And you are married to my sister Désirée?" Robert continued with only the slightest acknowledgment of the civility.

"Well, I had believed that to be the case."

"But it is I who have that honor," said the other man, rising from Désirée's side and bowing. "I am Etienne Freneau."

"What?" Robert glanced nonplussed from the enigmatic countenance of the Englishman to the Frenchman's stance of proud defiance. He then turned in unpremeditated accord with Amy to their newly discovered sister.

"By the way, Freneau, do you happen to have your marriage lines with you?" Sir Jason asked conversationally.

"*Bien sûr*—of course," M. Freneau replied with a tight-lipped smile.

When Fenton entered the room a moment later with a coffee tray, the rival claimants to Désirée's hand were discussing a document while the lady involved recounted the details of her marriages to her recently acquired brother and sister.

"Mr. Robert, you're home. Praise be!" the butler declared in heartfelt accents, looking like a man who had just had the weight of the world removed from his shoulders as he set the tray down on the big desk. He listened to Amy's instructions to pass on to his wife concerning a cold collation that could be set before their guests within the hour and left with a jaunty step.

After the door had closed behind Fenton and she had returned to the group to pour coffee for everyone, Amy, who had been looking grave since hearing Désirée's tale of her two marriages, addressed her stony-faced brother. "Robert, before we speak of the future, had we not better deal with the past? How came we—all three of us—to be raised in ignorance of our relationship?"

"Father's letter to me was quite brief, providing a terse recounting of his marriage to a young French *émigrée* who had lost both parents in 'eighty-nine, our births and his wife's desertion. I was born here, but the marriage was not a success. He swept his pregnant wife and child away to his mother's home in Northumberland where our mother gave birth to twin girls in 'ninety-two.

"By the way," he advised Amy, "you were actually christened Aimée Désirée, and Désirée has Aimée as her second name.

"Shortly thereafter, our mother eloped with the man she had fallen in love with in the south, taking one of the babies with her. When my father could not trace his wife, my grandmother somehow contrived to have a false burial service—no doubt private—and my father eventually returned to his estate as a widower with two 'motherless children.'

"He heard nothing of his wife, whom he never divorced, for a number of years until she wrote to him when her first lover married someone else and ended their . . . arrangement. She sought assistance for her daughter because the man with whom she next planned to enter into an alliance refused to accept the child. Our father paid for your schooling and support thereafter."

Désirée, seated within the protective circle of her husband's arm with tears running silently down pale cheeks during this recitation, flashed her eyes at her brother, declaring fiercely, "My mother loved me! She wanted me with her!"

"She must have loved you very much," Amy said gently. "She went to heroic lengths to keep her . . . irregular circumstances from harming your life."

"My father never cared a scrap for me—he never came to see me even once!"

"Our father was never a happy man, Désirée. I am persuaded he stayed away because he felt he could not take from your mother the one joy in her life. Considering the disaster that was their marriage, it seems clear that both our parents tried their utmost to ensure that their children's lives would not be clouded by scandal and bitterness."

Désirée's tears had ceased to fall, and she was listening intently to her sister's words. "Why did he not come to see me after my mother died?" she demanded.

"He never knew of your marriage or your—our mother's death," Robert assured her. "In fact, it is unclear at this point who died first. His letter requests me to make specific provision for you in the event of his own death."

"I fear the events of this morning, following on a long drive, have exhausted you," Amy said, rising and extending a hand to Désirée. "Let me take you to a bedchamber where you may freshen up and rest before luncheon. And I am persuaded you would appreciate the opportunity to shave at least, sir. My brother or I can supply anything you lack."

"Thank you, *ma belle-soeur,* in every sense of that word," Etienne replied gallantly, assisting his wife to her feet. "Désirée will be herself again shortly. I have some gear in my saddlebag, including another gown for you, *mon coeur.*"

"The maid will take your gown to be pressed when she brings hot water to the room. If you will excuse me for a few minutes, Robert, Sir Jason?"

The two men had risen and now bowed as Amy ushered the couple out. Before the door had even closed, Robert was rummaging in a cabinet behind the desk. He emerged with a bottle and two glasses. "I don't know about you, Archer, but I could use a brandy after that little session." When Sir Jason nodded in response to his gesture of holding up the bottle, he poured the glasses and held one out to his guest.

"I gather that my sister Désirée has treated you rather badly," he began bluntly. "Is that document Freneau produced worth the paper it is written on?"

"I have every hope that it is," Jason replied, handing over the paper from his inside pocket and swirling his glass meditatively while the other perused it. "They were Catholics married by a Jesuit priest who, Freneau tells me, still has ties to a small community outside of Portsmouth. That should make my task with the archbishop easier."

"I am relieved to hear it. A Frenchman," Robert said, in disgust. "At least I can be assured that he did not marry her for her fortune."

"From what Désirée told me during our mutual incarceration last night, Freneau's family has been raising grapes and making wine in Burgundy for centuries."

"Ah, the silver lining," the younger man said with a brief smile that was soon replaced by a frown. "I still wonder what he has been doing in this country."

"Much the same as you were doing in his country perhaps," Jason suggested blandly.

"Has Amy—" Robert stopped abruptly, his eyes hardening.

"Amy has held tooth and nail to a weak story about a trip to London on unspecified business, as has Tom Watkins, but you will forgive me for saying that you do not have the appearance of a man recently returned from a stay in the metropolis. There is a faint whiff of the sea about you."

"And I thought I had cleaned up rather thoroughly at Sim's before coming home this morning. I met Tom on the way here, and he told me everything he knew about what happened last week," Robert added, going on the offensive.

"It is all true. I abducted her by force and refused to believe her denials that she was my wife. I didn't ravish her, but if the story we concocted to explain her long absence is not credited, I will have destroyed her reputation beyond redemption."

"As for that, Tom has had his ear to the ground since they returned and he says there is no whisper of any impropriety, simply relief that she was returned unharmed, so you seem to be off the hook in that respect."

"Please know that it is not reparation. It is the dearest wish of my heart to marry Amy. Long before she ran away, I had realized that what I had felt for Désirée was mindless infatuation. In less than a sennight I discovered qualities in Amy that I had hoped in vain to find in Désirée."

"How does Amy feel about you?"

"I . . . don't know, but I have begun to hope."

"She must be warned that she could well be considered a figure of ridicule if she shows herself willing to accept what her sister rejected. That is how your marriage could be seen in society," Robert insisted, when Jason grew rigid with anger.

Amy walked in on them standing toe to toe before he could reply. Both men turned to her with quick smiles on their lips, and Robert said cheerfully, "I am going off to the kitchen to see if Mrs. Fenton loves me enough to add cream currant scones to the menu for this impromptu luncheon of yours, my dear."

"Yes, of course, but Robert," she began helplessly as he strolled past her, whistling a country air. "I have not had a chance of two words with him since he arrived," she complained.

"You haven't had a chance of two words with me either," Jason said, "but there are more important things than words, do you not agree?"

By the time he had posed this question, Amy was in no position to reply. She was wrapped within the compass of two strong arms, being kissed with shattering thoroughness. It occurred to the remnant of her dazed intellect that cooperation might be one of those items rated higher than words, and she proceeded to test this theory by placing her arms around his neck and snuggling closer still. By the time Jason ended the kiss, withdrawing far enough to gaze with wonder at her radiant face, Amy was able to speak again.

"Yes, I agree, cooperation for one," she said in dreamy tones.

"What?" Jason blinked in confusion.

"Something more important than words."

Comprehension dawned in his eyes and he laughed boyishly, hugging her to him again. "Thank you for the demonstration, my darling. You do care then?"

"Yes, of course. I've been so miserably unhappy since you left, Jason. I thought I'd never see you again."

"You would have seen me eventually. I would have provided for Désirée in any case, but after meeting you and loving you, I could never have lived with her again. My state was as wretched as yours, my love, because I could not in honor have spoken my feelings to you while still legally bound. I could not even ask you to wait while I conducted a search that might have lasted as long as your father's if she had left the country. The fear that you would marry someone else in the meantime would have been my constant companion."

She placed her fingers over his lips. "Don't torment yourself with what might have been, Jason. Today I feel I am the most fortunate creature on the face of the earth."

"No," he said firmly, his dark eyes lightening to pewter as they devoured her glowing face. "That position definitely belongs to me for having gained the blessing of your affection."

"We won't quibble over that distinction, I trust," she said demurely, mischief sparkling in her jeweled eyes.

"I hate to introduce a serpent into Eden, my love, but your brother is concerned that everyone will regard you as a figure of ridicule for marrying the man your sister discarded."

Amy was silent for a long moment, a frown pleating her brow. Jason had grown utterly still, and she surprised a look of pain in his eyes when she finally shifted her gaze from the horizon. "Don't look like that," she commanded, rising on tiptoes to kiss him swiftly before going on. "It strikes me that there need be no hue and cry about our marriage, indeed no notice at all if we marry quietly by special license in a place where we are unknown. I have no friends or relatives who will expect to be told before the event. Your household believes me to be your wife, and your relatives have met me already. You would have to explain my continued absence from Oakhill until we are married, at which time I may reappear with no fanfare. I can see no immediate pitfalls save that our anniversary might have to be celebrated on the wrong date at Oakhill and Glendale. The true advantage to this course is that there will be no scandal about the bigamous marriage if it can be kept out of the newspapers. Désirée will be living in France, so there will be no confusion on that head."

"She might return at any time," he said slowly, concentrating his wits. "There is also the school friend with whom she stayed at Portsmouth."

" 'Sufficient unto the day is the evil thereof.' "

This borrowed wisdom apparently struck Jason most forcibly. Amy observed with quiet joy as the strain and wariness that had seemed habitual, except for rare moments at

Glendale, faded from his countenance, replaced by an impression of peace. "Whatever comes, we will face it together. Is that what you are saying, my dearest?"

"That is what I am promising," she replied, raising her chin in what he was delighted to take as a clear invitation to seal the promise.